MAFIA FIRE

A DARK MAFIA ROMANCE

SHANNA HANDEL

WELCOME

Welcome!
Please consider signing up for my newsletter at my website
www.shannahandelromance.com
You will be emailed each time I have a new release.
xoxo Shanna Handel

Mafia Fire: A Dark Mafia Romance

Shanna Handel

Credits to my wonderful team:

Artwork by Pop Kitty Design

Photography by

WANDER AGUIAR PHOTOGRAPHY LLC

Editing by Jane Beyer

Proofread by Julie Barney

ARC Director Jess Bracewell

Welcome to the story...

Mafia Fire: A Dark Mafia Romance

By Shanna Handel

She never should have stepped foot in my club...

The little beauty came to my kink club, Fire.

Brought something she never should have touched.

I punished her for it and sent her on her way.

But I can't stop thinking of her.

How innocent yet sensual she is...

I have to be the first to have her.

She's in trouble with more men than me.

They don't just want to punish her.

They want to own her.

I can't let them have her.

She's gone from someone I can't stop thinking of...

To something I have to possess.

She's burning me up. Turning me to ash.

My little mafia fire.

1

SHANNA HANDEL

THEY'RE NEVER GOING to stop till they get what they want from me. And it's something I'm never going to give. With trembling fingers I peel the note off my front door. I have to read it one more time before my feet will let me go inside.

Your family owes us. You know what we want.

I stand on my stoop, still as a statue, and try to dissolve my fear. *Deep breath in, Kylie, deep breath out. You can and will get yourself out of this mess.* I open the door, fingers shaking less now, and make my way to our little blue and white kitchen. It's still spotless from when I cleaned it this morning, the electric teakettle sitting in the same spot I put it after I wiped the counters down. Nonna hasn't gotten out of bed yet.

Heat flashes over my face as I tear the paper into pieces, tossing them into the trash. I've got to find a way to fix this.

I will find a way to fix this.

I've already begun, haven't I?

I need money. Fast. A lot of it.

And not to pay for yardwork. It's to save my ass. If my current plan doesn't work… if I can't get the money… then hopefully my latest venture will offer me some protection.

But if my plan fails…

I sink down into a kitchen chair, staring out the large bay of windows that run along the back of the kitchen. I keep the glass spotless; the blue checkered curtains are freshly washed and ironed, but the patch of shaggy grass in the overgrown backyard tugs at my heart.

The lawn needs cutting but the mower broke. Another thing that will have to go untended. I wrap the end of a long strand of my dark hair around my finger, twisting and pulling it tight, a nervous habit I've tried to break but which lately seems to be happening more often. At least the wildflowers from the seeds my mom spread years ago came up this summer right on cue.

There's a rustling in the bushes… just past my mother's flower beds. My palms feel damp as I press them against the table, standing from my seat. Is it one of them? The man that left the note? Have they come to collect what is owed?

A mangy, orange-striped tomcat stalks out of the leaves. He glances up at the window, giving an ornery meow.

I fall back down onto my seat, willing my racing heart to slow. "It's just a cat, Kylie. Just a cat."

Today it might be a grouchy tabby, but in time, they will come.

I push the thought from my mind. I can't bear the thought of what I'll be forced to do. This is exactly why I found the new job. The pay is generous. Due to recent unseemly rumors finding their way around the village, my new employers have had difficulty finding home help. I'm hoping they'll become attached to me enough to protect me.

My grandmother calls to me from her bed. *"Tesoro,* sweetheart, is that you?"

"Yes. I just got home." I kick off my boots, neatly placing them by the back door. Padding down the hall in my socked feet, I head to her room. She's still buried in the piles of quilts I tucked around her this morning. Has she even moved? Is it possible she looks more frail than when I left her?

I hide the worry from my face with a bright smile. "Would you like some tea?"

"Tea is for old ladies." She shakes her head. "My spirit needs wine. *Pane vino e zucchero,* please."

Her favorite snack, bread covered in wine and dipped in sugar. I should make her eat some meat or cheese with it, but I haven't been to the store today.

I nod. "Bread and wine it is."

"Thank you, Kylie."

"Only the best for you, Nonna."

In the kitchen, I cut a slice of bread, putting it on my mother's beloved gold-rimmed china, little pink roses dancing along the plate's edge, a cherished possession she brought back from the States with her. Along with my short stature and round hips and a handful of photographs, the dishes complete the items I have to remember my mother by.

I sprinkle the bread with tons of sugar, the way Nonna likes it, and pour wine on top until the sugar is colored. I bring it to her on a tray with a fork, knife, linen napkin, and a jar filled with a bunch of wildflowers I picked from the backyard.

Time to tell Nonna the good news.

Her graying brow is perfectly manicured, and her silvery hair curls around her head like a halo. At sixty-two, she's still a beautiful woman with her sparkling blue eyes and high cheekbones. Even though she's spent the day alone, she's taken the care to apply a touch of rouge to her cheeks and a bit of gloss on her lips.

"Here you go." I set the tray down on the bed beside her, helping her to sit up to eat. I sink down onto the bed beside her.

She takes a delicate bite of the bread. "Perfect. Thank you."

"Nonna, I got a job today."

Her graying brow furrows. "Don't you have a job?"

"Yes, but working at the drugstore doesn't pay as well as this new thing I've found." I finger the soft petals of a wild orange lily. My stomach flips with nerves, wondering how much to tell her.

I don't want her to worry.

"But the pharmacy is dependable, no? You're the third generation of Barone women to work there. Your mother and I got by on what we made there." She gestures to her tray. "Look! We eat like royalty around here. We're doing just fine."

"Yes. You're right. It's dependable." My legacy... to work at the corner pharmacy in town, in walking distance from our tiny yellow cottage my grandmother was born in. "But I found a better one."

Her brow now knits with clear disapproval. "Where is this wonderful new job?" She runs the tines of her fork around the plate, collecting sugar crystals on her bread.

"It's as a housekeeper. For a very wealthy family." Prickles dance down the back of my neck as I get closer to revealing the name of my new boss.

"For who?" She eyes me, still not convinced I should quit the pharmacy.

A tightness forms in my throat and I clear it away. I hold her gaze. "The Accardis."

A look I can't quite read passes over her lined face. "Hmm... the Accardis. You say they are paying you well?"

"Yes. Why?"

She gives a shrug of her thin shoulders. "I thought they were broke. Spent up all their mom's money after she passed. Beautiful Bella. Those boys were lost after she passed."

A silence stretches between us as we think of my own absent mother. I can't help the guilt I feel. I know it's irrational, but the backs of my eyes burn with unshed tears when I think of her.

I blink them away. "Yes. But the Accardis have come into a new fortune. Apparently, they've got some new business deal. Pretty lucrative, from what I've heard."

Nonna makes the sound she makes when she disapproves of something. "Hmph." She shakes her head. "More like that generous dowry they got when they arranged for their daughter Emilia to marry one of those Bachman boys."

"The Bachmans are quickly becoming the most powerful family in Italy. Only my grandmother has the balls to call the men of the Bachman brotherhood 'boys,'" I laugh. "And I don't care where the Accardis get their money, as long as some of it gets into our pockets."

Nonna eyes me. "Well, you've got balls too and you know who you get them from. Now, are you going to tell me why you need more money? Do we have some bills I don't know about?"

I think of the threatening note, the cat in the bushes I thought was a dangerous man, and shake my head. "Nothing to worry about.

Just wanting, you know, some nicer things for us." I kiss her cheek, clearing the tray from her lap.

In the kitchen, I rinse the wine from my mother's china plate.

How do I tell Nonna that my uncle, her beloved son, my mother's only sibling, has stolen from the wrong men? She still thinks of Marco, now a middle-aged man, as her baby, buying the lie he sold her years ago that he's off traveling the world. In reality, he's most likely passed out behind the train tracks on the outskirts of the village, out of his mind from the drugs he bought from the Meralo clan.

Bought being an exaggeration.

The Meralos gave my uncle Marco an advance on his drugs, then a second, then a third. Their business is dirty: get someone hooked on their goods, feed them more and more until the buyer is in over their heads and then go to the family to collect the debt.

Marco owes them a lot of money. Money the Meralos have come to me to repay. They know I don't have the money and there's only one thing they are willing to take to clear the debt. I can't tell my grandmother the truth, it would break her heart. So I let her think Marco is still traveling the world.

And I hope to God she doesn't find one of the pretty little notes the Meralos have been leaving on our front door before I have time to tear it up and toss it out.

The morning brings gloom and rain, the perfect backdrop for walking up the gravel drive of the Accardis' haunted-looking mansion. Black shutters hang over peeling green paint. The over-grown brush has recently been cleared away from the house. The gardens are still in turmoil, weeds choking the late Bella Accardis' rosebushes as they struggle to survive.

My fingers grip the leather strap of my purse as I stand before the massive black front doors, deep rectangles in the wood. I take a closer look at the carvings in the doorhandle.

The carvings are angels.

Angels...

They have to be a good sign, right? Nonna says I'm always trying to find the good in the bad, the hope in the dark. I run a finger over the knob, tracing the wings of a tiny, long-haired angel.

"You're my good luck," I say.

The door swings open. I step back, snapping my hand away. An angry looking man about my age stands in the doorway, his dark hair hanging over one of his bright green eyes.

There's a growl in his voice. "You're late."

"Am I?" I glance down at the watch on my wrist, a delicate oval on a thin tan leather band. A gift from my grandmother. It's nine a.m. "I'm right on time—"

My words cut off as a glint of silver catches my eye. He looks right at me, dragging the sharp end of a metal hook down the frame of the door.

The hook is the man's hand. *Deep breaths.* I drag my gaze from the hook to meet his eye. So, the rumors are true.

"Antonio?" I ask.

He gives a grunt in reply.

I hold out my hand to shake his remaining one. "Pleasure to meet you. I'm Kylie. I did a phone interview with your father? He hired me, told me to be here at nine, and here I am." I repeat, "Right on time."

He looks at my hand and dismisses it with a deeper grunt. I pull it away.

"Kylie?" he says. "What kind of name is that? American?"

I shrug. "My mom lived in the States for a long time. She gave it to me."

His nose wrinkles with distaste. "You sound American too."

"I lived there till I was ten. Then...umm..." My voice feels shaky, and I pause to steady it before I speak again. "My mother brought me back here to live with my grandmother."

"I know. It's a small village. Everyone knows everyone's story." He eyes me. "And your mom is gone."

Okay, the tales of the Accardis' oldest son having no manners are also true. I try to smile. "Yeah. I heard something about that."

"My mother is gone too." Pain tugs at the corners of his eyes as he speaks. "But you know that. Everyone does."

"I guess we have that in common," I say, finding the perfect time to start forming that layer of protection I'm hoping for. "Motherless, and we both hate the Meralos."

"You hate them?" A nasty grin curls at his lips. "You don't look like you could hate anyone. Even after what they're doing to you."

"Maybe not." I don't want the story of my uncle getting back to Nonna. I hold back, giving a question as an answer. "What have you heard?"

His green eyes study my face. "Heard they got your uncle hooked on some nasty shit. Then stuck you with the bill."

So, people are talking. Does everyone already know? How can I protect the one person I love from finding out? I think of the notes. One every afternoon for two weeks now when I got home from the pharmacy, making demands of me. *Your family owes us. You know what we want.*

My stomach sinks. I try to keep my feelings off my face. "Yep. That's about right. But please. Don't tell anyone. If word got back to my grandmother, she'd be crushed."

His jade-green eyes flash. "Guess you're hoping for some protection along with that fat paycheck. Aren't you?"

Ice trips down my spine as he exposes my truth. My tongue feels tied.

"Well, am I calling it like it is?" He stares at me.

My answer is a whisper. "Yes."

He gives a nod.

"Maybe we can help each other out." He opens the door wider with his good hand. "Come on in, Cinderella."

I push past his dark ego, entering the dimly lit home. The place must have been gorgeous back in the days when Bella Accardis' money and elegant touch graced it with their presence.

Now it's filled with cobwebs and dust and grime. My little neat-freak heart bangs against my rib cage. I love to make things beautiful.

Time to get to work.

Antonio shows me where the cleaning supplies are, a cupboard just as dusty and neglected as the rest of the house. Then he leaves me to clean his house and wonder what he meant by *helping each other out*.

I know by the cunning look in his eyes it won't be long before I find out.

2

annon

I FEEL warm skin against mine as I open my eyes. Dread fills me as I roll away from last night's mistake. Who's in my bed this morning? I lift my head from my arm and take a glance.

Long blonde hair trails down the very bare back of a woman lying on her side, her waist dipping in a deep curve. Beautiful. She could pass for thirty but must be closer to forty.

What was her name? Cat? Kate?

Running a hand over my bare chest, I glance under the sheets. Naked as the day I was born.

I lift the comforter, moving across the mattress with stealth so as not to wake my guest. I've not had my espresso and am in no mood for the uncomfortable morning-after small talk.

Shower time.

Hot water washes over me as I scrub the scent of her perfume from my skin. I comb my hair back, trim my beard, and choose a button-down in my favorite color. Black. Pure perfection with no complications.

I return to the bedroom, hoping she's slipped into last night's wrinkled clothing and out my door.

Nope. Still here. Cat. I'm sure it was Cat.

"Um, sweetheart?" I lean down, touching her shoulder. A tattoo sits just below my fingertips. A swirling letter K. Now I remember. Kat with a K; that's what she said when I poured her a second shot of silver tequila at the bar.

I never sleep with members but will occasionally make an exception for a guest because it's likely I'll never see that person again. Each guest is only allowed one visit per year unless they're given a special exception—their member purchases them a key from me—but I rarely allow this, wanting the members to be our main focus.

One of the members of my club, an entrepreneur named Thomas, made his fortune creating an upscale American hotel chain. His wife thinks he's here in Italy expanding the business.

He's not. He's here for my club.

Thomas and Kat met in Rome and became fast friends. Thomas invests in upstarts and Kat's paired up with him to create her own hair extension line. I'm not so sure how much success they'll have; one of her long, fake locks got caught in my fingers last night when I was taking her from behind and tugged her hair too hard. Last night, Kat came as Thomas' guest.

I clear my throat. "Wake up."

"Hmm?" She blinks awake, stretching and yawning, her expensive, enhanced lips swollen from our night. Her gaze follows me from the top of my head, my wet hair combed back, down the plane of my chest to the tips of my boots. "Hey, baby. Last night was amazing."

She's not wrong. The sex was phenomenal. I'd never met this woman before but somehow our bodies acted as if they were familiar with one another. Instinctively, we knew how to please each other. There was a connection.

But now, it's behind us. Her time to be here in my personal space has long since passed. My skin starts to crawl. It always does on the mornings they spend the night and stay past sunrise. I didn't think she'd be one of those.

I've misread.

My business relies on my instincts, my sixth sense. I hate when I get it wrong. When I let her into my bed last night, I thought she was a one-nighter, just one of the women who wanted a one-time hook-up with *the* Cannon Bachman, owner of Fire, Italy's hottest kink club.

I usually have a pretty good read of people, but now she's snuggling deeper into my dove-gray linen duvet and calling me... *baby.* I was so tired last night from hosting back-to-back events that I don't remember much from the night, other than coming hard, right after her.

It's time for her to go.

"Sweetheart." The cool metal of my watch glides around my wrist and I snap the clasp. "I start my day at six sharp. Last night was amazing. But you've got to go."

She throws me a plump pout. "You don't even have time for breakfast?"

"Tell you what, make yourself comfortable. Take a shower. Call over to the kitchen and order whatever you want, then come up to the

Mafia Fire   13

main house and I'll have them call you a car. The espresso is better than anything you can get in Rome. I highly recommend it."

"K, baby." She pulls the covers up to her chin.

"Take your time. Enjoy the food. And one more thing, sweetheart—"

She rolls sultry, fuck-me eyes up to my face. "Yes?"

I give her a feral smile. "Don't call me baby."

Her gaze falls.

My brother Liam constantly tells me I need to grow a filter, that he despises rudeness, that I need to think before I speak. But some things just need to be said.

I'm nobody's baby.

There's only one woman in this world who I allowed to call me baby, and she's been gone for ten years.

I close the bedroom door behind me, leaving Kat and my memories behind me as I start my day.

The sun warms my skin, my boots crunching the stones on the path. Kat's little silver sports car is parked in front of the guesthouse I converted to be my current haven. Maybe I'll get a proper house one day. For now, I'm all about work.

I kick a tire. I'll be sure the next woman leaves before the sun comes up.

The path turns from loose stones to concrete as I wind through the garden to the front door of the club. I glance up at the giant black metal letters hanging from the stone wall of the hundred-year-old mansion I've renovated into Fire. At dusk, the sign comes to life, greeting our guests with real burning flames.

We bring the heat to Italy.

Fire is not your typical nightclub, not only for what we do inside, but for where it is. When I first had the idea for the club, I found a luxurious historic estate hidden in the mountains, a stone wall with iron gates protecting the property. When I first pulled up to the stone mansion surrounded by lush olive groves, I'd had one thought...

Sexy as hell.

Every time I lay eyes on that burning sign, I can't stop the grin that spreads across my face. My hand reaches out for one of the metal door handles I had commissioned, flames in the shape of angel wings. I start to pull on the heavy, dark-wood door.

Booker, a bouncer in his thirties with a smoothly shaved head and a solid build, beats me to it, holding the door open for me. "Morning, boss," he says in his South African accent, handing me my double espresso like he does every day at this time. The earthy scent of coffee hits me, the cup hot in my hand. "Thanks, man. What are we reading today?"

"Grapes of Wrath." He holds up the green, leather-bound novel he'd had tucked beneath one big-muscled arm. "One from Emilia's mother's collection. She said it's a must-read. A classic." My brother, Emilia's husband, turned a room in his house into her private library. He spares no expense when it comes to her.

"Emilia's a good woman." My open palm hits his in a high-five as I step over the threshold. "My brother's a lucky man."

"The luckiest. Emilia's the best." Booker gets a certain tone when he says her name, the one all the guys use when they talk about Emilia, like he'd kill for her if he had to. And he would. They all would.

"She is." My voice feels tight. Envy? I tip a stream of the hot espresso past my lips. "That she is."

Everyone loves Emilia.

Sometimes it's hard to watch her and my brother together. I get that familiar ache in my chest, just seeing the way he holds her... a feeling I felt for someone long ago, but haven't since and never will again.

Am I lonely?

There's a woman in my bed almost every night. I'm surrounded by the country's most beautiful women. I own a kink club for God's sake, gorgeous females ever at my service.

How can I be lonely?

Besides, I've got my baby to keep me company. Fire.

I pat Booker on the shoulder as I pass through the entryway, saying the same thing I say every morning. "Let's bring the heat tonight."

I look up at the gas-powered chandeliers hanging from the high tin-paneled ceiling, another one of my visions for the place. Each night they come to life, tiny flames licking the air, their reflections dancing against the metal ceiling.

Beautiful.

When people hear the term kink club, their minds drift to somewhere dark and underground, a palace of shame to be hidden from the world.

Not my club.

Hidden from the world, yes. It takes a full year to be vetted to join unless you have an in with me and my family. But dark and dingy and shameful?

Hell no.

I'm proud of my place. I started small, inviting friends and family to join first. Now, socialites from all over the world fly in, some only to experience one night at my club. It's a place so beautiful, you could bring your mother. Might be awkward as hell for you, but you could bring her. It's that nice.

My club is spotless. After every use, each room goes through a top to bottom clean and disinfect. And we're clean in more ways than one. No drugs. No smoking—which used to piss Liam off when he was a regular, before he met Emilia and she made him kick the cigarettes.

This morning, I'm conducting interviews. With every new member we accept, I hire an employee to cater to just that client and make sure each and every one of their needs is met. This team is called my one-on-ones and I need at least a dozen newbies.

I hire two of the twelve I interview. A tall man from Russia with perfect manners and an eloquent woman who's lived down the road her whole life. It took her two years to summon the courage to interview.

I take my lunch with Booker, the two of us going casual by ordering steaks at the bar, sitting side by side on barstools, him with his book open on the bar top, me with my laptop, looking over the schedule for six months from now.

"Hey, yo!"

"Hey yourself." I look up from my computer to find Tie grinning at me. He's a tall, thin man with blue-black hair and a striking smile. His nickname comes from his talent for shibari, the ancient Japanese rope-tying technique. He has a partners class tonight and came in early to prepare.

Tie pauses by the bar, eyeing me like he knows something I don't.

"What?"

"Cannon, you got company over at the guesthouse?" His mother, an American, raised him in Japan so he could be close to his father. His accent dips between the two worlds.

"This morning, but not anymore," I say. "Why?"

Tie gives me one of those big, teasing grins he's known for. "There's a silver Porsche parked outside the guesthouse. Last time I checked, that's your house."

"Damn. You kidding me, Tie?" I close my laptop, stand from my barstool, and slip the computer under my arm. Kat should have left hours ago.

He calls over his shoulder, "Nope. Saw it on my way in."

Booker's eyes leave the page, his gaze dragging up to mine as he raises a brow at me. "A woman staying at your place twelve whole hours?" He shakes his head. "That's some kind of record for you."

I pat my bouncer's shoulder as I leave. "Not by my choice, Booker. Thought I kicked her out this morning."

He goes back to his book. "Well, looks like you have some more kicking out to do."

"Yeah. It does, doesn't it?"

Kat with a K is in for another dose of my filter-less truth telling. I step outside. The afternoon is warm and overcast, clouds passing slowly by the sun.

When I reach the guesthouse, her car is already gone.

There's a note taped to my shiny black front door.

No man writes me off—

Not even the great Cannon Bachman.

I'll be back.

Kat

"Jesus." I rip the note off the door, crumpling it in my hand, wondering what her deal is. "Well, at least I got the name right."

It's very clear now. Kat with a K is going to be a Problem with a capital P.

3

K *ylie*

I PLACE the last bottle of window cleaner on the metal shelving unit in the little cleaning closet I found off the kitchen. I step back and smile, admiring the once jumbled supplies that now neatly line the shelves, their labels turned forward for easy identifying.

Time to mop.

I left this job for the end of the day, not only because it made sense to clean the floors after my dusting, but because I love saving the best for last. Oh, the reward of mopping these floors back to beauty! The wood is worn, yes, but removing the layer of grime and shining them up with my favorite oil soap is going to leave them lustrous and beautiful, bringing me peace and happiness.

I drag an old mop bucket out from behind a pile of brooms. At least it has wheels; I'm going to need them. This house is huge. I turn the rusty old spigot and clear, warm water runs out. As the bucket fills, I grab discarded mops and brooms and hang them on their rightful hooks on the wall.

Bootsteps lure me from my meditative organization, signaling an Accardi man is passing my closet. I find myself holding my breath, waiting for him to pass. They've left me alone all day, and now I cut the water, hoping against hope.

No such luck.

A brother with gray eyes—Silas, I think—pops his head into the open closet door. "There you are. I've looked everywhere. I'd accuse you of hiding out in here all day, but the entire house smells like lemon so I'm guessing you have been working."

I roll the now-filled bucket to the center of the closet, indicating I'm ready for him to leave.

"Just getting ready to mop." I push a strand of hair that's loosened from my ponytail back from my face with the clean back of my hand. "Can I help you?"

He moves out of my way, letting me pass into the hall. He glances around at the polished wood, the sparkling glass on the family picture frames. "Nicely done."

"Thank you."

His back facing the cleaning closet, his broad shoulders fill the doorframe. The hairs on the back of my neck stand on end. I repeat myself, eager to have him gone. "How can I help you?"

He tilts his head in the direction of the front of the house. "Antonio wants you. He's in the dining room."

Antonio. The man with the hook for a hand and bright green eyes that promised me we would be helping one another out. The time for me to pay back the favor of employing me has already come.

"The water is still warm," I stall. "Would it be okay to mop first?"

Silas' dark brow knits over his storm-cloud eyes. "This house has eleven rooms in it. Besides the fact it will take you the rest of the night to mop, my brother hates to be kept waiting, and he already has been while I've been looking for you. I'm sure he's tapping that hook against the dining table right now, agitated as hell." He gives a laugh.

There's an edge to his joke that makes my skin feel prickly. "Okay. Let me just wash my hands and I'll be right there."

"Maybe skip the handwash and just head on in."

"O...kay." I wipe the dust as best I can on my apron.

He steps aside, letting me pass. I turn left, my feet softly moving along the threadbare carpet runner. His gaze feels heavy on my back as I go, making the hairs on my arms stand on end.

The dining room door is closed.

Knocking feels like a job on its own. I lift my hand but before my knuckles can hit the wood, a gruff voice calls to me.

"Come in."

I thought I'd moved quietly down the hall, but I guess not. I open the door. Antonio sits at the head of the long, gleaming table I earlier brought back to life with lemon polish.

His dark hair hangs over one eye, down to his shoulders. He tilts his face up from his paperwork, green eyes penetrating mine. "Cinderella. We finally found you."

My throat feels tight and I swallow hard, forcing my words to come. "Yes. Sorry for the delay."

"You can start by walking into the room. I don't bite." He taps the sharp hook against the wood table. "But I do scratch."

I hold in a nervous giggle, hoping it was a joke. "How can I help you?"

"That's a phrase I like to hear." He eases back against his chair, slinking an arm around the back of it. The silver hook hangs down, shiny and bright against the crimson velvet. "With this job—we pay more than you could dream of getting elsewhere. Let me be blunt. We pay so well because our money is buying your discretion. What you see or hear within these walls is never to leave here. Understood?"

"Yes." The hook catches my eye. The silver around the cuff is tarnished. A simple fix. "Sir."

"Great. So we are helping you and now, I need you to help me." He beckons me with the hook hand. "Come closer."

I eye the sideboard to his left. The one that holds the family's collection of silver flatware. I glance back at his hook.

Impatience storms into his tone. "Am I that scary that all you can do is stare at my hook and act as if it's taken your tongue? Say something."

"No. Sir. It's just... it's just that I noticed your hook." I can't believe I'm doing this as I nod to the appendage. "It's made of real silver."

He furrows his brow at me. "And?"

"Well, sir, it's a bit tarnished. And I just think it's a shame not to care for the metal properly. There's a simple paste in that cabinet right behind you. I found it this morning when I was polishing the wood. It'd only take me a minute. I hope I'm not overstepping, but I could shine it right up."

"Oh." For a beat of a second the hardness leaves his eyes, the edge disappearing from his tone. "Fine then. If you feel you must."

I dash around his chair, finding the silver polish and a white rag, the cotton clean and soft in my fingers. I move to the chair beside him, prepping my cloth.

He eyes me.

I hold out my hand. "May I?"

"Just. Be careful. It's sharp." The concern in his voice surprises me. He lays the cool metal in my open palm.

I hold it gently, working the polish over the silver. Each time I wipe it away, the pewter haze disappears, leaving behind gleaming metal.

Satisfied with my work, I lay the rag on the table. "See? Good as new."

He withdraws his hook from my hand. There's a soft gruffness to his voice as he thanks me. "Thank you."

I can feel his eyes on me as I move to the sideboard, putting the polish back. The cloth I'll add to the mountain of age-yellowed linens I'm preparing to bleach and wash.

I hover by the chair. "And what was it you wanted me to do for you?"

"Sit."

I sit.

"There's a club that the Bachmans own. Fire. Have you heard of it?"

My virgin heart pitter-patters, heat rising in my face as I think of the things I've heard about the secretive sex club hidden behind huge iron gates at the top of a mountain. "Um... a little. Why?"

"I need you to go there tonight. To deliver a package for me. Can you do that?"

"I thought only members were allowed to step foot behind that stone wall. How will I get in?"

"I have a guest pass for you." From the breast pocket of his shirt he pulls out a black skeleton key tied to a gold ribbon. He slides it across the table to me.

I stare down at it. Seems harmless. It's just a key. But I feel its sensual energy, the danger behind accepting the request.

"Go on. Take it."

I pinch the ribbon between my finger and thumb, lifting it. It dangles in the air. Are those real black sea pearls set into its curving handle? The bit at the bottom that fits into the lock is shaped in a flame, its top breaking into two tips.

I run a finger over the metal. "It almost looks like angel wings."

"There are no angels at Fire. Only sex-obsessed devils—" He pauses, eyeing the blush rising in my face. "Never mind. You'll be fine. You only have to deliver this package." From the seat beside him, he lifts a rectangle the size of a brick, wrapped in brown paper. He slides the package across the table as he did the key. "A man will meet you by the first-floor elevator."

"How will I know which man is the right man?"

"You'll recognize his face. He's the Head of State."

The Head of State? Is he serious? I look up from the package to Antonio's stoic face. He's not joking.

I lift the package. It's lighter than I anticipated. I know better than to ask what's inside. They pay me for my discretion. I hold it in my palm, my fingers curling around it.

I have questions that do need to be asked if I'm going to succeed in this mission. "What do I wear? What time do I go? Do I just deliver and leave, or am I supposed to fit in somehow?"

His gaze travels from my lips to my full hips. "You'll fit in fine. Just wear something sexy. Red would look good on you."

"Sexy?" I think of my wardrobe of jeans and sweats and casual tops. I took the job at the pharmacy right out of school. My grandmother is my roommate. Caring for her is my only social event at the moment. "I'm sorry. I don't think I have that."

"My sister, Emilia. She left a few dresses in her bedroom upstairs. There's a red gown with a slit up the side. She brought it back here to store it. Didn't want it at her house." His eyes meet mine and the anger, the hardness in him returns. A mean smile curls at his lips. "Said she couldn't part with it because she has wonderful and terrible memories of that dress."

Something tugs at the back of my mind. A memory of some story Nonna was telling me months ago over a pizza Margherita I'd made for us. A red gown. A brother who touched his sister where he shouldn't have. The revenge of a Bachman husband.

I can't stop the loud, gasping intake of breath that rushes into my lungs. I'd written off Nonna's story as town gossip and completely forgotten about it, but now...

The real devil sits across from me. Antonio Accardi. Rumors fly around the village about the man who taunted his sister, Emilia, when she lived here with him, touching her where he shouldn't, and of how her new husband, Liam Bachman, cut off Antonio's hand in revenge.

I blurt the words out. "It's true?"

"It's true. Liam didn't like the story my sister told him. And now, I have this." He waves at me with the shiny hook.

I nod, looking away from him and the hook I just polished.

Why had I not put this together before? Antonio Accardi, the oldest brother who touched his sister's breasts, then when her husband

Liam found out about it, he came to this mansion, maybe even in this room where I sit now, and... cut... this man's hand off of his body.

A shiver runs through me, my spine tingling. I polished that hook...

Heat washes over my skin. The prickles are back. The spacious room suddenly seems very small.

Still... there's something in his gaze, the way his tone was softened by my kindness. He can't be all bad behind those hard green eyes, can he?

I stand, clearing my throat. "We all make mistakes, I suppose." My knees feel weak. "May I go get the dress?"

"Yes. Why don't you call it a day. Head home early and get ready. I'll have one of our cars pick you up at seven."

Seven. Nonna goes to bed early, but at seven, she'll still be awake. "I care for my grandmother, and I'd prefer not to leave the house at night until I have her tucked safely in her bed. Would it be alright to make it eight? Please?" I ask.

He nods. "Fine. She's lucky to have you."

"Thank you." See... he's not all bad. I leave the cloth on the table. My hands are shaking too bad to pick it up. I clutch the package in the other hand, my palms growing damp against the brown paper packaging.

My fingers curl around the polished banister, a lingering lemon scent in the air. I grip it for support as I make my way up to Emilia Accardis' old bedroom. This is where he may have touched her. Hurt people hurt people. What went on within these walls after their mother died? I've heard their father is a harsh man. Without a loving parent... no child comes out unscathed, but still...

I've taken a job working for one monster in the hopes of gaining protection from another. Now, I have to deliver a package to the Bachman club, a place run by dangerous men.

Hand-cutting-off kind of men.

Monsters surround me.

Have I gotten myself into deeper waters, trying to tread out of danger?

I give the bed a wide berth, unsure if it's where the crime took place. I open the closet door. The bright red gown grabs my eye at once, putting every other item hanging here to shame.

"My God." I take the hanger off the rack, holding the gown high, careful not to let it brush against the floors I haven't cleaned yet. The silk feels like cool water as it slips between my fingers. "It's gorgeous."

My stomach tightens. This is *the* dress. The one her brother touched her in, the one that led to his gruesome punishment.

And tonight, I'm going to wear this dress to walk my virgin self into a kink club, when I've never even been kissed, and deliver a package I'm pretty sure has something illegal in it, to our country's Head of State.

The knot in my stomach twists, hard.

I have no other choice.

I need to get Antonio Accardi on my side so when the time comes, when the Meralos come to collect the one thing I can't give them, I can ask for his protection.

I can't let the Meralos win. The consequences would be devastating. I'd surely drown.

The antique full-length mirror that stands in the corner of Emilia's room sends my reflection back to me. My face is a mask of determination. I hold the dress in one hand, still holding the package in the other.

My cloak and my weapon. I'm going to war.

As much as my heart hurts for whatever messed-up childhood these Accardis had, I'm feeling very certain I've chosen the wrong alliance.

Maybe I need to swim in a new direction.

4

annon

GRACE, the curly-haired favorite of my Events Coordinators, looks to me. "Blue or black napkins for Extravagance?" She holds up two paper napkins, the club's emblem stamped in the center of each in gold leaf.

"Black. Always."

"That's what I thought." She smiles, tucking the samples back in her massive binder, colorful tags neatly lined up down the side. The girl is organized. Anally so. So much so I've had to bite my tongue to keep from jokingly suggesting she play in the plug room on one of our staff play evenings. But...

I don't cross that line with my employees. Jokingly or otherwise.

"I'll leave this with you." She slips a photo from her binder, passing it over the bar top. She taps the polished wood with the tip of her glossy red nail. "I need to know by tomorrow whether you're going with the decorative chains or whips for the event. It's in two weeks, you know."

I slide the picture back. I don't need to see it. "Easy. Both."

"Of course you would say that, sir." She gives me a smile and a giggle, taking her photo back as she leaves.

I watch her walk away, curves hugged by a tight black pencil skirt. Shame I don't play with employees. She'd love the feeling of a cold metal toy inside her. I'm sure of it.

A member of my undercover security team hovers in the corner of my eye, dressed in plainclothes: a black suit, the top three buttons of his collar undone, his dark hair gelled back in a ponytail. As soon as Grace is out of earshot, he leans down, his voice low in my ear. "We have an issue."

I turn to him with a sigh. "You know how much I hate to hear you say that." Of course there're kinks when running a kink club, but I prefer my nights to run smoothly. "What do you have for me."

"A girl."

"A girl?" I glance around the room. We're surrounded by dozens of beautiful women, their clothing ranging from none, to barely-there lingerie, to floor-length evening gowns. I don't see anyone who could be described as a girl. "What girl?"

"About three minutes ago, a young girl dressed in street clothes came to the door with a black pearl guest passkey. We'd never seen her before and she wasn't with a client so we knew to keep an eye on her. She went straight to the elevators and removed a package about the size and shape of a brick, wrapped in brown paper, from inside her sweatshirt. She stood there for a moment, then hid the package behind the pots of one of our Monstera plants."

She better not have hurt my Monstera. Those things cost a fortune. I run a hand over my brow. "Did you retrieve the package?"

He shakes his head. "We can't right now. The Head of State is there, lingering, waiting on someone. I have someone posted by the elevator bay, eyes on that plant, ready to retrieve the parcel as soon as he leaves."

"Good. Where is the girl now?"

His finger goes to his ear. He presses the button on the hidden device, then waits, his lips pursing as he listens.

He looks at me. "Headed this way."

"Let me know when you have the package."

"Yes, sir." He nods. "And the girl?"

"Take care of her." Speak of the devil... A curvy little brunette comes dashing down the hall. Something about her makes me change my mind before he answers me. "Actually, I'll take care of the girl."

"Yes, sir." He takes his leave.

The girl spots me behind the bar and rushes over.

"Is there a manager here? I really need to apply for a job." Her heart-shaped face turns to me, hazel eyes filled with innocence begging me. Her short bubblegum-pink nails tap the bar as she shifts her weight on white sneakers. "Like, yesterday."

She doesn't look a day over twenty. And her clothing—jeans and a loose sweatshirt—tells me she doesn't understand the first thing about this club or what we do here. My job applicants wear their sexiest, very best couture knockoffs to apply here, knowing if I accept them, they'll soon be able to afford the real thing.

"You want a job?" I ask.

"Yes," she nods.

I take in her fresh-faced innocence. "Here?" I ask.

She gives me a flash of a nervous look. "Yes, sir."

I laugh, wiping down the bar. "I think you'd better head back to town. I think there's a children's clothing boutique that might be hiring."

She slaps a palm on the bar top, pleading eyes grabbing mine. "I need a job. Here." The desperation in her voice makes me stop.

I drop the rag, washing my hands in the bar sink. I dry them on a fresh towel. "Come. Sit. Tell me why you're really here. Who told you about this place?" Perhaps the friend that sent her with the mystery package, that best not be poisoning my plant?

Her eyes dart right, then left as she sinks onto a stool. "I, um, don't know. Just a friend, you know. They said the pay was good."

"What's their name?" I know every single employee by face and name. I do all the hiring, male and female dancers, bartenders, scene masters. I handpicked each person on my diverse staff. They all have three things in common. They're hard working, they want to improve their station in life, and each has an almost inhuman ability to be discreet.

Discretion is *everything* in this business.

The housewife of a prominent mobster should be free to come to my club and be a pretty little kitty for the night, complete with a tail and velvet ears—with her husband's permission of course—without fear that she'll later bump into someone in town who will taunt her about her kink.

"Who sent you?" I ask again.

She shakes her head, looking away. "Oh, they said not to say."

She's a terrible liar. I get the feeling she's not very practiced at it. I like that.

"Is that so?" I ask.

She nods. "Yes."

"Can I tell you what I think?" I ask.

She looks like she's trying to hold in a roll of her eyes. "I guess you're going to."

"Yes, I am." I move in closer. I bring my face a beat away from hers. Now I have her attention. Her hazel eyes lock on mine, her rosebud lips parting.

She hangs on my every word.

"I think you're a little girl who's somehow gotten herself into some trouble and you heard whispers of this place and how we protect our own. You want a job here to be able to hide out, as a way to protect yourself."

The color drains from her face as I speak. She looks away.

I'm dead right.

I slide a few fingers under her chin. Her skin is smooth, cool to the touch. Her eyes brighten with heat as I tilt her gaze up to meet mine.

"Answer me," I demand. "Is that why you're here?"

She shakes her head again, preparing to tell another lie. "No. I... um... I..." Her face falls, her lips trembling as her eyes fill with tears. "Yes. Okay? I'm in trouble. And I have a job, but I... the boss and I don't see eye to eye on things."

I let my hand drop as I stare at her, debating whether to kick her out or ask her further questions. Right now, my gut is telling me to show this curvy brunette the door. Send this gorgeous damsel in distress on her way. To not get further involved.

But my cock is stirring as she sinks pearly white teeth into that full bottom lip of hers. And he says...

Game on.

I stare at the girl before me, wondering how the hell she got tied up in whatever mess she's in. The naivety radiates from her. She doesn't belong in a place like Fire. It'll be fun to play with her a bit as I find out exactly what she's doing here.

I grab a polished apple from a bowl of fruit on the bar, its skin smooth and cool in my hand. "Walk with me."

"Alright." She trips to keep up with my long strides as we make our way deeper into the mansion.

Her gaze wanders as we go along. The long halls are wallpapered in a red brocade, gold and silver patterns rising from the silk. Persian wool rugs, their patterns of deep reds and blues and yellows, protect the gleaming wood floors. Black-and-white photographs of sexy models line the walls, not a speck of dust on their shiny black frames.

"You think you could work here?" I ask. "What do you want to do?"

"Um, I, ah..."

I glance down at her curves. Gorgeous body under that hoodie. "Dancer?"

"Huh?" She's distracted. Her gaze takes in the photos, flawless photography that captured an evening of magic, bodies contorted in acts of pleasure. "Say again?"

"I asked if you are a dancer. We have two troupes. The Beautiful Men, *Hombre Hermoso,* and The Beautiful Women, *Mujer Hermosa.*

They greet our guests, dancing on my balconies. Naked. Is that why you came?"

"No." She shakes her head, color rising in her cheeks after I said the word naked. "Um. I can't dance but—"

"What job are you here to apply for, then?" I shove open the heavy gloss black door to one of my offices. I hold it open for her, gesturing for her to enter. It's too fun to play with her. I continue my lewd business talk. "To be one of my Clamp Tramps?"

She snakes a glance up at me as she dips past me into the room. "I'm sorry. A... what?"

"It's a nickname we have for a beautiful woman who dresses in fishnet tights and a leotard and places clamps on a client's nipples while they're strapped down."

She stands in the center of the wood and leather room, looking around. "Oh, um, I don't have that kind of... experience, but I could learn."

"Looks to me like you don't have any experience at all." I love watching the rosy hue on her cheeks deepen. "Is that what you've come here to sell?"

Her gaze snaps up to meet mine. "Sell what?"

"Your virginity." I toss the apple from my right hand to my left.

She shoves her hands in the pockets of her sweatshirt, shifting her weight from one sneaker to the other. "Who said I'm a virgin?"

"Your face."

"What do you mean?"

"You're blushing." It's too fun, making her blush.

"I... um... okay, look." She shakes her head, her dark hair falling over her shoulders. "Obviously, I'm in over my head here. I came to you, hoping for a job. I'm a hard worker. I don't have a lot of sexual, um, experience, but—"

"You don't have any sexual experience." I take a bite of the apple, my teeth sinking into the crisp flesh.

She raises a brow. "I didn't say that—"

"I did. You're vanilla. A little vanilla bean."

"Okay, maybe. But I'm a quick learner." She persists despite her discomfort. "I can work nights, weekends, whatever."

She said she doesn't see eye to eye with her boss. Is that who she's in trouble with? "Who do you work for now?"

"I'd rather not say." She looks away.

"I'd rather you didn't ignore my question." I move in closer, putting my hands on her, my fingers lightly trailing down her cheek to her chin. I capture it between my finger and thumb, forcing her gaze to meet mine. "Answer me. Who do you work for?"

"The... The A—ccardis."

The Accardis. My sister-in-law's thug family.

Trash.

I release her chin. "What are you doing working for them?"

She shrugs. "They pay well."

"What do you do for them?" I ask.

"Clean." Her face brightens. "I love to clean."

"Why didn't you say so?" I take another bite of my apple, a bright burst of tang tickling my tongue. I'll bet she tastes twice as sweet as this apple. Intrusive thought... *Focus, Cannon.* "We can use cleaners."

She gives me a suspicious look. "What do cleaners do?"

"Clean."

"Like... just clean?" She takes a hopeful peek at my face. "In their clothing?"

"Yes. Clean in their clothing. Well, uniforms, of course. I have to have everything sexy, beautiful. But the cleaning uniform is..." I think of the cute little French maid costumes I have for the women on my first shift cleaning team. "Modest?"

"I really love to clean. And I love to make things look beautiful. Like, I'm kind of obsessed with it. If I see something that could be made prettier, I can't help myself." Her gaze goes distant like she's remembering something. "The idea nags at me till I fix the thing, whatever it is. And I'm good at doing it on a budget. You know—a few wildflowers in a jar really pretty a place up."

"True. But we don't do tight budgets at Fire. We're a spare-no-expense establishment. My clientele deserves the best. And cleanliness is next to godliness."

"I couldn't agree more." She nods. "I keep my house spotless."

She says it with such conviction, it's the first thing she's said that I believe without question.

"You're hired," I say, ignoring my instincts once more.

How much trouble can this tiny girl be?

Her face brightens. She looks like she wants to burst into applause. "Really?"

"Yes."

She smiles. "Godliness. Funny. I knew I had an angel looking over me today."

"What do you mean?"

"Nothing." She shakes her head. "It's nothing."

I can't help the wicked grin that spreads across my face. "Now for the good part."

"Which is?" she asks.

"You seem to struggle finding words to answer simple questions," I say. "As your new boss, I'm going to help you."

Her gaze shifts, her hands tucking into her pockets. "How?"

She thinks she's gotten away with her botched secret delivery. That I have no idea what she's done and just gave her a job.

Time to close in for the kill.

I move toward her. "I'm going to interrogate you. Find out exactly what you really are doing here tonight. And what was in the package you hid behind the plant and why exactly the Head of State was waiting around our elevators right around the time you were there."

Her skin pales. She didn't know I knew about the package she brought onto my property. She takes a step back. "I don't know. I'm just their cleaner."

Closer. I'm only inches from her now. "That's what you said. But we both know you've lied to me tonight. I want the truth. And I'm going to get it. My way."

"But—"

I hold out the untouched side of the shiny red apple. "Open your mouth."

Uncertainty washes over her face but she parts her lips. I press the untouched side of the fruit against them.

"Bite."

Wide-eyed, she obeys, taking a bite of the apple, her teeth slicing through to the flesh, chewing delicately.

I won't let her play the part of the innocent, unknowing victim when she's not. She made her choices. And now I want to find out why.

"Your eyes will be open, your innocence lost." I take the apple, holding it to my lips, tracing the tip of my tongue over the place she's bitten. I reach for the owl carving on the shelf mounted on the wall, giving it a tug. "Welcome to the Garden of Eden."

5

K *ylie*

THE WALL IS MOVING. I try not to choke on the bite of apple in my mouth. The wall is... *moving?* Why is the wall moving? The shelf, the one with the owl on it, stays in place but everything to the right of that slides like it's on tracks, a stretch of it tucking into itself one panel at a time.

The room revealed is dark, sensual black leather and mahogany wood. The back wall is covered in black leather squares, padded like cushions, tufted with large buttons covered in matching leather in the center of each square.

Potted plants line the right and left walls, filled with lush, green leafy bushes and long thin branches with narrow leaves and bright red flowers. An indoor garden. The garden walls are deep rosewood panels, a redder shade than the glossy brown floors.

On the wall on the left hang all shapes and sizes of brass handles. A few rows of industrial-looking rectangular ones run vertically down the center of the wall, then some more artful pieces, devils' tails and angels' wings. A chandelier hangs from the ceiling, the metal painted a glossy black, its bulbs filling the room with a soft, warm glow.

Above the chandelier there are smoky glass panels. I stand in the center of the room, staring up and watch as the glass comes to life, sliding apart with the quiet whir of a motor, revealing the starry sky above us. The cool night air rushes over me, chill bumps rising on my flesh.

Where am I and how did I go from working at the pharmacy counter only a day ago to being here, in this room, the Garden of Eden... a sex dungeon? Only "dungeon" doesn't give the respect this magical place deserves. What is this room? Why has he brought me here?

A nagging voice plucks at the back of my mind. He brought you here to interrogate you, to punish you. He's a powerful man and he brought you here to teach you a lesson for coming into his club, for doing what Antonio asked.

And I didn't even follow all of Antonio's instructions. I couldn't wear that dress. I brought the package but then I couldn't deliver it, not without knowing what was inside. All this led to my moment of insanity, rushing to who I assumed was a bartender, begging for a job.

Only this man isn't mixing drinks. Feeling his commanding presence beside me, I sense the tall, broad-shouldered man standing so close is very powerful.

His voice is calm but deep, and it awakens something in me as it fills the room. "Take a moment to take it in. What you see. What you feel."

I see him. He's one of the most handsome men I've ever met—there's no questioning that—the kind of man you can't help but to take a second or third glance at. His dark hair is thick with wave. He wears it a touch longer than most men, curling around his ears. His short, dark beard is neatly trimmed, not so much as a speck of lint marring his crisp black shirt. He's built tall, much taller than I am, with a strong, athletic frame.

His open gaze holds mine.

Along with his voice, it's his eyes that captivate me.

They're a deep, dark brown, expressive, naked. Looking in them I get the sense this man lives his life speaking with brutal honesty. He looks right at me now, demanding I speak the truth to him.

"You want to tell me what you are doing here?" He leaves me standing alone in the center of the huge, echoey room as he walks to the back wall, pushing one of the leather buttons in the center of a square. There's a quiet hum as two metal cuffs come out of the wall, one on either side of the square. He glances back at me. "Or am I going to get to have some fun?"

"I—I can't." My heart hammers hard, the sound of blood pumping loud in my ears. Panic fills me, my palms going damp with perspiration. I start to back away.

Do I run? Scream? Cry for help?

Or tell the truth and try to avoid whatever it is those metal cuffs are for?

Antonio pays me for my discretion. He may be a monster, but I feel I owe him some cover from the Bachmans for whatever it is he's doing. I don't know what was in that package. And I don't want to tell this man about my uncle, the Meralos, how I came to work for the Accardis in the first place, then flipped my loyalty from them the moment I walked in the doors of this club, and in my cowardice begged for a job.

My feet seal to the floor, ice forming at the top of my head, working its way down over my entire body. I stand there, frozen.

Are those cuffs for me?

He makes his way back across the room to me, his steps as sleek as a panther's in his all-black outfit. He takes my hand in his. Electricity snaps up my arm at the feel of his strong fingers circling mine. "Cannon Bachman. Owner of Fire. Come this way."

My God... he's the... owner?

He doesn't even know my name, yet he's pulling me, breaking me free from my frozen status, tugging me across this... room. This black leather room with torture devices that pop out of walls. He grabs my shoulders, turning me to face him and pressing my back against the padded leather.

His eyes stay locked with mine as his fingers circle my right wrist. I should fight him off but there is no rise to defend in my body. I just try to breathe. He lifts my arm, placing my wrist in the cold metal.

It closes around me with a *clink*.

He does the same with my other arm.

I stand there, staring at him, my arms stretched above my head, my wrists testing the clamps. My sweatshirt's ridden up, cool air caressing my midriff.

I can feel the heat coming off him, a calm anger he's well in control of. His deep voice vibrates through me as he speaks. "Tell me. Why are you here and what was in that package?"

I think of the parcel I hide behind the plant, not wanting to go through with the transfer to the Head of State. I shake my head. "I don't know what was in that package. That's the truth. And that's why I hid it behind the plant. Because I didn't want to be responsible for delivering something when I didn't know what it was."

He stares at my face a beat. "I believe you."

"Thank you." A slight sense of relief wiggles its way into the tightness knotting in my gut.

"I can only imagine it was your employer, one of the Accardis, who sent you with the package. And judging by the way the Head of State was lingering by the elevators, I assume it was for him. Is that true?"

My teeth sink into my bottom lip. My loyalty to and sense of pity for Antonio is strange, impossible to understand, but still there, underlying my decision-making. "I'm sorry but I really don't want to say."

His gaze darkens. "This is the way this is going to go, little girl. I'm going to ask the questions and for each one you don't answer, there will be a punishment. And that was two questions just now. We're already rolling."

He walks across the room to the wall of handles, tugging one of the rectangular pulls. It is a drawer hidden in the wall. He takes what he wants, leaving the drawer open. In one hand he holds what I can only imagine is a black silicone sex toy.

My spine tingles, ice tripping over my skin. I look away. This is not happening.

Bootsteps make my knees go weak as he returns to me. His hands go to my waist, skin hot and ticklish against the bare flesh of my midriff.

A whimper rises from me. "What are you doing?"

He undoes the button of my jeans, lowering the zipper, exposing the fabric of my pink cotton panties. White heat rushes over my face at his actions. This is not happening...

"Punishing you."

I get a better look at the toy. It's shaped like a scoop. He pushes it down the front of my jeans, over my panties. His fingers are dangerously close to my pussy, but they don't touch me, only the toy does, the pressure of my jeans capturing it against me.

It presses against my clit, the tightness of my half-zipped jeans holding it in place. The eyes I first found so captivating now scare me. He holds a remote in front of my face. And pushes a button.

The toy comes to life, vibrating against me, a shocking, raw sensation that travels to the center of my core, hitting me hard. My eyes close, the back of my head resting against the padded wall. "Oh my God." It feels good but overwhelming, my mind going to liquid, my limbs heating.

The vibrations stop, leaving me dizzy, breathless. I open my eyes. I don't know what to say.

"That was your first punishment for the first of your two unanswered questions." He holds up the remote. "I owe you more."

I don't want more. I plead, "No!"

He pushes the button.

Twice.

The vibrations are much stronger this time, making my jaw go slack, my head going back against the cushioned wall. My clit pulses against the toy, throbbing, clenching, wanting, needing more, but everything inside me wants it to stop.

"Uhn... umm... please..." Again, it stops. My arms start to ache as they stretch above my head. I take in fast, short breaths. I don't know if I want to beg for more or plead with him to never push that button again. My confusion results in one whimpered word. "Please."

"Please what?" His face comes close to mine as he leans over me. He's tall, so much taller than I am.

What do I want? I tilt my head back to look up into his eyes. "I don't know."

"Finally. A little truth out of you." At my words, a slow grin spreads over his shapely lips. How had I not noticed those lips before? The man is beautiful.

And evil.

He stares at me in a way that makes heat flow to my core, the echoes of vibrations still humming there. I can't tear my eyes from his. What's this crazy connection I feel? How has this moment, me chained to a wall, my body under complete control of this striking, intriguing stranger, come to be?

His mouth is a beat away from mine. He moves closer. Is he going to kiss me? My lips part.

This is madness. Chaos. It can't be real.

He moves back, pressing the button. He's turned it on even higher, the waves of electricity shocking my body, making my pussy clench and dampening my panties with arousal, my clit humming like it will burst. I teeter on the edge of the Earth, my entire body tightening, my wrists tugging against the cold, hard metal cuffs.

Will this madness end? Am I going to come?

"Any business with the Accardis ends when you begin your employment here. Understood?"

A whine rises in the back of my throat. I'm so, so close. I don't want the humiliation of climaxing in front of this stranger, but I desperately need the relief.

He ups the power. "Answer me."

Strangled words fall from my mouth. "Y—yes! Yes, sir!"

The toy goes silent, still. It's the best and the worst feeling in the world, all at once. My heart races, my skin feels damp. My knees are weak, my legs like jelly. I stand there, my arms above my head, my breath coming in pants.

He's staring at me. Those dark eyes do something to me. I want to tear my gaze away from his and can't.

He closes in. "I look forward to having you on board," he says, his lips a beat away from mine.

He's going to kiss me.

I need to stop this.

"Don't." The choked whisper leaves my throat. "Please. Don't."

"Don't what?" He pulls back, his brow creased.

I whisper the words. "Don't kiss me."

He looks down at me with those deep brown eyes, demanding more words from me.

"The other stuff, you've already done. You've punished me... but..." The words are silly, babyish, lame, but I force myself to say them anyway. "I've never been kissed before and... my first kiss..." I shake my head, my voice trembling. "It shouldn't be like this."

"Fair enough. Fuck." He studies my face a moment. His gaze lowers to the floor, then drags back up to mine. He makes his decision, giving a nod. He turns on a bootheel, facing away from me. When he turns back to me, he's calm, cool, and collected once more. "I don't know what came over me."

Relief washes through me, but on its edges lies a hint of disappointment. Did I want this man to kiss me?

He gives a growl, running a hand through his thick hair as he mutters, more to himself than me, "What the hell am I doing? I never mess with employees."

I release the breath I didn't realize I'd been holding. I'm grateful for the job even though my interview ended in torture. Trying to be helpful, I offer, "Technically, I'm not yours till tomorrow."

He glances at me. "True."

The sound of a bell rings through the room.

Already on edge, I startle at the noise. "What's that?"

He walks to the drawer as if he needs space between us. His boot-steps sound heavier than before. Frustrated almost. He drops the remote inside. "Dinner."

"At ten at night?" Living with Nonna, I'm used to having dinner before the evening news comes on.

"Why not? We start late around here. Well, the fun starts late. My day begins with the sun."

For a moment he just stands there, his back facing me. I take in the beauty of his silhouette, his height, the way the fabric of his shirt pulls across his broad shoulders. I watch as he runs a hand through his dark hair once more.

He's contemplating something.

What to do with me?

I glance at the toys hanging from the wall. They look... *sting-y.* My stomach flips.

He catches me staring.

Those eyes hold mine.

What is he going to do with me?

His voice fills the room once more, making my knees go weak.

"Are you hungry?" he asks.

Hungry? Of all the plans he might have for me...

Relief and confusion intermingle. Is that what he was deciding? Whether to feed me? This man has me chained to a wall and now asks me if I'm hungry as casually as if we're acquaintances on a lunch break. But I take stock of my nervous body and realize I can't remember the last time I ate.

His bootsteps return quieter than they left me. As he gets closer, I feel my temperature rising. He stops a respectful distance away. "What's it going to be, kid. You want to dine with us or not?"

This is crazy. What am I even doing here, chained to this wall? I should go home. But...

I am hungry. And I find this man... captivating. "Um... okay? I guess?"

"Great. I'll have someone come get you prepared."

"Prepared?" I give a choked laugh. "Am I the dinner?"

His eyes drag over my body in a way that has heat rising between my thighs all over again. "No. But I wish you were. Maybe I'll taste you for my dessert." He gives a shake of his head, like he can't believe what he just said.

Taste me? My clit pulses at the idea of his warm tongue, those shapely lips doing things to me that have never been done. I should say something but I'm too overwhelmed to speak. My tongue feels useless, my mind going hazy with clouds.

"Good. See you there." He gives me one last look, and turns on his bootheel, walking away from me.

"Help?" I whisper to the empty room.

How long will I stand here, my wrists in shackles? Who will come to my aid?

Why did I agree to dinner?

Moments later as I'm diving deep into worry, a woman arrives. Gold sparkles on her eyelids and in her short, tight, dark curls. She's dressed in a black leather corset, black stockings, and a long red-to-orange ombre silky robe that flutters behind her like flames licking at the air. Her glossy black stilettos click against the floor as she makes her way to me with her determined stride.

She's got black medical gloves in her hands and she puts them on as she walks, covering her sparkly, black-painted nails. She goes right to the handcuffs, undoing them. "Pleasure to be seeing you. I'm Keisha and I'll be your goddess for the evening."

The cuffs open and I lower my aching arms to my sides, rubbing at my wrists. Then I remember the half-zipped state of my jeans and the toy tucked inside. Humiliation wells in my chest as I quickly pull the vibrator from my jeans, zipping and buttoning them.

"I'll take that." Without a word about my situation, she plucks the toy from my hand with her gloved fingers.

I can't help but stare at her—she's breathtaking. What did she call herself? "Did you say you're my... goddess?"

"Yes. Of course! Any guest of Cannon's is assigned a personal assistant for the evening, and I'm happy to be yours. Your goddess." She takes a long look at me. "Or in your case, maybe you'd be more comfortable with a... oh, I don't know. Fairy godmother, I guess? I have wings I can put on if you'd like."

I don't know if she's teasing or not, but I don't want her going to any extra trouble on my behalf. "No, no. Goddess is fine."

"Alright. Just a minute then."

Click clack across the floors she goes, pulling a coiled whip brass handle in the wooden wall, this one opening a small door, a hinge on its underside like the one on the book return at the town library where I spend my days off.

I think of the *No Talking* sign and the strict librarian with her steely gray bun and thick glasses. I hold back a nervous giggle. This place is nothing like the library.

Keisha drops the vibrator inside, letting the door close shut. She takes the gloves off, finding another handle, opening another hinged door, and drops them in. Reaching up over her head, she grabs a gold bar, sliding it across the wood paneling to reveal a sign that says *The Garden of Eden is closed for cleaning.*

They do take their cleaning seriously. Maybe I could fit in here... have a job here... but working for Cannon? Just thinking of him floods me with heat. I press my thighs together. I was crazy to beg for a job. I'm probably safer at the Accardis'.

My goddess returns to me. She grabs my hand in hers, warm and comforting amidst this strange, other world that I've entered.

"Come, come." She eyes my worn sweatshirt. "We have work to do. Cannon gave me very specific instructions for you."

Her accent is clearly American. "You're not from here, are you?"

"Nope. Good ol' Cannon recruited me when he first opened the club. I knew him way back when, before the Bachman Brotherhood snatched him up. We worked together in a bar in New York City and always kept in touch. When he told me he was converting an old mansion on a mountain in gorgeous Italy into a sex club, yeah, I kinda jumped at the chance to join the team."

My clit is still humming as I walk. I'm still being punished by the dampness between my clenching thighs, my body wanting to be filled. I press my thighs together harder as we wait for the elevator, in an attempt to stop the pulsing. No luck.

We ride the elevator to the second floor. She pulls me into a room with a red door. There're dressing mirrors in gold frames hung along one wall, with black and silver diamond-patterned wallpaper hung behind them.

The opposite wall is lined with doors. She goes to them, pushing them to the right, and they slide open on tracks, folding into one another to reveal a magnificent closet. Filled with clothing. Each garment hung neatly, an equal amount of space between each item.

"Hmm... let me see." The hangers click gently as she glides outfits across the metal bar, searching for the one she wants. "Aha! Here she is!"

She pulls a black garment down from the rack, bringing it to me.

It's a black one-piece pantsuit; the thin straps of the top are made of thin gold chains. I've never worn anything like it. I reach out to stroke the material, cool silk between my fingers. "It's gorgeous."

She flashes me a stunning grin. "And it's going to look gorgeous on you, my dear."

Gold metal catches my eye, lines running up the inner legs of the pants. "Are those... zippers?"

"Mmm hmm... Now, time to get dressed and I hate to be the one to tell you, you're gonna be naked under this gorgeous garment. And it's a little tricky to get into so I'm going to have to help you." She gives me a soft look. "Is that alright?"

Naked...

I've never been naked in front of anyone.

But I'm unsure of this place, this night, those zippers, and I need help.

My words are locked in my throat. I give a tiny nod of consent.

"Come here, ladybug." She helps me out of my sweatshirt, which is not necessary, but my hands are shaking so badly I let her. I fumble with the rest of my clothing and Keisha is kind enough to fold it, setting it on a chair.

Moments later, I'm standing naked in the center of this vast room, a stranger's eyes on my body. The cool night air caresses my skin, combining with the nervous energy I feel, chill bumps rising on my flesh.

She looks away, slipping the chains of the pantsuit from the hanger. "I'm not trying to stare, not to be rude, but damn, girl. You've got gorgeous curves."

My hand goes to her shoulder to steady myself as she helps me step into the pantsuit. "Thank you?"

It takes her a minute to get everything in place like she wants it. I stand obediently, arms at my sides as she works, unclasping the chains and crisscrossing them over my bare back. The fabric is silky, tight across my ass and bare breasts, but the legs are loose, flowing as I move. Keisha swipes a bit of mascara on my lashes, a pale red gloss over my lips. She leaves my hair down, running a brush through it till it's glossy and smooth.

She steps back, eyeing her work. She shakes her head. "I don't want to do much more. You just don't need it. Take a look." She gestures to the wall of mirrors.

The strappy shoes she put on me tap against the floor as I walk. I stare into the reflection of a gold-framed mirror. I don't look like myself, the blushing virgin from the pharmacy. I look... sexy. I feel powerful and beautiful, like a woman in control of her destiny, but somehow, I'm still me.

A woman very much out of control...

There's a knock on the door.

"Come on in, Bastian!" Keisha leaves me wondering, clipping her heels across the floor.

The door opens. A man wearing nothing but a black bowtie, tight black shorts and combat boots stands in the front of the room, holding a silver tray in his hands. His chest and arms are covered in eye-catching tattoos of colorful flowers.

He gives her a friendly grin, holding out the tray. "Here you go, K." His eyes drift to me, offering me a professional smile and nod.

Suddenly shy about my new look, I quickly nod, then duck into a cushy black velvet chair.

I can't see what's on the tray from where I sit. I only see Keisha pick up something, a flash of black and gold. She leans over, kissing the man on his cheek. "Thanks, B. See you later."

She strides over to me. What's she carrying? My ass clenches. Is that...? A small black leather paddle rests in her hands, a gold rope hanging from the hole it's been tied to in one end of the handle.

"What," I ask with a shaky breath, "is that?"

"This is a cute little toy. Feel it." She holds it out to me.

The leather is cool, the paddle has give to it, it's not hard like solid wood. Kind of like the cushioning in the black leather wall of the room I just left. I imagine the feel of it against my bare skin, stinging, warming my ass. More damp heat creeps between my thighs.

"What is it for? More importantly, *who* is it for?" My voice shakes.

"Any tool that's black and marked with this," she points to little gold flames forming wings stamped in the handle of the paddle, "belongs to Cannon. Stand, please."

Cannon. Obediently, I rise. I run a finger over the pretty embossed wings. "But... why? What does this mean?"

"I guess he's not done with you yet." Her words send a shiver through me, uncomfortable and electrified but not altogether unpleasant. She brings the golden rope belt around my waist, saying under her breath, "Lucky girl."

"Lucky?" Was it luck? To be punished so shamefully at the hands of a stranger?

But if I'm honest with myself, I wanted the earlier punishment, and I want more. My body comes to life under his hands.

I've never felt more powerful, and powerless, all at once.

It was thrilling.

Keisha loops the ends of the rope, tying a knot so the paddle is secure around my waist. "Cannon doesn't play with the staff. Or clients, for that matter. Otherwise I'd be at the front of a long line of women begging to make it to his list."

"Play?" I ask. "What does that mean?"

She laughs. "You're joking, right?"

I don't answer.

She stops in her tracks, her head slowly turning toward me. Her brow furrows. "Haven't you been here before?"

"No. I... ah... I don't really know anything about this place." Or sex, or kink, or... even kissing, really. My first physical experience with a man was up against that leather wall just now.

She studies my face. "I should have known you hadn't been here by the way you tiptoe around, like a spooked kitten. No offense."

"None taken," I say, feeling shaky at the sight of the paddle around my waist.

"It's just I've never actually seen Cannon mess around with someone at the club like he did with you tonight. It's super out of character—" She cuts herself off with a shake of her curls. She pulls me down onto a black leather bench, sitting beside me and pats my thigh. "Never you mind, ladybug. I've got your back. I'll give you a quick rundown, tell you as much as I can in the next two minutes before we're expected at dinner. But you'll have to keep the questions to a minimum. We don't have much time. Got it?"

"Got it."

"Okay, so here's the basics. Sex." Her eyes brighten at the word. "Everyone loves it, right? Some people are ashamed of it—well, others love the shame of it but that's a convo for another day— anyway, some hide it away, only do it behind closed doors with the lights off. Others fully embrace their sexuality, find out what turns them on, explore the world of physical pleasure. That's where this place comes in. We give them a safe, exciting place with knowledge- able staff to carry out those desires."

I know she said no time for questions but mine comes out in a burning whisper. "What kind of desires?"

"Some people just like to come and look, have a drink, and relax at the end of a long day, you know? We have a lot of beautiful dancers and they're a joy to watch. The human body, it's just a miracle, isn't it?" Her voice lowers. "Others want an experience. Some like pain with their pleasure. They liked to be spanked or whipped. Other like the control of inflicting the pain. Then there's the kinkier stuff." She takes one look at the blush on my cheeks and shakes her head. "But I don't think you're ready for that conversation yet. Let's just get you to dinner."

"And this?" I touch the black leather paddle hanging from my waist and snap my hand back like it's a snake that could bite me. "Where does this fit in?"

"That. Is wonderful, baby. Give it a chance. I got the feeling when Cannon gave me his orders, he—" She looks away.

"He what?"

"Just, um, try to relax and breathe. You'll be fine."

Her words only make me feel more on edge, panic flashing through my chest, my muscles tightening.

Why is he not finished with me? What is the dark-eyed man going to do to me?

And why on Earth am I staying to find out?

6

C *annon*

SHE WALKS into the banquet hall, nervous as a kitten, her eyes darting right and left as she takes in the room. Chandeliers with real candles hang from the ceiling, their wicks glowing soft orange. Gold-plated sculptures of two flames forming wings hang from nearly invisible wire, giving the impression they float in the air unaided, the candlelight glimmering against the gold.

Keisha lightly touches the girl's shoulder, and she relaxes.

But she's not *the girl* anymore. Is she? She's Kylie Barone and she lives at 10 Fiore de Campo, Wildflower, in the village at the bottom of the hill, in a small yellow house she cares for on her own, along with assisting her grandma. As of yesterday, she was a third-generation Barone woman working at the pharmacy on the corner.

No information could be found on her father. Her mother's name is on the birth certificate, Kathalina Barone, but not much could be found on her, either. Today was Kylie's first day working for the Accardi family as their housekeeper. She did an excellent job, paid attention to detail, and made large improvements with little to work with. They pay her well.

At approximately four this afternoon, Antonio gave her specific instructions to wear a sexy red dress from his sister's old closet, come to my club in his car, and deliver a package to the Head of State by the elevators.

She agreed. Working for the Accardis was her first mistake. Agreeing to do their bidding was her second.

She went home, made soup for her grandma, dined beside her, played a game of cards, and they watched the news together. Afterward, she took her grandma into a room, presumably to put her to bed, drew the curtains, then came back out alone.

She sat at the small table in the kitchen, drumming her fingers against the wood.

When the long hand of the clock on the blue wall hit eight, a black Town Car, one in the Accardis' fleet, pulled up outside the house. Kylie came outside, not wearing the sexy red dress, but instead sneakers and a sweatshirt, locked the door behind her, and dipped within. The rest I was mostly present for. The package is accounted for and I know exactly what is inside.

The contents were no surprise to me.

The only thing I haven't figured out yet is where Antonio got that guest passkey.

I have eyes and ears everywhere on this mountain, in this club, in the village. The Bachman name is gaining respect and I've been able to purchase a few of the men of our enemies as spies. I have no need to interrogate the girl.

I find it fun.

The one thing I don't know is how she came to work for the Accardis in the first place. I'll find out tonight. She comes toward me, twice as beautiful as I knew she'd be in the outfit I chose for her. Keisha left Kylie's face natural, and I highly approve. Kylie wears my paddle around her waist. It gently swings against her hip as she walks.

My pants are suddenly tight, my cock demanding what he wants. It was his foolish idea that started this whole thing anyway. And I tried to... kiss her? It was bad enough I played with her in one of our rooms. What was I thinking? I never break my own code. I shift against my leather dining chair, seated at the head of the long table, my fingers gripping its wooden arm.

This girl has some kind of hold on me.

Kylie's hazel eyes meet mine, a look caught somewhere between fear and desire. Her teeth sink into her full, glossy bottom lip. I can't take my eyes off her as she slips into the open seat to my left. She leans down to adjust the fabric of her outfit and as she does, a lock of her silky hair falls over her shoulder, brushing against my forearm as it rests on the arm of the chair. Electricity races across my skin.

Why is my heart beating so hard, my breath tight in my chest?

Why is this girl having this effect on me? I've had at least a dozen beautiful women this month alone. But none have altered the rhythm of my heartbeat. I haven't felt this... feeling... in a long time.

Ten years long.

I realize I'm so caught up in my reaction to her presence that I have yet to acknowledge her. I lift a crystal pitcher filled with ice and water, filling her glass myself. "Hello, Kylie. Thank you for joining me."

"Thank you for having me." She takes a small sip from the glass and shoots me a wary look. "You know my name?"

"I know quite a lot about you. You think I'd let you stay for dinner without a little background check?"

She grows uncomfortable, shifting in her seat. She gives a shrug. "There's really not much to know. I told you. I'm a good girl."

"To be determined, I'm afraid. From what I've seen tonight, I wouldn't say you're an angel."

At the word angel, her eyes light, a tiny secret smile rising on her lips. I have to know what thought it is that makes her face illuminate like this. "What? What did I say?"

She shakes her head. "It's nothing. I just... like angels."

Again, like in the Garden of Eden when I had her cuffed to the wall, frustration fills me. She tells me nothing. Yet she had the audacity to come in here with Accardi trash and then dared to hide it by my precious Monstera. I feel anger well in me and I push it down.

Control.

"You don't like to talk. You might change your mind after dinner." I eye the little paddle hanging from her waist. "I have plans for you."

"Is that so?" She lifts her glass to her lips, this time taking a gulp of the water.

"Yes. I want to play a little game with you."

"A game?" Her skin is soft and as I touch her, her lips part, her eyelids grow heavy, but she keeps that burning gaze locked with mine.

"Would you like that?" My fingers dip beneath her chin.

"I don't know. I know I shouldn't want to, I shouldn't even be here, but I am, aren't I?"

"I'll take that as a yes."

The tension between us is almost visible, our heads bowed together exchanging heat-filled whispers. I feel the eyes of the room on me. I've never shown a woman this type of public attention. And I hadn't planned on doing so.

She... does things to me.

I don't know what possesses me but now I'm brushing the pad of my thumb over that full, lower lip I came so close to kissing in the Garden of Eden, her arms stretched helplessly over her head, a bare sliver of her belly peeking at me, her eyes bright and bold yet filled with fear...

I wanted to kiss her then.

I want to kiss her now.

Her trembling words come back to me. *Please. Don't.* I drop my fingers from her face.

What makes her different?

Liam's words come to me. He fell for his wife during the process of trying to find brides for us single brothers. He was never going to marry himself. When I asked him what changed, he shrugged and gave one of his rare full smiles. He said *the heart wants what it wants.* And it can't be denied.

My heart seems to want her, this girl that I've known all of what? An hour? Am I foolish enough to think that there's something different about her, that she isn't just another beautiful girl?

Trust.

That's the only thing that would make me change my single status, and this girl has already shown me, without a doubt, that I cannot trust her. So why am I wasting my time punishing her, teasing her, hell, dressing her to my liking, feeding her?

Luckily, food arrives, offering me a delicious distraction. *Primi Piatti*, the first course, a small portion of a creamy mushroom risotto. As the antipasti trays of nuts, meats, and cheeses are being served, I notice a familiar flash of blonde hair taking a seat two down from Kylie.

Kat with a K. My little problem. Looks like she garnered herself a guest pass for tonight too.

She leans over the table, waggling long red nails at me. "Ciao, Cannon! Lovely to see you. Again, thank you *sooo* much for last night. It was, in one word, *stupefacente*, just amazing!"

"To hot nights and chilled wine." I lift my glass of Pinot to her, offering a tight, false grin.

She raises her own glass, shooting me a seductive look as she runs the tip of her tongue over her lips before taking a sip. She puts her glass on the table, tossing her hair over her shoulder, a move I'm guessing is supposed to lure me in. The massive glittering stone in her ring catches her hair as she performs, pulling away a long thread of her hair extensions.

Benita, her goddess for the evening, quickly helps her detangle the hair from the ring, and leaves the table to dispose of the strand.

"Prototype. Still working on the actual product, but we'll get there." Kat takes an artichoke from one of the wooden charcuterie boards, sucking the oils and spices from it before popping it in her mouth, another move meant to make me squirm. "Delicious. Just like you."

I am squirming, but not in the way she's hoping. Nausea pools in my stomach. How had I gotten her so wrong? "Enjoy your meal."

She's licking her lips again. They're going to chap if she's not careful. "I will but not as much as last night. Ah-mazing. It was like we knew one another in another lifetime or something."

Benita returns, saving me. "More wine, chica?" She pours Prosecco into Kat's glass till it's almost full, drawing her into a deep conversation about her new hair extension business.

God, I've got to stop sleeping with guests of members. I go back to my food, grumbling under my breath. "Last night was about as amazing as your audacity to hang around my place till noon."

Kylie's been hiding her face behind the curtain of her dark hair, but now takes a peek at me. She dips the tines of her fork into the risotto. The corners of her lips curl as she slips the food in her mouth.

Is she... *laughing* at me?

"What," she leans over, whispering to me. She raises her brows. "Not a love connection?"

"Not exactly." I lean back, giving the waitstaff room as they remove my shallow bowl, replacing it with a steaming plate of pasta. "Her hair came out in my hand last night. Then she wouldn't leave."

"Just a prototype. That'll happen." She smirks, taking a delicate sip of her water. "So, I'm guessing she's not going to be the mother of your children then?"

"No. She's not."

Kylie goes back to her meal.

I look over at the girl beside me. She's beautiful. Strong. Brave. She must be kind, caring for her grandma, cooking for her. The type of woman you want for your wife, to raise your children.

What the fuck is wrong with me tonight?

I down the rest of my wine, refilling the glass. "Wine?" I offer to pour for her from my personal bottle of Pinot.

"No, thank you." The smile drops from her lips. "I don't drink much."

"Don't like the taste?" I take a long sip of the smooth bright wine.

Her gaze clouds. "I don't like to... make poor decisions."

I go to correct her, to harass her further for her poor decision-making tonight, but she stops my words with a gentle hand on mine.

"I'm sorry. I shouldn't have come here, and when I realized that, I tried to correct it, but I didn't know how." Her hazel eyes capture mine. There goes my damn heart again, racing in my chest. "I really am a good girl. I'm an honest person. I don't make a habit of lying. I don't like it. It makes me feel bad and cringey inside and... and I just... I just..."

Her words trail off as her hand slips from mine. Worry creases the corners of her mouth. I believe her.

So what is going on to push her to make these choices? I thought maybe she just came across a little trouble and went to the Accardis for some help. Whatever she's gotten herself into, it's deep. She's really scared of something or someone. Isn't she?

I twist the stem of my wineglass between my fingers. "You're not just in trouble. You're in danger. Aren't you?"

"Yes." She nods. She takes the linen napkin from her lap, dabbing at the corners of her eyes. My God. Are those... tears? My breath does that funny thing again, my chest closing in on itself, tightening.

"But you won't tell me. Will you?"

She shakes her head, still dabbing at her eyes.

I will find out what kind of danger she is in. "We'll have to see about that. We still have our game to play."

Her eyes reach mine, that fearful hint of desire playing in her irises, making my cock grow hard once more.

I want to know the truth. And I know how to get what I want.

7

K *ylie*

HE HOLDS my hand as we make our way from the banquet hall. The experience of walking through the halls at his side, with his confident swagger and his big, warm, strong hand around mine, sends butterflies through my belly.

All eyes are on us, and I mean all. Dozens of beautiful strangers pretend not to stare while openly staring. Nerves flood me and I focus on my steps so I don't trip over my own feet. I smooth my hair with my free hand, then straighten the chains at my shoulder.

The staff tries to remain professional, but I catch their sneaky glances. The clients and their guests are all out gawking, some with envy in their eyes. I remember Keisha's words about there being a line of women wanting to be with Cannon... *Lucky girl.* The club really is acting as if they aren't used to seeing him with someone on his arm.

What makes me different?

He takes me to a new room, a small room off the main entrance of the mansion. It's a coat closet, furs and trench coats hanging from a wooden rod. There's a long wooden bench covered in, of course, black leather. He takes a seat, his legs wide, casual-like. I stand there, clasping my hands, unsure of what to do with myself.

His smoldering eyes roll lazily up to meet mine. "Do you want to play?"

"I..."

"Let me guess." He smirks at me. "You don't know?"

I nod.

He stares at me, spreading those muscular thighs. He grabs my hand, pulling me over his lap, his patience used up. He's made the decision for me.

"Oh!" My legs hang down, my arms stretching out over the long bench. I tuck my elbows in at the outside of his thigh, pushing my chest up a bit. His thighs are hard under my belly. My swollen clit presses against his lap. I want to rub against him, my body demands friction.

I'm laying over his lap like a naughty little girl. He's in total control over me and all I ever seem to be able to do around him is stutter out three words. *I don't know.* One thing I do know, my body is curious, aching for him to do something about it.

His hand glides over the silky fabric of my outfit. With no panties on underneath, the material so thin, I can feel the warmth of his skin. He cups the bottom curve of my right ass cheek in his palm.

Shame fills me as dampness spreads between my thighs. Why am I so needy for him?

"Now for a question I think you'll actually answer." He gives my ass a squeeze. "Have you ever been spanked?"

I shake my head. "No. I told you I was a good girl."

"Well, that's changed, hasn't it?" He gives a chuckle, the laugh vibrating against my side.

"No. Not really. I'm good. I just... got into some trouble."

Not even of my own doing...

Should I tell him? That it was my uncle, not me, who got me into this trouble? Maybe spare myself some punishment? No. I have to keep this family secret. The more people who know, the bigger the chance it gets back to my grandmother.

He leaves his hand resting, heavy, on my curves. "But you agreed with an Accardi to bring a package here. Didn't you?"

"Yes."

"And you knew, you had some idea that was bad. Didn't you?"

I think of the knot in my stomach, pushing my decision to hide the package. "Yes. I guess so."

"And don't you think that means you're naughty? That you're a naughty girl who needs to be punished?"

Does it? The weight of his palm against me, the idea of his big hand spanking my ass, it makes me clench with need. I shift my weight on his lap. "I—I don't know."

"It does. You're a naughty girl who came into my club, ready to do something very naughty, something that could cause a lot of trouble. And now I'm going to paddle your ass for it."

"What?" I flip my head to look over my shoulder, staring up at his face to see if he's serious. I mean, I know he ordered this thing to be tied around my waist in the first place, but now that he's actually threatening to use it...

His gaze is stern, his jaw set.

He's serious.

He unties the paddle at my waist, holding it up for me to see. "What did you think this was for?"

I groan, laying my head back down. "I know what it's for but I just kinda ignored it all night."

He slips the paddle into his shirt pocket for safekeeping. "It's going to be pretty hard to ignore it now." He leans over me, heat and muscle against me as he reaches for my ankle. He finds the end of the zipper there, tugging it up my leg. "Spread your legs for me, naughty girl."

Can I? He remains always in control, but I sense he isn't a patient man. *Deep breaths.* I force myself to part my legs. He goes to unzip my outfit. His fingers cruise up my inner thigh, brushing against my skin as he unzips. The light touch of his fingers barely making contact sends a shudder of electricity through me, my shoulders tensing. This makes him give another deep chuckle and I feel his laughter against me.

The fabric of the unzipped pantsuit lays over me like a skirt. Cool air rushes up and over my bare skin, traveling over the heat of my naked pussy.

He has total access to my sex, my ass, the entire lower half of my body. I squeeze my eyes shut tight as shame fills me. I want his touch, yet I'm terrified to have him touch my bare skin, have his hands and fingers places no one has ever been.

I wait, frozen.

His rumbling words shock me. "Ask me to touch you."

I thought he was going to do what he wanted, that I was going to lie here, swallowing my shame, and take it. My finger strokes the leather of the bench. "What?"

"You heard me."

Silence hangs in the air between us. My mind wars with my body. He's woken curiosity, desire, and shame inside me. My throbbing core demands he follow through, that he continue to play this wicked game he's begun.

Now he wants me to drive this thing forward? Wants me to ask, to beg for this game to keep going? No way.

The tips of his fingers stroke the backs of my thighs.

God... that feels so good. If his touch on my thighs feels this good... I want to know what it feels like to have a man touch me... there, to make me come.

I cave. "Please. Touch me."

I tremble as, for the first time in my life, a man's fingers stroke my naked pussy. His finger dips into my arousal, then traces downward, the slick pad of his finger circling my clit. "Oh, God." It's terrifying and electrifying all at once, overwhelming waves of pleasure tearing through me.

"Before I punish you, I want some answers. The trouble you're in, is it with the Accardis?"

I take a deep breath, trying to focus on answering his question as his finger continues to swirl around my tight bundle of nerves. More waves of ecstasy shoot through me, making my voice tight as I try to speak. "No. It wasn't. But now that I didn't do what they asked, I'm guessing I'm in trouble with them too."

"I'll take care of the Accardis. You can let that worry go."

"Oh... okay?" I hold my breath as he leaves my clit, his finger trailing upward. He pushes a finger into my tight entrance, my skin burning as it stretches. Oh my God. It feels so good to finally have something inside of me, the empty aching now clenching around his thick finger. I'm so wet from all his talk, the dark looks from his captivating eyes, lying over his lap like this, his rumbling voice.

He pushes a second big finger inside me, filling me. "You work for me now."

"Huh?" My eyes close, my mind hazy, my only focus the feel of his fingers entering me, filling me, pressing into me, then dragging back out only to be thrust further inside. My hips buck against his lap, my fingertips digging into the buttery leather of the padded bench as he strokes me deep inside.

Did he say I work for him? "Come again?" I manage to choke out.

He pumps his finger in and out of my sex, faster. A moan drags up from my gut, deep and animal-like. I try to be ladylike but it's no use, I'm humping my hips against his thighs, pushing my ass back to let his fingers deeper inside me.

"You took a job here cleaning. Remember, you begged for that job."

Job. Cleaning. I clean for a job. "Oh, yes. I forgot."

More, more, more, please! My muscles tighten around his fingers as a spring coils in my belly, growing taut. He moves his finger inside me again. A whine rises in my throat, my fingers clutching the edges of the bench.

I'm getting close to something, I'm reaching for it with my mind, with my body, the promise of tumbling off the edge of the Earth...

He pulls his fingers from me. My empty pussy clenches with need. No, no, no! I try to hide the whimper that settles on my lips but it's no use. I need those fingers back inside me. I need to reach whatever pinnacle I was climbing toward.

I'm not above begging. "Please, don't stop!"

"Do you want my fingers inside you, pretty girl?"

My body demands it. "Yes."

"I'll put my fingers inside you. But you'll have to be a good girl to get what you want. You'll have to be obedient and tell me what I want to know."

"Um... okay?" Honestly, I would tell him anything right now, just to get those fingers back inside me. I wiggle my hips helplessly against him.

"I'll start naming families. When I get to the one you're in trouble with, you don't even have to tell me. Just squeeze."

Huh? "Squeeze? With what?"

His fingers are back on me. Thank God. I melt into him at his touch. He strokes my clit with his slick fingers, sending me into space. Stars spark in my vision as delicious tremors travel through me.

"With your pretty pussy," he says.

Shame fills me at his dirty words.

"Okay. I'll try."

His dancing fingers are gone from my clit, his palm offering a sharp slap on my ass.

I ricochet off his lap, the sting spreading across my bare skin. "Ow!"

"Don't try." He brings the tips of his fingers to my mouth. "Obey."

I catch the faint scent of my pussy, my shame going into overdrive as he brushes the fingers that have just been inside me against my lips. He forces a slick finger inside of my mouth, the earthy tang of my sex lighting my tongue. "Taste."

Oh my God... I'm dying, the humiliation too much to bear. He leaves me no choice, stroking my tongue with his finger, making me taste my own sex.

"There's a good girl. Obedient. We're finally getting somewhere."

His hand goes back to my ass, cupping it with his palm. His fingers dart between my thighs as he shoves his fingers inside me, hard and fast. It's more than I can take. I gasp, clutching what I can of the bench as he fucks me with what must be three of his fingers.

It's deeper, harder than when he first entered me, my skin and muscles stretching to accommodate the thicker girth. It burns, the pain edging on the precipice of pleasure but not quite there.

"It hurts..."

"Good. I want it to hurt. I want you to focus." He fucks me deeper. He pulls his fingers back, then gives a name, "Ricci," leaving a long pause before he says another one. I'm careful not to clench my muscles as he fucks me. The onslaught of the next thrust comes, hard and deep. The pain turns to need, my sex wanting more stimulation, to be fuller, to be entered even harder, faster.

It's almost impossible to keep from clenching as I lie limp over his lap, panting. The names keep coming. "Bianchi... Rossi... Russo... Romano... Meralo..."

I tense. He said it. He said the name.

His fingers are all the way inside me, waiting, as if he already knows the answer, his palm cupping my ass. Shame fills me as I force myself to do what he said. I squeeze my muscles, clenching my pussy tight around his thick fingers.

"That's what I thought." He pulls his fingers from me, leaving me empty and aching with desperation.

"Wait!" A cry of desperation bursts from me. "I thought if I obeyed, you'd give me what I want..." I'm too shy to say "come," or "orgasm."

I glance over my shoulder, searching for his face, to see if he knows what I'm trying to say, but he's not looking at me. His hand goes to his chest, to his shirt pocket.

My ass cheeks clench as he grabs the black handle, his embossed emblem catching my eye as he pulls the paddle from his pocket.

"Meralos," he says absently, dragging the cool leather of the paddle over my curves. "I thought so."

"If you knew, why play the game?" I give a wriggle of my hips, the paddle making me curious, my poor pussy still begging to be taken to that next level.

He taps the end of the paddle lightly against my right ass cheek. "For my enjoyment. You owe me a little fun after the trouble you caused."

"Fun?" My voice is weak, my limbs slack, while my core remains burning and tight.

He pushes the fabric of my clothing away from my skin. I tremble as he drags the leather paddle over my bare ass.

"Time for our second game. I'm going to paddle your ass while you answer my questions."

My body is so frustrated. The pent-up energy he built inside me provokes my desire to fight back. "Don't be so sure I'm going to tell you what you want to know—" His big open palm cracks against the center of my ass, choking off my words. "Shit!"

His hand leaves my ass, finding my lips. He shoves his fingers in my mouth, the sweet taste of my sex against my tongue once more. "Watch your language. It's 'yes, sir,' or 'no, sir' from here on out. Understand?"

He pumps his fingers in my mouth, leaving them there. He forces me to answer with his fingers filling my mouth, pressing against my tongue.

I answer the best I can, the words coming out lisped in my humiliation. "Yes, sir." But it comes out jumbled, sounding silly.

He takes his fingers, wet with my spit, and pushes them back inside my pussy. He leaves them there, filling me, but doesn't move them. I let out a deep moan of despair, wanting to move my hips, to make him fuck me, but I don't dare. Not after the spank that still burns across my ass.

His paddle hand strokes the toy against my curves. He lifts it, bringing it down in a sharp smack. It stings just like I knew it would. My sex clenches around his fingers as the fire spreads over my skin. The warmth from the paddle strike creeps between my thighs. He pumps his fingers inside of me.

His voice is low, husky with the pleasure he gets from his play. "Tell me. Are you in danger because of something you did..." The paddle comes down, sharp and sweet, and I suck in a sharp breath. "Or something someone else did?"

I can no longer protect my grandmother's feelings from the truth. I need my own protection. And this position he has me in, the power he wields over my mind and body, has me as weak as I've ever been.

I lay my forehead against the cushion of the bench, defeated.

I break, telling the truth. "Someone else, sir."

"Now we're getting somewhere. You said you don't like lying. Is that true?"

"Yes, sir."

He smacks the paddle right at the spot where my ass meets my thigh. Once on the right side, then on the left. The wonderful stinging warmth spreads.

"Thank you for telling me the truth, babygirl."

Babygirl?

Where did that come from and why does hearing him say the pet name in that deep, rumbling voice of his make another pool of arousal rush over his fingers?

He gives a dark chuckle, the sound vibrating against my side. He feels it. I'm going to die of shame right here, over his lap. R.I.P. Kylie Barone, who died with a kink club owner's fingers inside of her.

"You like that?" he croons "You like being called babygirl?"

I don't answer. I can't.

"Oh, naughty girl. I thought we agreed you were going to start telling me the truth." The paddle comes down harder this time, the pain lingering longer before the pleasurable heat spreads.

Defeated, I hiss between clenched teeth, "Yes. I liked it, okay?"

"Good girl, babygirl. That's what I like to hear. The truth." He taps the paddle against my ass, moving his fingers in and out of my sex. "I get the feeling you don't like to lie. So don't."

"Um... okay..." I try to keep my sex from clenching around his moving fingers but I can't, my body demands more from him. I feel weak. Confused. Needy. "I won't."

"You promise that you won't lie to me again. And then,"—he brings the paddle down hard against my ass, once, twice, a third time, while simultaneously thrusting those fingers deep inside me—"I'll let you come."

"Oh my God... please." He's going to take care of me, finally putting an end to this aching need inside me. "Deal. Sir."

"Good girl. That's what I like to hear. Now, kneel on the bench a little and lift your hips up off my lap."

I obey, lifting my hips from him, my bare bottom sticking up in the air in the most shameful way, my elbows digging into the padding of the bench. The unzipped fabric of my pantsuit dangles down over my body.

"Now, reach down your belly with one hand."

One shaky palm presses into the leather, balancing my weight as I nervously reach the other hand down to my stomach. It hovers by my waist while I await further instructions.

"And slip your fingers between your legs."

I freeze. "What?"

The tone of his voice is pure, sensual evil. "I said I would let you come. Not that I was going to do all the work. You're going to have to help."

I've lived a sheltered life. Work, home, library on the weekends. Sure, I've fumbled around under my quilt some, but... I can't... touch myself, especially not here, not in front of him.

I collapse against his lap, my legs falling down behind me. I rest my cheek on the back of my hand, letting out shaky words. "I—I can't."

His tone softens into almost too-sweet baby talk as he rubs circles over my lower back. "Don't you want to come, babygirl?" he croons.

"I can't," I whisper. "It's too much." I want to whimper, to cry, to beg. But I can't do what he asks.

"Have it your way."

I sigh, knowing I'll never get to that heavenly place I've only tasted the edges of. But now... what's this? His fingers are fighting their way back between my thighs. He finds my clit, circling the tender, aching bud.

Sweet relief! Stars explode behind my eyelids. "Oh my..." It feels so good, a heady rush washes over my mind, tendrils of pleasure easing their way through me. Release. It's coming. He's going to give it to me after all!

And then, he stops. He pulls his hand away from me. He pats my ass. "Let's get you dressed and get you home. You have a long day ahead of you tomorrow. First day on the job."

My eyes snap open, my jaw dropping to protest. "But..."

"I'm sorry, but the deal was you help. And little girls who don't obey don't get to come. Now get off my lap."

He can't be serious. I sneak a glance at him over my shoulder.

"Now." He's staring right at me. He's dead serious.

8

K *ylie*

I scramble off his lap, backing away from him and the bench. He presses his palms into the bench behind him, relaxing, watching me. I try not to look at him as I bend down, grabbing the zipper at my left ankle. It's a struggle, but I manage to get the thing zipped all the way around, wishing I had a pair of panties to hide the slickness between my throbbing thighs.

I stand there, wrecked, my face flushed, my bottom stinging, my hair wild around my face, my sex aching. I press my back against the coolness of the wall, avoiding his gaze.

What now?

He stands. He comes close. So close. He looks down at me. I look at the sparkling sandals on my feet.

His breath is hot against my cheek. His rumbling words reverberate through my ear, but really, I feel them in my core. "I'll give you one more chance, little girl. Do you want to come? Or go home in the state you're in right now?"

"I..." My teeth sink into my bottom lip. My body burns with desire. The discomfort runs so deep, it creeps into my soul. I want to come. So badly. But I can't do what he asks. It's too much. I rarely touch myself even when I'm alone. The thought of doing it in front of him makes my stomach flip over. My aching pussy begs me to comply.

I'm torn.

"Don't know?" he guesses.

I nod.

"I'll trade you something. I'll do all the work—"

"Oh, please." My eyes snap up to meet his, begging, my body begging.

"In exchange for something you don't want to give me."

Jesus, if I get to come, I'd give him almost anything right now. "What?"

His eyes capture mine. "Your first kiss."

"Oh..."

His hands snake around my waist, and he pulls me even closer. His lips brush against the soft skin of my cheek, sending tingles dancing over my face as he speaks. "Say yes, babygirl. Give me what I want—"

"And you'll give me what I want," I finish for him.

"Exactly."

We're pressed together so close, the heat from his body emanates into mine. Who have I been saving this kiss for? There is no Prince

Charming coming to tear down my door, to save me from this world. I'm surrounded by men who are monsters.

If there is no prince to kiss, I may as well give my kiss to a beast.

I shift my weight to my other foot, my pussy crying out, still throbbing, my clit aching. My body demands the deal be made.

I choke out the word. "Fine."

He pulls back until he can see my face, demanding our eyes lock. "That's not what I want to hear. This is the last time I'll ask you. Do we have a deal?"

I know what he wants. I force myself to say it. "Yes, sir."

"Good girl." And with that, he drops to his knees on the floor of the coat room.

"What are you doing?"

"Giving you your first kiss." He just looks up at me with a wicked grin as his fingers tug at my zipper, raising it up my right leg, curving it over my sex, and bringing it back down my left leg until it's fully undone, the coolness of the air rushing over my heated skin once more.

My heart races in my chest as he parts the fabric, throwing one leg of the pantsuit over each of his shoulders. His eyes are on my naked pussy, his strong hands parting my thighs, making my feet spread apart over the floors.

"Oh my God." I close my eyes, my head lolling back against the wall. My hands instinctively wind into his hair. It's soft and thick and I hold onto him, wondering what it will feel like when his mouth finally makes contact with my pussy.

But he takes his sweet time. He's been doing that all night. I should have anticipated the torture, but I didn't, and now the tip of his hot tongue is lashing against the soft skin of my inner thigh, driving me mad with need.

One of my hands stays in his hair, the other trails down to his shoulder, my fingers digging into his flesh. "Please."

"Please what? You've never had a man kiss you on the lips, so I know you've never had one lick your pussy. You don't even know what you're begging for, do you?"

The shame of my inexperience clouds my desire for a moment, but I push it away. "My body knows what it wants. Now make good on your promise to me."

"Bossy girl. Let's see how bossy you are when I slip my fingers back inside you." He cups my ass with one hand and I give a gasp as he pushes two fingers inside my tight entrance with the other, filling me. The pad of his thumb parts my sex, cool air rushing over my buzzing clit.

Then, heaven appears.

His tongue flattens against me, warming my skin, pressing against my clit. He leaves it there a moment, just letting me experience the feel of his mouth against me. It's wonderful, so wet and warm, pleasure flowing through my body. My knees go weak.

Slowly, he starts to move his tongue up and down, lapping at my pussy.

"Holy... shit." He laughs, and as he does the sound vibrates against me, reminding me of his punishing toy from earlier and sending me into an even higher realm. My hand tightens in his hair, my fingers around his shoulder.

He murmurs against me, "You taste just as sweet as I knew you would."

He's thought about how... I would taste? He really is drawn to me...

But my thoughts are lost as he pumps his fingers in and out, moving faster with his tongue, the strong tip now swirling figure eights around my ever-throbbing clit. A heady sensation I've never experienced comes over me, like my entire body is being covered in a warm, velvety blanket.

Finally... finally... *Deep breaths... deep breaths.*

The tightening I experienced over his lap on the bench comes back, only now, I fully embrace the sensation, knowing this time, the tension will finally be released and I'll be set free. I move my hips in the opposite direction of his tongue, finding the steady rhythm that I know will take me where I need to go.

The pleasure mounts, rising and filling me till I think I will burst... heat flushing my skin, my heart racing, and then I do, an explosion of white lights in starbursts against my lids. I cry out his name, "Cannon!" and it feels as familiar on my lips as any other. A soul-nourishing wave of ecstasy fills me, elating me, and I call his name once more.

I collapse against the wall. He gives my pussy a few last teasing lashes as the final shudders of my orgasm wrack my shoulders. All the tension melts from my body and I feel as if I'm sinking down into a warm bath, my body loose, my limbs liquid.

He glances up at me. "Now I want my other kiss."

I'd forgotten our deal. The loose relaxation in my body leaves; nerves and excitement fill me. What will it be like to be kissed?

He rises. My breath catches as he comes near, bending down to bring his lips to mine. The fact that my first kiss will be tinged with the taste of my own sex has heat washing over my face. He closes his eyes and I do the same.

And his mouth is on mine. His kiss starts off soft, slow, but it grows demanding, possessive, taking my breath away, bringing my head back up to the clouds. The feeling is magical, electric, nothing I could have anticipated.

He pulls away too soon.

There's a catch in his voice as he speaks. "I don't like the idea of you going home tonight. It's not safe."

Is he asking me to stay? I shake my head, my lips still buzzing from his touch. "I have my grandmother at home. I've left her alone too long already. I hope to God she's sleeping safely in her bed."

"I can't let you go alone." He slips a finger down my face, dipping under my chin to tilt it up in the way I've noticed he does when he wants my eyes on his. I obey, looking up into the deep depths of those soulful eyes.

"I'll get you a ride home. There will be a driver as well as two guards in the car. Tonight, there will be a guard outside each door of your home. The driver will wait on the road. If there's any trouble with the Meralos before morning, you'll be protected. I start my morning at six. Be ready to get in my car by seven."

There is no arguing with Cannon.

Moments later, I'm sitting on the buttery tan leather back seat of a car that probably costs more than our house, squished between two giant men. A South African named Booker who is flipping through the pages of a book, the light on overhead so he can read, and Carlos.

Carlos is a tattooed man who can rock a black leather vest even though, judging by the lines in his tanned face and the silver threading through his hair, he looks to be in his late fifties. Multiple silver chains hang around Carlos' thick neck.

We make small talk about the weather, how warm it's been.

When we arrive at the house, Carlos immediately goes around to his post at the back door. Booker escorts me from the car to the front stoop. My heart sinks. There's already another note. I try to snatch it away before Booker sees it.

Booker gently takes the piece of paper from me. "Boss's orders." He moves his big brown eyes over the paper, reading the same threat that is there every time.

Your family owes us. You know what we want.

Booker tucks the note into his book like a bookmark. "This is our concern now, not yours. Okay?

God, if only that could be true. Have I found the help I need? I take a deep breath. "Yes, sir."

"You hear anything, see anything you don't like, you come get me. Okay?"

"Of course." I look down at his book. "I'm really sorry you had to come out here. It must be a bother to stand here all night for me..."

His smile is bright and genuine. "It's my pleasure. Now you get inside safe and sound. Get some sleep. And don't worry about Accardi. In the morning we'll explain to him that you work for Mr. Cannon now."

"Yes."

I go into the house, peeking out the front curtains to see him take his stance beside the front door. I do feel much safer. But how am I going to explain this to Nonna in the morning?

I rush to her room to check on her. Her light is out, her chest rising and falling slow and steady in the pale moonlight. Relief washes over me and I take a deep breath.

I go to my room and take a long shower, scrubbing between my legs. No luck. It doesn't make him or what he awoke in me disappear. I try to forget him, to relax, to get ready for some much-needed sleep.

It's no use.

There are too many questions in my mind. I go to the dinosaur of a desktop computer on the small white desk in my room, booting it up. I need to do some research. Keisha left way too much to the imagination.

I spend the next hours deep diving the internet, hitting Google with all kinds of naughty questions. I give myself an education on all sorts of things I didn't know existed. When I'm so exhausted I feel like I can't keep my eyes open, I finally shut the computer down.

"Tomorrow is my first day at a kink club, huh? Can I really do this?" I lie on my bed, staring up at my ceiling, still in disbelief at the turn of events tonight.

Many of the things I read about on my computer I want to try. Some I do not. I fall asleep with visions of ropes and whips in my mind. But there's one image that stands out the most from my crazy, unexpected night.

His face.

I can't do this... I can't do this...

I wake to my grandmother's shrieks. "Who is that man at our front door!"

"Oh noooo!" She's found Booker.

I've slept in. I meant to get up before her to fill her in. I fly from the bed, rushing to the living room where she stands in her nightgown, her hand clutching at her chest. I put my hands on her shoulders, guiding her to the kitchen. "Just a friend, Nonna. He's... he's just hanging out. Let me make you some tea."

She's not convinced. "What friend? Why have I not seen him before and what is he doing? And why didn't you tell me sooner? I've not even put my makeup on yet."

"Don't mind him. How about some of those blueberry scones you like? I can make those." I steer her toward the chair facing away from the back door. No need to scare her further with Carlos.

She takes a napkin from the stack on the table and unfolds it over her lap. "With butter?"

"Of course! And extra sugar on the top."

I get her settled with her book, put on the kettle, and start the scones.

A while later, there's a knock on the front door. Shoot. I look up at the clock. Seven.

"Nonna, stay here."

"Okay, sweetheart." Thank goodness she's engrossed in her shows on the small kitchen television.

I rush to the door. The driver stands on the stoop, Booker and Carlos behind him. "Ciao, Signorina. Are you ready?"

"I, I'm not going." Three sets of very serious eyes stare at me. The silence in my front yard is deafening. "I'm sorry, but I'm not taking the job. Please tell Cannon, Mr. Bachman, I mean, please tell him that I thank him for... dinner, but I'll be declining the position. Have a good day."

I close the door before they can protest.

I return to the kitchen, sinking down into a chair. My heart is racing. I just couldn't do it.

I just can't take the job. I'm a third-generation employee at a pharmacy counter, a virgin, and I'm not going to work at a sex club for a man who puts his fingers inside of strangers. It was a twisted whirlwind of an evening, almost impossible to believe it was real.

It has to end there.

I just can't.

I slather my scone in butter, letting it melt into the sugar-encrusted crevices.

I can't go back to the Accardis, not after what I did with their package last night. And I'm not working for Cannon. It won't be long before the Meralos stop leaving notes and take what they want.

Me.

9

annon

I GROWL INTO THE PHONE, "What do you mean, she said she's not coming?"

Booker clears his throat. "Just that, sir. Not coming. She's in there eating breakfast in her pjs right now and she said she's not coming."

"Well, grab her ass and drag her to the car. How hard it is to tame a girl her size? What does she weigh? Half of what you do?"

Booker stands firm. "I can't. She's got her *Ouma* here, her grand-mother. She seemed pretty set on not taking the job."

"I don't give a fuck what she's set on. Doesn't she know what kind of family she's wrapped up with? What they'll do to her?" I run a hand through my hair, trying to cool the anger I feel at the thought of the Meralos' hands on her. I won't let that happen. "What does she think she's going to do? Go to the Accardis and beg for them to take her in? There's no way they'll even let her step foot on the property after what she did last night."

Booker stays quiet, letting me work the problem out the way I want to.

"So you're not going to throw her over your shoulder and shove her in the car?" I say.

"No, sir," Booker says, very respectfully.

"Fine. I'll do it myself. I'm on my way. Stay put. Keep your guard up."

"Yes, sir. Happy to do it. I don't want anything happening to that sweet girl." He pauses. "She's gotten under my skin too."

His words stop me in mid-stride. "Too? What do you mean, *too?* You think that girl is under my skin?"

Heat flashes through me. Fuck. What am I doing? I knew last night when she walked up to my bar I needed to let her go, to not get involved.

She didn't give me much of a choice, though, did she?

That's what I tell myself at least.

"She's not under my skin," I reiterate.

Again, Booker remains silent on the other end of the line, refusing to engage. Booker will never allow himself to get in an argument with me. When he feels enough time has passed, he says, "I'll be here when you get here. She's in good hands."

I take my little green Maserati, the car hugging the curves of the road as I tear down the mountain. One hand grips the wheel, the other taps against my thigh, wanting to smack that perfect ass of hers. How dare she defy me like this?

I didn't ask her to get in the car at seven. I told her to.

Finally, I spot the little yellow cottage. The house is small, modest. The paint is peeling, the yard in need of cutting and a good weed killer, but the windows are spotless, the front porch swept, and well-cared-for flowers sit in window boxes.

Booker stands at the front door, eyes watching. My driver is sitting in the parked car that brought her here. He sees me through the windshield, giving me a shrug. I can't see Carlos, but I know my men. He's at his post at the back door, keeping watch.

I throw the car into park, slamming the door as I leave it. "That little girl's got some explaining to do."

Booker opens the door for me. No smile this morning. He knows I'm not in the mood.

"Kylie! Kylie, get out here." My hands go to my hips. I pace the small porch. Booker wanders down the front path, giving me some space.

Her pretty face pops in the doorframe as she appears at the open door, her hair drawn up in a ponytail that makes her look impossibly cute. It's... frustrating. She narrows her brow at me. "What are you doing here?"

"Why didn't you come with my men this morning? I told you, very clearly. Be in the car at seven."

"I'm sorry. I told Booker." Her ponytail swings as she shakes her head. "I can't take the job."

I stop pacing. One hand on my hip, the other pointing at her. "You begged for that job."

"I know. And I'm sorry."

I cross my arms over my chest, planting my feet, my stance wide. I'm not leaving this porch without her. "You owe me an explanation. The truth. Why didn't you get in that car this morning?"

"The job, the club... it's just not... me. I'm... I'm scared. I didn't know what to do."

Her voice is small and the sound of it does something to my chest, that tugging sensation coming back.

I lower my tone. Drop my arms to my sides. "What are you scared of?"

Her gaze drags up to meet mine. "Of you."

She's scared of me? Why? "Me?"

She nods.

I feel anger building back up. This girl is in serious need of another trip over my lap. I think of my black riding crop at Fire, and I want to reach for it. "I'm trying to protect you. It's the Meralos, the Accardis, you need to fear. Not... me. Explain."

She takes a deep breath and whispers, "Last night. It was... overwhelming. I've never done anything like that before, or had anyone do things like that to me."

I think of that pretty, perfect, sweet-tasting pussy of hers. "You were so wet. You loved it. You wanted more."

A pretty rose blush blooms on her cheeks. "I can't deny that. But it scared me all the same."

"What do you think you're going to do? Go back to the Accardis?"

"If they'll have me. I was good at that job. I'd like to see that house clean. I'll apologize, beg them to take me back—"

Fury floods me. It takes every ounce of my self-control to not grab her, shake her, shout. "Do you want to know what was in that package? The one your precious Accardis gave you to deliver?"

"What?"

"A kilo of cocaine."

I let that sink in for a moment, taking a deep breath, trying to calm myself. "You think they're protecting you, sending you out with something like that? To take to the man in charge of the entire country. Send you into my club—" *Breathe, Cannon.* I lower my voice. "Send you into my club, when everyone in Italy knows that there are no drugs allowed in my club, with cocaine. They were using you. They were using you to irk me or send me some kind of message. I don't know why they did it, but they knew, Antonio knew when he sent you to Fire with that poison. He knew there was no way in hell it was going to get by my guys."

She looks past me, staring at the road, her brow knitting in thought. A look akin to disappointment covers her face. Did she have some kind of attachment to Antonio? The thought irks me to no end. "I guess... I guess I don't really have a choice. I'd better go with you, then."

"Yes, you'd best. And you are going with me. Right. Now."

She gives me a look.

"Tell your grandma you've got to go to work. I'll change out the guards, leave two here so she'll be safe while you're working. Go now. I'll wait here. Leave the front door open. I don't want you out of my sight."

She obeys, leaving me and Booker on the front stoop as she goes to her grandma.

I can hear their conversation with the door open.

"Nonna, a man is here. Cannon Bachman. He owns the club, Fire, the one on top of the mountain?"

Her grandma's face peeks out from the curtains. "What on Earth is one of the Bachman boys doing at our front door?"

"He's offered me a job, Nonna, cleaning for him. I turned him down at first, because it's at the club, you know, and—"

"Does it pay well?"

"Yes."

"And it gets you away from that Antonio, hook-for-a-hand, Accardi? He touched his sister. You know that, don't you?"

"Yes, Nonna," Kylie says. "I remember you saying something about that."

"Well, good for you, *tesoro!* And don't be shamed by working for the club. A good honest day of work is something to be proud of."

"Yes, Nonna, but... you do know what kind of club it is, don't you?"

Kylie wasn't lying about being honest. I'm surprised she's going there with her grandma. I hold in a laugh.

"I know more than you think," Nonna laughs. "Well, you don't know this, sweetheart, but your Nonna was a sex kitten back in her day. I worked at the pharmacy during the day, yes, but my nights were my own. I loved to go to the club, wear pretty dresses, drink liquor, smoke cigarettes and dance with all the boys." Her voice falls to a hushed whisper. "I was quite... progressive... in my day, if you know what I mean."

I can practically see Kylie blushing. "I didn't know that."

"I'll show you pictures of my younger days, sometime. You'll be shocked. But now, go. Don't keep a Bachman man waiting. I've heard they get firm hands when they grow impatient, if you know what I'm saying."

Kylie gives a nervous giggle. "I hear you, Nonna."

She understands her grandma better than Nonna will ever know. My hand is currently pressed against my thigh, waiting for Kylie to get her ass out here.

"Listen," Kylie says. "There are going to be more men outside the door. They want to keep us safe. I know it's strange, but they won't bother you. Just go about your day and pretend they're not here and that everything is like normal."

"Yes, sweetheart. You can tell me later what that's all about. Just go. Now. You don't want to be late for your first day of work."

"Thanks, Nonna." Kylie comes to the door, cheeks flushed just like I knew they'd be, her eyes soft. "I'm ready. Unless you want me to bring anything?" She looks down at her leggings and tee shirt. "Oh God, I'm not even dressed. Can you wait one more minute?"

"No." I'm done waiting. "You have clothes at work. Come as you are."

She follows me to the car. I open her door for her. I go to close it but notice she hasn't buckled her belt. "Buckle up."

"Oh. Yes." Her fingers shake as she fumbles with the clasp. This little girl is scared of me. I lean over her, fastening it for her. I pull away, my face so close to hers, I feel that familiar draw luring me in, wanting to press my mouth against her lips.

I don't.

I close the door. By the time we pull away from the curb, her grandma's standing on the front porch in her nightgown, handing Booker a plate.

"What's she doing?" I ask.

"She was a little unsettled by our visitor this morning, so I baked her some scones she likes."

"Of course you did." I glance over at Kylie's fresh-faced innocence. She got up and baked homemade treats for her grandma, after the night she had.

"Looks like she's sharing them." Kylie smiles, giving Booker and her grandma a wave as we pass the house.

I turn around, heading west. I don't take the turnoff for the road to Fire. Instead, I head toward the forest behind the lake. To Accardi country.

"Where are we going? You missed the turn for Fire." She points a pink fingernail at the window.

"We have a stop to make on the way."

She knows before I tell her. She looks at me. "Don't... don't hurt him. Please."

This girl is something else. Any of the other women I tangle with would be egging me on to kick his ass. "He put you in harm's way, used you, and you tell me not to hurt him?"

"I just... I don't fully believe that was his intent." She stays silent, having said her piece.

"You're more naïve than I thought."

She cringes at my words. I think of Liam. Right now, he'd tell me to grow a filter. Still, the girl is too closed off about the world. If she's going to be working for me, she's going to have to open her eyes.

I pull through the open iron gates onto their drive. The dark green mansion's paint is still peeling, its dark shutters in desperate need of a wash. But the bones are good. It could be a beautiful home. I can see why she wants to rescue it.

My usual mode of operation would be to blare the horn. Yell for Antonio to get his ass out here and face me. I glance over at Kylie.

She's got the end of a lock of her dark hair twisting around her finger, her teeth sunk into her bottom lip.

I'll go inside.

"Wait here," I command.

She doesn't say anything.

I grab her shoulder, giving it a shake. "Wait here and do not touch that door handle. Do not get out of this car. You sit here and you wait for me. Do you understand?"

"Yes, sir." She looks away, turning her gaze out the window.

I lock the door to the car, taking the keys with me. I take the front steps two at a time and bang my fist against the front door.

One of their men opens the door. Dimitri. A tall man with a neck tattoo of the three of clubs, but no one knows why. "Cannon. Who are you here for?"

"Antonio. I'm here for Antonio." I shove my way past Dimitri. Sensing I'm in no mood to converse, he steps aside to go get their other men, I'm sure. "Antonio! Get your ass out here."

I wait. Ten seconds. He's taking too long. I fill my lungs with air, ready to bellow his name again. He comes slinking out of the dining room, a damn apple stuck in the end of his hook. He lifts it to his lips, slowly taking a bite.

"Bachman. What can I do for you?" He stands in the foyer, eyeing me. He takes the apple from his hook, offering it to me. "Hungry?"

"Fuck you." I take the apple, throwing it against the wall. "You know why I'm here?"

"I know why you're here. But I don't think *you*"—the little shit has the audacity to tap my chest with his hook—"know why you're here."

I grab him by the neck, shoving him right up against the wall where the apple hit. "What the hell is that supposed to mean?"

Dimitri's gathered the men and now they surround us from all angles. I don't care. I'll fight them all.

Antonio holds them off with a raise of his hook. "Leave it."

He settles his gaze on mine. I'd forgotten how bright his green eyes are, their color unnerving.

"You have it all wrong," he says. "Did you even check to see if what was in the package was what you assumed?"

"What do you mean?" My face is so close to his I could give him a good headbutt and knock him out right now.

"Typical, pigheaded American." He scoffs. "You didn't even test the goods."

"What the fuck are you on about?" Kylie's doe eyes pop up in my mind, pleading for me to not hurt the bastard.

"I know why you are here, I know what you think, but you have it all wrong." A sly smile creeps over his face, like he's won this fight.

"Then help me understand." My fingers slide up from his chest to his throat, pinning him in place. "Let's start with the guest passkey. Where did you get it?"

"Kat. She's a friend of mine. She was pissed off at you for kicking her out. She texted me, complaining. I told her the way to pay you back, to get your attention, was to steal a guest passkey. That way she could come back to the club, to surprise you one night. She's cunning. I wasn't shocked when she actually pulled it off. I told her to let me borrow the key first, before she used it. That I'd find a way to get your attention with it."

So that's what Kat was doing at my place all morning. Sneaking around, looking for a key so she could get back into Fire. I keep a few at my place, ready to sell for members' guests, but I rarely permit them.

I tighten my hold on his throat. "Alright. You've got my attention."

"Kat's slightly obsessed. Not sure why." He eyes me like I'm nothing special. "But she is and so she brought me the key. I lied to her. I used the key to focus your attention on Kylie, not Kat. But I'll figure something out to tell Kat. Though she's going to be disappointed to find it's out of my hands now. I'll make it up to her. Buy her something. She's easily distracted by shiny things."

The mystery of the key behind us, I move on to my next question. "Why send the girl to my club with your filthy drugs?"

He could claw me with his hook, but he doesn't. His voice is raw but fearless as he struggles to speak. "I—I did it for her. I did it for Kylie."

What the hell is he talking about? First, telling me he used the key to get my attention onto Kylie, now saying he planned this whole thing for her? The Accardis only look out for themselves. But something in Antonio's gaze makes me take enough of a pause to hear him out.

"Explain." My hold loosens. I release his neck, shoving his chest as I draw away.

His green eyes glint. "Do you really think I'm foolish enough to think I can send drugs into your club without getting caught? It was powdered sugar. The Head of State was there to collect it as a favor to me, but I heard she didn't get that far. I'm just glad she made it as far as she did so you'd notice her. It was all a ruse."

Powdered fucking sugar. God, I look like an ass, not having someone check out the powder. He's got me cornered. He knows my security detail. Hell, he probably even knows...

"You know I have a plant here, in your house, don't you?" Every detail that was reported back to me about her afternoon with Antonio, Antonio planned. "Did you make sure he was in earshot when you gave Kylie your instructions?"

"I figured word would get back to you. And I knew if I sent her with something of ours, you'd catch her and... the girl... When she came to my doorstep yesterday morning, she was just so damn sweet. I liked her. I knew you would like her." His gaze holds mine, accusing me, leveling me, baring my truth. "I knew you wouldn't let her go."

Antonio might be a shit, but he can read people. I've heard Emilia say that of him. And I see it now. The little fucker is right. I couldn't let her go.

Could I?

"How did you know I'd get... attached?" I ask.

He shrugs. "I just had a feeling the moment I saw her. Then later, she did something for me."

"What did she do?" I ask.

"She... polished my hook. No one can even look at the damn thing, much less touch it." He looks away from me. "She... helped me. And I wanted to help her."

"She... *what?*" I shake my head. Kylie Barone, polisher of hook-hands, who the hell are you?

"I told you." He gives an unexpected half-grin. "She's sweet. Good. Kind. She doesn't belong here. My plan wasn't foolproof, but I hoped that somehow, someway, you'd get involved, take her in, give her the protection she needs."

"Why didn't you just come to me, ask me to help her?" I ask.

"I knew she wouldn't go willingly. She's innocent. A virgin." He says it simply, a statement, a fact. He says it... with respect. "You think she'd march off to a kink club looking for help? She's a cleaner."

Here I've judged him for what he did to his sister, but a prickle of shame dances along the back of my neck. *Please. Don't.* I stole her first kiss not only on her lips but on her sweet pussy too. And I want to steal her innocence.

All night, all I could think about was how my fingers felt inside her, what it would feel like to be inside her. The desire burned through me, turned me into a pile of ash in my bed, leaving me unrested and in need of extra espresso this morning.

I feel like Antonio is looking through me, seeing all of this.

I step back. Run a hand along the back of my neck. I'm still not sure what the hell is going on in his mind. I wait for him to speak.

He reiterates his point. "The only life she knows is living with her grandma and working that pharmacy. Getting help from the owner of a kink club? It'd be too much for her. She was perfectly content to clean our house. Look around. I knew she'd try to come back."

With my anger at bay, I can focus on my surroundings. The place smells of lemon and pine cleaner. The banister has been polished. The mirrors and windows are spotless.

I believe him. I know what he says is true. Because now, I feel I know Kylie. She's just that damn sweet.

"Then we're good. I'll take good care of her." I eye him. "Do you know why she's in trouble with the Meralos?"

He gives a nod. "She doesn't want anyone to know. Her uncle owes them drug money and they've been coming to her for payment. That's why she wanted to work here, to earn more money, to get some protection. She's trying to keep it to herself, to not let the story spread any further than it has. It would break her grandmother's heart if she found out what's happened to her only son."

The Meralos want money. Something they have plenty of. How much can her uncle possibly owe? A rank feeling flips through my gut. They know she has only enough to cover her meager expenses. They must be after something other than money as payback.

I nod. "Fine. Thanks. For the information."

His gaze steels, the softness he had when speaking of Kylie dissolving. "I've told you everything," he says. "Now get off my land. I've got things to do."

I leave him with a long look before I decide to leave, my boots tromping over the rickety boards of his porch.

Kylie's in the car right where she should be. I unlock the door, sliding in beside her.

Antonio stands in front of his house, arms crossed over his chest, the hook glinting in a sliver of morning sunlight that's made its way through the thick trees. He stands his ground, watching us as we leave.

"He looks okay." She eyes him, probably looking for bruises.

My fingers tighten around the wheel. "I can't believe I'm saying this. You were right."

Finally, she releases the twist of hair from her finger, turning to me with wide eyes. "What do you mean?"

"It was sugar in the package. The whole delivery was a front." I turn the car around the circular drive. "He did it for you."

Her eyes widen. "He did?" She glances over her shoulder at the forlorn Antonio.

"Yes. He set the whole thing up for you. So you could find me and get the protection he knew you needed."

She turns back around, shaking her head in disbelief. "I had this feeling that he... I mean, I didn't know what was in his head when he sent me, but I just couldn't believe he would... you know?"

Does she like him? Am I... jealous? I run an agitated hand through my hair. "No. I don't know."

She gives a happy sigh, settling back against her seat. "I knew it. I knew he had some good in him. I could see it in his eyes when I sat with him."

"Seriously?"

She shrugs. "His mother died when he was young. I imagine his father was hard on him. I know what it's like to grow up without a mother, it really messes you up, trust me, but at least I had my Nonna." She looks to me. "Who did he have?"

The pureness of her kindness makes my throat feel tight. I clear it. "Well..."

I leave it at that, cruising along the mountain roads. It's not lost on me how different the feeling, the energy, in the car is with *her* here beside me. Something deep inside me loosens, a knot I've kept tied up and buried for a long time.

Kylie... this girl... she's... *undoing me.*

What she does to me is going to be a problem. A major one. For once in my life, it's a problem I don't know how to solve.

10

K *ylie*

"THIS CANNOT BE what he means for me to wear." I stare in the mirror, disbelief reflecting back on my makeup-free face.

I'm dressed in a white minidress with molded, ruched bra cups that are edged in black ribbon. The same ribbon is ruffled into thin bra straps, not that I need them to hold the contraption up, because over the dress is a black, lace-up corset-like bodice.

There's even a black silk garter around the top of my exposed thigh. Keisha had to tell me what to do with the stretchy, ruffly band when she gave it to me.

I had no idea what it was for. I stare at what is basically a scrunchie wrapped around my thigh for no reason. Still don't.

Keisha stands behind me, a hand covering her mouth to hide her laughter.

I smooth my damp palms down the front of the skirt. "I mean, could he choose something a little more sensible? I'm going to be cleaning, for goodness' sake."

"Sensible? It's a kink club, baby." Now she's not even trying to hide her laughter.

"Why are you laughing at me? Is the outfit that ridiculous?" I tug at the edges of the lacy white apron.

"Have you seen the stuff I wear? I love this kind of clothing. You look hot. So sexy. Like, really gorgeous. I'm laughing because you're so damn modest. And you're working here." She tugs at the garter, letting it snap back against my thigh.

I'd be offended by her brashness, but the woman has seen me naked. Besides, I like her. A lot. There's no way I would be able to get through this first day without her.

She's staring at me, a funny grin on her face. I tug the hem of the microskirt, willing it to grow longer. "What?"

"You're just such a—"

My ponytail swings over my shoulder as I face her to finish her thought. "Virgin?"

"Yes! I'm sorry but it's true. And Cannon hired you to work *at Fire,* the country's, and what has to be, quite possibly, the *world's* hottest kink club. It's just too funny."

I shrug. "Well, I'm a really good cleaner."

"And you're going to be hella sexy while you scrub those toilets." She pecks a kiss on my cheek. "Come, come. Your boss awaits."

"Oh God." The thought of Cannon seeing me in... this?

The only decent article of clothing I wear—my white sneakers—are glued to the floor.

She hooks her arm in mine, dragging me from the staff dressing room. "Come on, let's go, Kylie V."

"Kylie V? Is that like my work name now? V for virgin?"

"You got it." And she continues to laugh as we walk down the hall.

Cannon's sitting behind his desk when Keisha pushes me into his office. Prey delivered to her predator. Keisha leaves me with a grin.

Cannon looks up from his computer. He can't hide the desire in his eyes when he sees me in this ridiculous outfit. He clears his throat. "Nice."

"Thank you." I hold out my apron and do a little curtsy, then start a nervous rant. "Now, where are the cleaning supplies? I'd like to get started. I really don't need any instructions or anything. On my way in, I spotted some chrome that needs my attention. No fingerprints on my watch."

"Wow. You're raring to go. Have at it." He points behind me. "Supply closet is behind the kitchen."

"Thank you." I take my leave, painfully aware of his eyes staring at my barely covered ass as I leave.

Now, to find the kitchen.

Too shy to ask for directions, I follow the scent of bacon, my eyes taking in all that surrounds me. A parade of scantily dressed men and women are going about their day. This truly is another world. It's staff-only in the morning and the place smells of breakfast and coffee.

I catch snippets of conversations as I wander the halls. Lush, a woman in her forties with pink hair, is worried about one of her shyer clients backing out of the orgy tonight, even though it's the dream of the quiet finance guru to participate. Clever has a sick cat and wants to reschedule her bondage session with a very famous actress tonight but knows Cannon would flip.

Kinda siding with Cannon on that one.

When you take away the whips and chains and leather and sexy lingerie, or just plain nudity, it turns out the staff here are just normal people with problems and families and responsibilities they worry over. And like me, they love food. They are obsessed with the meals that are being served. What time they'll sit down to eat, what it's going to be, where the meat and produce came in from.

Speaking of... I've found the kitchen. An industrial place with gleaming stainless steel appliances I'll happily be polishing. A man dressed in a white chef's hat and coat stands behind the stove, working with a cast iron pan. He tosses two slices of bacon and some scrambled eggs on a plate.

"Hungry?" He holds the plate out to me as I pass him.

"Oh, that's so sweet. I've already eaten." The bacon is perfectly crisped, the eggs light and fluffy. I take the plate. "But I could be tempted."

He nods to a stainless steel bar lining the far wall of the kitchen. "Take a seat and have a bite before you go. And welcome to the crew."

"Thank you." I take the plate to the bar, slipping onto a barstool. There're napkins and silverware here, everything ready for staff to eat. I eat quickly, taking care of my dishes afterward. I thank the chef again, asking him to point me in the direction of the supply closet.

There's no door, just an opening in the wall, arched and decorated with a pretty molding. It's not a closet, but an entire room of the mansion. I step inside. I've found my heaven. The floors are large black-and-white square tiles, freshly scrubbed and spotless. The walls are lined with shelves, each one labeled, items neatly placed, labels forward, cloths and towels folded properly. Everything here just makes sense.

I inhale the scent of cleaner. I touch the clean, soft cloths. I do happy twirls in the center of the room, spinning on the toes of my fresh white sneakers.

"Somebody sure likes to clean." Keisha's voice grabs my attention.

I stop, mid-spin. "Sorry. Didn't realize anyone was here."

"Just came to check on you, ladybug," she says. "Looks like you've found your happy place."

"Yes. It's amazing." I grab a stack of cloths, ready to get to work.

"See you at lunch?" she asks. "I'm meeting a couple of the Clamp Tramps by the pool for lettuce wraps at one. Sound good?"

"Yeah. Sure. Of course."

I spend the morning happily cleaning alone. This place is just about spotless, but I find a few areas that need improving. At one, I dine by the pool, happily chatting away with a number of underdressed, beautiful women. I find I have more in common with them than not.

I'm on the pre-clean day shift and at five, Keisha comes to tell me I'm off the clock. I go to the staff desk in the room behind the coat closet, blushing from memories of last night as I pass by it. I follow Keisha's directions for signing out from my shift. There are strict protocols, and I focus, following each set.

Heavy bootsteps come my way. *That* voice fills the small room. Just the sound of it and heat trickles down my spine. "What are you doing?"

I don't dare take my eyes off the screen, tapping the numbers Keisha gave me. Can't screw this up. "I'm clocking out. Then I'm going to go change. Then I'm heading home."

I think over what I've got in the fridge to make for dinner. Not much. I still haven't been to the store. Looks like I'll be making Nonna egg frittatas tonight. I feel guilty after the wonderful meals I've eaten here today, wishing I could bring her some of the chicken lettuce wraps we had for lunch. She's never complained, though, only thanked me for each meal I've prepared.

I'm so engrossed in my clocking out and my dinner planning, it takes a moment to realize he's standing before me like a locked gate, his hands planted on his hips, his stance wide, blocking my exit from the room.

There's a growl in his voice now. "You're not going anywhere."

"What do you mean?" I say. "Keisha said my shift was over."

"You're not leaving. You're not going home. It's not safe."

"I thought you had guards, I mean, not that you have to do that for me, I hate that they have to be there for me, but—"

His gaze dares me to defy him. "You are not going back to that house."

I think of my grandma, our frittatas, our nightly routine. "I have to. For Nonna."

He takes a beat to think but his dark eyes don't leave mine. "You will come stay here at Fire. And you'll bring your Nonna with you."

Two women from the dance troupe *Mujer Hermosa* pass by, feathers fluttering over their bare asses, hung from sparkly belts tied around their bare waists. They too, have dinner on their mind, chatting over what's on the menu tonight. Steak. I wave politely as they pass by.

I hiss at him, "Are you... serious? You want my Nonna *here?* She may fancy herself a sex kitten, but Fire is a whole different world than the one she grew up in."

"There is no other option." He shakes his head. "I want you where I can have my eyes on you. You'll stay with me in my guesthouse. And Booker's been looking for any excuse he can find to complete his 'read a hundred classic novels before you die' challenge. Nonna can have the carriage house with him. It's a one-minute walk from my place. We've converted it into a four-bedroom home. I think there'll be plenty of room for the two of them and Booker can keep an eye on her too."

This is crazy. My precious grandmother moving in with the bouncer of a sex club? I mean, I know things are friendly between them, nothing inappropriate, but still... "She's only ever lived with me."

"I spoke to Booker. You've been replaced." He gives me a look of victory.

I shoot him one back of denial. "Can't be."

"Turns out your grandma kicked his ass in poker today and he's demanding a rematch tonight," he says.

"Well, he should know better than to play with her. She's the best. But wait—Nonna is always in bed by eight," I say.

"Not tonight. They're having a poker tourney. Sounds like Carlos and a few of the other guys were invited."

"And I wasn't." My Nonna is having a party. Without me.

He nods his head. "Looks that way. And tomorrow they've already made plans. Booker's taking Nonna to Emilia's library to borrow a few books and meet their house manager, Marta. They've hatched a plan to sweet talk her into giving them some of her famous cinnamon rolls to take home. Apparently, they're going to spend the day stuffing their faces with sweets and reading by the pool."

They're even friendlier than I thought. Nonna and Booker sound like they're quickly becoming BFFs. I think of the frail woman tucked into her quilts, asking me for bread with sugar and wine. This is not my grandmother that Cannon is talking about.

I need to hear her voice. "Can I call her?"

"Of course."

The only phone I can afford is a cheap flip phone. I never use it, it's just in case Nonna needs me if I'm not at the house. She's never even called it once. I pull it from my pocket, dialing the landline at the house. It takes ten rings for her to pick up.

She's laughing as she says, "Hello!" into the receiver.

There's loud music playing in the background. Polka? I press my finger against my ear, hoping to hear better. "Nonna, is that you?"

"Booker, put that down! It's a doily, not a hat. Oh, you are a funny man, aren't you? Kylie, my darling. How are you? How was your first day?" Before I can answer, she's talking again, but not to me. "Carlos... Carlos? I thought you said we have to soak the corn husks?"

"Nonna. I heard you are moving in with Booker? You really don't have to, I promise, we can figure something out—"

"No. Sweetheart, please. Go. Go and have fun. Stay with your man and I'll stay with mine."

I turn away from Cannon, hissing into the phone, "He's not my man, Nonna!"

"This Bachman boy has been a blessing to us. You've taken care of me long enough, and let's be honest, we've gotten ourselves into a rut, haven't we? I hate to cut you off, *tesoro*, but Carlos is teaching me how to make tamales for the poker game tonight. He's an expert, been making them for over forty years! It's a very tricky process. I need to pay attention or otherwise the boys will be very disappointed in the food tonight. Love you!"

"Okay, Nonna, if you're sure—hello?"

The line is dead. Unbelievable.

He's eyeing me as I flip the phone closed.

"Told you." The way he looks at me makes me feel like all my clothing has slipped off my body. "Tonight, you're all mine."

A tremble of fear and thrill tear through me. My Nonna is heading up poker night for a bunch of men and I'm spending the night... with... him?

He just stands there, staring at me with those deep brown eyes I can never seem to tear myself away from. He crosses his massive arms over his toned chest, lifting a hand to his short beard, running his fingers along his jaw, eyes still on me.

Is his smoldering gaze an open invitation to change my life, to truly, physically step into his world? To join him tonight as more than just a roommate? Does he want to be more than a safe place for me to land?

Since graduating from school, I've spent every night of my life doing crossword puzzles and making tea and watching the news. Yes, there was an occasional card game, but who is this Nonna that's making tamales for a poker game with a group of kink club bouncers?

A thought hits me.

Hard.

What if...

What if I'm not the virginal, routine-driven person that I am today because of living with my grandmother?

What if... *it was me...*

What if *I'm* the one who made our lives predictable and sheltered and boring?

I've always kept our routine, playing it safe, never taking risks for fear I'd end up like my mother, making one mistake and dashing all of my dreams. But the truth is, I've never even dared to dream for myself or my future.

My mother has an adventurous streak and look at how she's lived her life. Going after what she wants, even at the cost of others. My grandmother now tells me she went against the grain in her younger days.

What about me? Doing crosswords and baking for fun. Did the gene for excitement and adventure pass me over?

I'm... the scaredy cat.

And I've encapsulated my Nonna with me, wrapping her up in our safe, boring, predictable world. Didn't I just this morning try to turn down a fantastic job and crawl back to the Accardis out of fear? I need to make a change. I need to embrace this blessing, this second chance at life, the excitement, the new experiences.

Maybe even embrace... *him.*

He still has yet to speak. He just stares at me, waiting for me to speak, but there are no words for him in my hazy, heat-filled mind.

Again, he says, "Tonight, you're all mine." The tenor of his tone leaves no mistake; he's not looking for a roommate. He uncrosses his arms, offering me a hand.

Do I slip my hand in his? Change the entire course of my predictable life with one innocent gesture? If I go with him, I know...

I'll never be the same Kylie.

I take his hand.

He offers me a shower at his place. Needing a moment to breathe, I take him up on it. As the hot water glides over my body, I wonder what it will be like, to be with him... what it will feel like to have him inside of me.

Will it hurt? Will I like it?

Will he find me... sexy?

I scrub every inch of my body with the softly scented soap in his shower. Is it okay to borrow his razor? Deciding I'd rather use it and dispose of it rather than be self-conscious, I take it from the shelf, removing every hair from my body, shaving my pussy bare and clean.

As I press the soft towel against my skin, it feels as if every nerve ending is wide-awake, wanting touch, warmth. Desire floods through my body at the thought of the man waiting on the other side of that door.

Waiting, for me.

annon

I start innocently enough. "How about a shower? You've been working all day."

"Sounds good." Some of the tension leaves her face at my proposal. "Thank you."

I show her where everything is, handing her a stack of clean towels. I go to the living room to wait. The sound of the water tempts me, but I give her her space.

She comes to me from the shower, fresh and pure as the water running through the mountain. Her hair is damp, her face bare. She wears nothing but sweats and a tee, and I can see the outline of her peaking nipples through her thin shirt.

She's a vision. A thing of beauty. Staring at her makes that familiar tug pull in my chest.

It's her first time. My little vanilla bean. I should lay her on a bed of roses or some shit and murmur in her ear while I take her gently.

But I'm not that man.

And I'm beginning to get the feeling from the sultry way she keeps looking up at me through those hazel eyes, she doesn't want gentle.

She wants to play.

I run a hand over her silky hair. "Tell me, Kylie. How do you want this to go down? You want music and flowers and lovemaking? Or do you want me to do what I do best?"

"Which is?" There's a lilt of nervous curiosity in her voice.

"Fuck," I answer. "I'm really, really good at fucking."

I watch that pretty flush rising in her cheeks, my cock rising with it. "Um... so, I've never done this before. That's obvious. But I think I'd like to try things your way."

Her eyes stay with mine, the tip of her pink tongue dragging over her full bottom lip. I have to hold in a moan. This girl is going to wreck me. I'm already throwing my rules in the gutter by messing around with one of my employees. What will I do next? How far will I go for her?

I lean down, brushing a kiss over her lips. "Are you sure you want to do things my way? Because once I start, I won't want to stop."

She gives a shy nod. "Yes."

Hell to the yes. Game on. Time to take this spark and start a wild-fire between us.

I grab her face in my hands, kissing her the way I wanted to when I first clamped her to my wall in the Garden of Eden. My tongue swirls against hers as she kisses me back, hungry for all the things I'm going to show her.

She's so responsive, it turns me on even more, how into this she is. A soft sigh leaves her lips, entering my mouth, her breasts pushing against my chest, her arms winding around my neck, hands tangling in my hair.

I'd never know she was a virgin, the way she kisses. Some people just have an internal fire burning, ready to embrace their sexuality, to let go fully and chase their pleasure. She's one of those. I can show her all the things she needs to learn. I can teach her how to find that pleasure, how to leave this Earth and shoot above the clouds, grasping for her own piece of heaven.

I run my hand over her breast, cupping it in my palm. I kiss her neck, nipping at her delicate flesh. I find my way to her ear, whispering against her soft skin, "Are you ready?"

"Yes." Her head lolls back, her eyes closed. "I'm ready."

I grab the hem of her shirt, breaking my kiss only long enough to raise it over her head. She's not shy of her body, there's no shame in her pretty eyes. She stares into mine, a small smile on her face, watching me as I take in her beautiful body.

Her hands go to my shoulders, holding onto me as I tug the loose band of her sweatpants down over her hips. She steps out of them and stands before me, fully nude.

I lose my breath as it catches in my throat, my heart skipping a beat. I want to tell her she's the most beautiful woman I've ever seen but the only word I can manage is her name.

"Kylie."

I go back to kissing her, my hands smoothing over her bare skin. It feels amazing, to touch her, to caress her perfectly laid curves. Her nipple responds to the light brush of the pad of my thumb, going taut.

My mouth goes to it, licking and sucking. Her fingers tighten in my hair, and she gives a soft sigh of satisfaction.

This isn't me. Next, I'll be singing her sweet serenades and offering her wine and cheese. What's gotten into me?

She has.

I force myself to break away from her. Running a hand through my hair, I tell myself to get my head back in the game. I'm in control, showing her my world. *Not* getting lost in her.

I give her a command to get myself back in the headspace I need to be in. "I want you bent over my bed. Your legs spread."

She gives me a naughty glance, a nervous smile. "Okay." She moves to the bed, hips rolling as she walks. Her tempting curves beckon to me as she lies over the bed, her ass on full display. I stand, staring as she slowly spreads her legs, showing me everything.

Her full, untouched beauty is on display for me. Just for me. I'm the only man to have had this privilege and I don't take the honor lightly.

She glances over her shoulder. "Like this?"

I move to her, running the tips of my fingers over her lower back. "Yes. Just like that. Now close your eyes and just relax against the bed."

She obeys, slipping her hands under her cheek and closing her eyes.

I go to the black lacquered cabinet in the corner of my room, opening its doors. My collection of toys beckons to me, sparkling clean and neatly hung inside the cabinet. What to choose, what to choose?

My spreader bar calls to me from the back of the cabinet, black and shiny and ready for playtime. She'll be new to everything and keeping herself open to me, bared to me the way I want her to be, will be hard for her. So this will help.

I grab the bar and it rattles as I move but she doesn't let the sound tempt her to open her eyes. Good, good girl. She was born for this lifestyle.

I move to her, kneeling on the floor behind her. "Just relax." I grab her delicate ankle, small in my hand, and cuff her with the soft velvet interior of the clamp.

"Oh! Is this like some kind of handcuff for your ankle?"

"Something like that." I move to her other ankle, clamping it in the second cuff. I run a hand up the back of her bare leg, enjoying the sight of chill bumps rising over her flesh. "It's called a spreader bar and it will keep your legs spread for me if the things I do to you make you want to snap them closed."

I bring my fingers up high between her thighs, dipping them along her sex, feeling her wetness. God, she's already so slick, so ready for me. I haven't even touched her.

I leave her, going back to my cabinet. I choose my little black oval-shaped flat disc vibrator, something that will remind her of that first night in the Garden of Eden.

When I return to her, I kneel down between her legs. "Look at me," I say, my voice thick with desire for her.

She presses her hands into the bed, turning over her shoulder to eye me.

"See this?" I raise the vibrator to show her.

She gives a nod. "Yes, sir."

"I'm going to use this to make you come. You're already wet for me but since it's your first time, I want to be sure your pussy is as ready for my cock as possible. Get comfortable."

Her cheek returns to the back of her hand and she gives a shuddering sigh. She shifts her weight, adjusting her legs, testing the bar. It's locked in place, firm and in control of her body, just as I am with her.

I turn the vibrator on, at the lowest speed. From where I kneel, I can see every inch of her beautiful sex, already glistening for me. I bring the vibrating disc to her pussy, pressing it against her vulva.

She gives a gasp, shooting up from the bed, the spreader bar holding her wide. "Oh my God."

I hit the button again, increasing the strength of the vibrations. She pulls against the restraints as she moves, and they hold her in place. I run the vibrator over her smooth lips, up and down, up and down, until her hips start rocking back toward me, her beautiful ass open to me.

"Tell me... do you want to come for me, babygirl? Are you ready?"

"Yes, God, yes." She gives a strangled moan, her fingers clutching at the bedding.

I hit the button once more, turning the vibrator on as high as it goes, and shove the disc against her clit. "Come for me, babygirl. Come, right now."

She has no choice but to obey. She gives a loud cry. "Cannon!" Her legs want to clench together but the bar keeps her open for me. Arousal glistens at the entrance of her sex, spreading between her thighs. Her upper body shudders as she cries out my name again. "Oh my God, Cannon!"

I hold the vibrator to her, making her come again. She can't take much more, a whine rising in the back of her throat.

I have to take her. Now. I toss the vibrator to the floor, greedy hands unlocking the cuffs from her ankles. The bar collapses to the floor with a rattle. I grab her hips, turning her over onto her back. She lies there spent, her breaths coming in pants.

I kiss her and the kiss reawakens her, the heady cloud of climax leaving her and the whole process starting over. My fingers find her slick sex and she's just so wet, I can't wait any longer.

I stand up from the bed, unbuttoning my shirt. She lies there, a hand lazily resting on her breast as she watches me undress. I can tell she likes what she sees as I slip out of my shirt and pants, her tongue wetting her lips before her teeth sink into her bottom lip in anticipation of what's to come.

My cock is hard, so ready for her.

I have to be inside of her. Now. "You ready, babygirl?"

She gives a nod, her arms reaching up to wind around my neck. I slide my hand under her ass, pulling her up higher onto the bed. I leave my arm under her lower back, holding her close to me as I guide my cock toward her entrance as I kneel on the bed, rolling on a condom.

"I want your eyes on mine when I enter you."

She stares up at me, her gaze full of trust, her lids heavy with desire. "Yes, sir."

I press the head of my cock against her slick entrance. She's so tight, and I'm huge and throbbing, so fucking turned on by her. I ease the tip of my cock inside of her.

"Are you okay, babygirl?"

She nods, biting her lower lip.

I push further into her tightness, going slowly, easing her into her first time. I'm going slower, being softer with her than I thought I'd be but there's so much trust in her eyes I don't want to do anything to hurt her or taint the memory of her first experience.

I hold her tighter, closer, kissing her shoulder, her neck, her ear as I inch my way into her tight pussy. "God, you feel so fucking good."

"You do too. But you're so big. I don't know if I can take all of you."

"You can, babygirl. You can, and you will." I roll my hips, thrusting in her further. She tightens even more, her muscles locking around my cock. Her fingers clutch at the muscles in my shoulders as I thrust again, then once more.

Finally, I'm all the way inside of her. "Does that feel good, baby?"

"Yes." She gives a gasp. "Yes. It hurts, but it feels good at the same time."

I cup her ass in my hand, lifting her hips. Rolling mine, I build a steady rhythm, going slowly at first, thrusting inside her and pulling back, then entering her again.

Her hips start to move with mine. Her smooth legs pull up along my outer thighs, her legs wrapping around my torso, her ankles crossing over my lower back. She tightens her hold around my neck, her eyes closing, her head lolling to the side.

I stare at her face, enraptured by the look of pleasure that's taking her over. Her body responds to mine, moving with mine, her hips bucking to meet each of my thrusts.

"Oh my God. That feels so good. So this is what all the fuss is about..."

"Yeah. Sex makes the world go round." I give a chuckle, my laughter getting lost in her hair as I lean down over her. My lips find hers and I kiss her as our bodies rock together. An orgasm clenches at my gut, rising in my core, my entire lower body tightening as the impending eruption builds.

She tightens around me, moaning into our kiss as I come inside of her, my balls rising into my body as my cock spurts and jerks, filling the condom with my semen. She hasn't yet come again so I pull out of her, kneeling down and lapping at her clit with my tongue.

She curls her body around me, hands in my hair, thighs locking around my shoulders. I shove two fingers inside of her and lap at her clit as she shudders. "I'm coming. I'm coming again."

I don't stop until she pushes me away, collapsing against the bed.

I wipe my mouth with the back of my hand, staring at her flushed face, a sheen of perspiration glistening over her brow.

"Oh my God! My goodness," she pants.

"How was it, babygirl?" I push her hair back away from her face, staring at her, entranced by her afterglow beauty.

"That was amazing. I just need you to know..." She glances down, her dark lashes fluttering. I'm not prepared for how hard her gaze hits me when she drags her eyes back up, locking them on mine.

"What?"

"This was great. Amazing. The best first time a girl could probably have. But I need to be clear with you, right now. I need you to know, I can't... be with you. I can't be in a... *relationship.*"

The afterglow hasn't even hit yet. Why is she saying this? I don't even do relationships. So why are her words tripping a cold prickle down my spine?

I clear my throat. "Who said that's what I wanted? Besides, I never mess around with my staff. It's a rule of mine."

She raises one perfectly arched brow. "Never?"

"Okay, well, with one exception. You. Tonight."

She gives me a look of reprimand. "And last night. Twice. In the Garden of Eden and the coat closet. Though technically, I hadn't started work here yet."

"Okay, so I've made three exceptions in the entire time I've run the club. But it won't happen again." I stand from the bed, needing to leave her presence before I grab her naked body in my arms and take her again. "You can have my room tonight. I'll take the spare."

"You don't have to do that." She stretches, yawning, and snuggles down into the pillows.

"It's fine." I grab a few things and leave the room, pausing only a second by the door to stare at her beautiful face.

"Okay. Thank you. I'll take a shower in a minute but right now I'm so cozy." She nestles down, satiated in her satisfaction.

God damn, she looks too good in my bed to be a one-night stand.

"Goodnight, Cannon." She gives a little sigh, closing her eyes.

And just like that, our evening is over.

I've been dismissed.

12

K *ylie*

I WAKE with a soreness between my legs I never want to go away. A smile like the cat that's got the cream covers my face as I stretch, lazy and not ready to begin my day.

I'm no longer a virgin.

I'm a woman. I know most first sexual experiences are two teens fumbling under blankets, or in the back seats of cars, but that was not my experience.

What I had last night was, in one word...

Phenomenal.

The Cheshire Cat grin spreads further. Did I expect anything less? Cannon is hot with a capital H, all lean muscles and tanned expanses of smooth skin, hair that your fingers can get lost in, and a cock that—well, I've nothing to compare it to but after last night I'm certain it was an appendage formed by the gods.

One night of sex and the only thought in my mind is: I want more.

I want to feel like this every night of my life, my senses tuned to overdrive, my heart racing in my chest, my sex pulsing like a goddess demanding the pleasure that is owed to it. Now my smile is more than I can bear, hurting my cheeks and making me feel silly, because I realize...

I work in a sex club. The most prestigious sex club in all of Italy and possibly the world. Everything, anything I want to try is right here at my fingertips. Willing staff will help me, guide me, show me the way. Awaken my body and make me feel that pulsing vibration that is the purest form of life energy, a feeling I'd forgotten, thrown away, pretended didn't exist within me.

But it does. Oh, but it does.

My pussy aches for more, my fingers wanting to slip between my thighs and rub away the desire, but that's never been my thing. I want the heightened sense of someone else pleasuring me.

I want... Cannon.

But I know that's a slippery slope, a tricky, edge-of-your-seat ride down a hill when you're only waiting to crash. You know you're going to crash, but still your fingertips dip into the armrests of your chair and you hold on for dear life, thinking, *I'm going to make it.*

You're not.

Trust me, I know.

It's much, much safer to play with the staff at my disposal, to keep my attachments light, friendly. Because the way I feel when Cannon looks into my eyes while entering my body with his perfect cock, it makes me wonder if our babies' eyes would be hazel, or dark like his.

And that, my friends, is very, very dangerous territory. I should know. I've lived through the pain of other people's mistakes and I choose to learn from them. *Not* repeat them.

Cannon comes to me, cutting through the soft yellow morning light that beams through the windows, fresh from the shower, his hair still damp and his skin scented with spicy soap. He leans down, kissing me, perfectly content from our night together.

"Hello there, you little taste of heaven." He drops a kiss on my lips, dragging the towel around his waist.

He might be content.

But for me, the games have just begun.

"Hello, yourself," I purr, knowing that there is a whole world of pleasure ahead of me and he is the key that has unlocked the desire to experience it. "Thank you for last night."

"It was my pleasure," he murmurs between kisses. "Every single moment."

I need to be fair, to be clear, to reiterate what I told him last night.

Cannon's reputation precedes him and from what I've heard there's a different woman in his bed almost every night of the week. I know I won't offend him by what I'm about to say, but still, I'm one of those people who likes to be honest, who abhors being led on or leading others on when I know my intentions.

"This was great. I had a wonderful night," I say. "But I just want to be sure we're on the same page. About the relationship thing."

He looks away, folding a shirt to tuck in a drawer. "We're on the same page. It was one great night, and now it's over and I'm your boss."

The conversation continues and he says all the right things, the words I need to hear to know I'm not leading him on, but there's something in his tone, a bristling or anger dancing just around the edges of his words.

Like he's not on the same page as me.

But this is Cannon. Cannon Bachman. Owner of Fire and owned by no one. I'm imagining the discomfort in his tone. I must be.

Every evening at Fire, there is one hour. One blessed hour when all the chores and prep work are done. When the day crew has done all their cleaning, scrubbed the place of every particle of DNA, set the scenes, made sure everything is perfect for the guests... After all that work, that's when the shift changes from the daytime cooks and cleaning and prep crews to the sensual teachers and leaders of the rooms, the professionals who know how to bring every inch of your flesh to life.

And that's when the staff gets to play.

Cannon, wanting to reward his hardworking employees as well as ease his evening workers into the mood of the club, had the brilliant idea for the staff's paths to cross in this way, for the day crew to blow off steam and the night crew to have an hour after their busy day, filled with the worries of ordinary life, to get to play and ease into the sexy work ahead.

He chooses a few rooms each night to close, leaving them available for the staff hour.

I'm staff. I'm no longer a virgin. I'm ready to play. The morning after my exquisite evening with Cannon, I make a decision. Tonight, I will play. With trembling fingers, I go to the sign-up sheet in the room we clock in and out of. I scan the piece of paper, trailing my finger over it as I read. There're so many options.

Across the top of the page in bold it reads: **Play with equal parts respect and liberation.**

I like that. Cannon's made it clear there's nothing going on in this club that isn't one hundred percent consensual. And as far as problems arising, so far in the employee gossip chain, I've heard of none. His meticulous vetting of staff and clientele seem to have avoided conflict.

There're codes for everything, and everything must be agreed to before the scene. *FN* means full nudity, and *FP* means full penetration. I think of Cannon and blush. Let's see, let's see... I don't even find the need to remind myself to breathe deeply as I scan the list. I find there's not an apprehensive bone in my body.

I think Cannon cured me of that last night.

I sign up to be a recipient of a full-body erotic massage. The masseuse, Ricky, a man with a thick accent and a deep olive complexion, wants to practice on someone before his billionaire tech boss babe client arrives.

"Yes, Ricky, I'd be happy to be your guinea pig," I say, swirling my name across the paper with an inky pen.

Twenty-three minutes later, I'm lying flat on my back on a table of black leather. I wear nothing but straps of black leather studded with silver metal circles, wrapped around my rib cage, my belly, my thighs.

My breasts and pussy are fully exposed. There's an audience hovering around the edges of the room. That's one of the rules with staff playtime—it's never a private event, anyone may come and watch.

I can't believe I'm lying here naked, my nipples standing on end, perfectly on display from my full breasts that heave as I take a deep breath. I love the feeling of people watching. There's got to be at least a dozen sets of eyes on me, including one dark pair that seems to delve straight into my soul whenever I look into them.

Cannon stands in the open doorway of the green room, named after its dark green wood paneling, arms crossed over his chest, sipping a drink. I can't quite read the look he's giving me. Caught somewhere between anger and desire maybe? I can't focus on him now. I've got Ricky's smooth, sultry voice beckoning me.

"Kylie, Kylie, Kylie. What a beautiful body you've offered to me to tonight. I give my deepest gratitude for your trust and enthusiasm." He stretches his open palms over my shoulders. "May I?"

"Yes, you may."

I close my eyes as his warm, oiled hands make contact with my skin. Every nerve ending stands at attention as he touches me. Oh my God, the feel of his strong hands working the knots out of my shoulders—

My relaxation is interrupted by a cough coming from the doorway of the room.

"Sorry. Just got a bit of my drink down the wrong way. Please, continue." It's Cannon's deep voice giving the apology. I would recognize it anywhere.

I close my eyes once more, settling back into the cushion.

Ricky continues to massage my shoulders, moving down my arms, thumbs massaging the tense muscles in my forearms. He's grabbing one of my hands in both of his, and the feel of him kneading my palm then rising up and tugging on the ends of my fingers. It's close to the orgasm I experienced with Cannon last night, and it's only my hand in Ricky's.

"God, you're good," I say. "Really good. Tasha is going to love tonight's session. I swear your touch is like reaching into heaven."

"Thank you," he says. "I aim to please. And when my playmate is as beautiful as you, I can't help but enjoy every moment of my job."

"Thank you," I say, but my words melt in my throat as he lays my hand flat on the bed, moving his touch to my waist. His oiled fingers move higher, rolling over my ribs, finding my breasts, encased between thin lines of black leather. He takes a nipple between his slippery fingers, rolling it until I feel the touch deep within my core—

A familiar voice booms through the room. "Enough."

Ricky's hands leave my body. Nooo!

"Would you look at the time? Madam Tasha always arrives early. She's one of our most important clients. We can't provide excellent service if we're just standing around here playing when she shows up, can we?" Cannon throws back the rest of his drink and turns on the heel of his heavy boot, leaving the room.

Ricky shrugs. "Guess we'll have to cut it short."

I shrug off my disappointment. After a quick shower I take the softly lit path to the carriage house, garden pebbles crunching under my feet. I spend the rest of the evening playing Scrabble with Nonna and Booker, a familiar game for Nonna and me, but with the added pleasure of whiskey and a saucy South African, it's double the fun.

The two of them have become the best of friends. Booker, missing his own grandparents back home, has slipped into calling Nonna *Ouma*, the South African equivalent of grandmother. Nonna's afghans are spread over the backs of the couch and armchairs, and a few of her crocheted doilies protect the wood of the side tables from drinks.

Nonna wins with her last two words, fornicate and threesome. She laughs herself all the way to bed. Booker walks me home and I crawl into Cannon's bed, half-hoping he'll crawl in after me. He doesn't. I wake to the soft close of the guest room door when he comes in hours later.

The next day Cannon gives me an additional duty of ordering the fresh flower arrangements for every room each week.

He hands me the crisp order form, pinned to a clipboard, each room labeled neatly in an empty rectangle. "I think you have an eye for this kind of thing. And we've had late deliveries in the past. I can tell with you everything will be right as well as right on time. Just as I like it."

"Of course, sir." I take the board from him.

He stares at me a beat longer than a boss might an employee before turning on his heel and leaving the room.

I exhale a long breath I didn't even know I'd been holding. "Peonies for the Pink Room, red roses for the Garden of Eden, orchids for the Black Leather Room, hanging ivy for the Green Room..." I go down the list, easily filling in my vision for each space. I call the vendors, chilling my tone a bit as I inform them that I'll be holding them to their promised delivery times.

After placing my orders, I can't help but to go back to that naughty list that hangs in the staff room, tempting me at all hours of the day. I sign myself up for a half-hour long session with Rapture, a six-foot-seven-inch (according to Keisha's American measuring) man who wields a long black cat-o-nine tails, remembering how warm and stinging Cannon's paddle felt landing across the curves of my ass.

Keisha dresses me in a pair of black leather, full-cut panties and a matching high-cup bra for the evening. Fishnet stockings and patent leather stiletto-heeled boots complete the outfit. I drag my long hair up into a high ponytail, smoothing it back before securing it with several hair bands.

Keisha gives a wolf whistle of approval. "You're no longer Kylie V, that's for sure."

She has no idea...

"Thanks for your help." I slap her a high five as I strut out of the room.

"Get it, girl! You're on fire tonight, Miss Kylie."

"Thanks, Keisha." Confidence radiates from me as I clip-clop down the hallway on the heels of my fuck-me power boots.

After making very pleasant introductions and exchanging our thoughts on today's mild weather, Rapture secures my wrists in the cuffs in the wall of the Garden of Eden. This time, I'm facing the black leather wall.

I can hear the crowd of people behind me, murmuring about their days, my clothing, the way Rapture commands the respect of a room. As soon as the swish of his cat-o-nines is heard, the room falls into a silent hush.

"Ladies and Gents. My deepest gratitude goes out to you tonight for joining me and Miss Kylie in our half-hour adventure into the land that borders pleasure and pain. Or not borders, exactly, more brings the two together, fusing them as one into the body's memory."

I grit my teeth, readying for the impact of the leather tails to come screaming across my backside. Instead, there's the soft sound of a swish in the air and the pleasant sting of several strands landing softly over my curves.

"That wasn't too bad," I say.

"It should never be bad. It should either be pleasure or invited pain. I like to warm my clients up first," he says, dragging the leather across my panties.

I hear a hiss from the crowd as if someone else has been hit by this thing, much harder than I was. I glance over my shoulder. I only see the happy faces of my fellow staff members.

I turn back around, training my gaze on one of the black buttons on the leather wall. Will it hurt? Will I cry out? *Deep breaths, deep breaths.* But I find I don't need them. There's a calmness in the unknown, the uncertainty of what's to come. I trust Rapture to guide my body in this experience.

The delicate ends of the lash come down again, this time harder than the first. Bright sparks of pain dash over me. I suck air in between my teeth, fast and sharp.

"I think it's time we remove these leather panties. What you say, Fire?"

There's cheering and wolf whistles from the crowd.

Rapture moves to me, whispering in my ear. "And what does Miss Kylie say?"

"Yes, of course." My commitment comes quick, but after my words escape me, I'm left with that electrified moment of doubt before the deed actually happens. Exposing my ass to the club, having them all stare at whatever red marks the whip raises on my flesh—

"Nope." Cannon's booming voice echoes through the room. "No. I'm afraid we don't have time for that. We're actually going to have to wrap this session up now." There's an audible sigh from the crowd. He continues, "Madam Funai is flying in from Japan, and I've just gotten word she'll be arriving a little early. Seems like the theme this week, early birds. Sorry, everyone, but we need to be ready."

I stare down at my black leather bra, at my legs wrapped in the sexy fishnets. Disappointment comes over me. I was so looking forward to seeing where this would go, how it would feel, but I know clients come first.

Keisha strides over to me, undoing the clasps around my wrists. "You did great, ladybug."

"You really did. Next time, we'll go all the way," Rapture tells me with a grin.

"Thanks to you both," I say, lowering my arms to my sides. I turn to face the crowd, but my gaze only searches for Cannon's face. He's already gone, making his final round of inspections.

Rapture slides a big, heavy arm around my bare shoulders as we make our way from the room. "You're amazing to watch. So responsive. Everyone loved you."

"Thank you. That's kind of you to say. I'm sorry it got cut short," I say.

"No matter. Tomorrow night we'll more than make up for it." His eyes light up. "We can't wait to play with you at ASAG."

"ASAG?" I ask.

"All Staff Anything Goes. Once a quarter, Cannon shuts down the club to clientele and guests and gives his staff free rein of the place. He hires outside help to host, and we basically get to act like the millionaires for the evening. There's no sign-up sheet." Rapture gives a devilish grin. "Whatever happens, happens."

"Really? That sounds incredible." A thrill runs through me at the thought of such an evening.

"It is." He gives a naughty wiggle of his brow. "You're going to love it."

I go to the staff room, pulling a pair of loose sweats on over my tights and slip my arms into the lightweight jacket I brought with me. The walk from Fire to Cannon's is short. It's a dark night, no moon, and not a star can be seen. A breeze blows by, rustling the leaves in the bushes as I walk down the stone path, my way lit only by the little fake flame solar garden lights Cannon's had installed.

The little brick house is painted white; shiny black shutters gleam in the soft light. It's quaint and beautiful, a homey cottage. A place I'd be happy to never have to leave.

"Signora." A voice with a thick, local accent startles me. "Signora Barone?"

I glance over, finding a man I've never seen before standing just off the path. I look around to confirm my fear — I'm alone out here with him.

"Ciao?" My heart races faster. "Do I know you?"

He shakes his head and smiles. "No. I'm afraid not. But I'd like to make my introductions. I'm Max. Max Meralo." He holds out his hand for me to shake.

Maxim Meralo. Mad Max Meralo.

They call him Mad Max for his temper and the fact he's supposedly a genius, crafty and highly intelligent, with a short fuse. He's the head of the Meralo family. My blood turns to ice. I shake off the chill, willing my tongue to thaw in my mouth.

I don't offer my hand.

He pulls his back, giving a grin. A wild look rests in his eyes. "I'm not here to cause trouble. I promise."

I cross my arms over my chest, trying to bring warmth back to my shaking body. "Then why are you here?"

"I just wanted to take one look at you. To see you in the flesh. The woman who's owed to me to pay off the debts of her family." His grin turns menacing. "My bride."

"I'll never be your bride," I say.

Ignoring me, he reaches out to stroke my face. His hand is cold, his touch icy. "I'm not disappointed."

I snap my head away. "I'm not going to marry you. You need to speak to Cannon. He'll take care of everything."

Max gives a nod, a slow grin creeping across his face. "I'll do that. I'll do just that." He gives me one last look, then turns on his heel, disappearing into the bushes.

I waste no time. I run down the path, letting myself into Cannon's place, locking the front door. Leaning my back against the solid wood, I close my eyes. *Deep breaths, deep breaths.* I will my racing heart to slow.

What do I do? Text Booker? I don't want to frighten Nonna. Do I tell Cannon? I've already caused so much trouble for him. Does he even need to know about this visit? It was a harmless enough exchange, wasn't it? He didn't hurt me or anything, he didn't even threaten me.

I shower and change, debating with myself the entire time. I finally land on telling Cannon what happened. Just not now when he'd just moved me and Nonna in, given me a job, and made Booker Nonna's personal guard. It'll only put him out further, probably by giving me my own guard or, God forbid, not letting me work and keeping me locked up in his house.

I'll give things a few days to settle down, then I'll tell him. Unless something else happens. If something else happens, I make a promise to myself to tell Cannon about the strange visit right away.

Exhausted from my day, I crawl into bed, thinking of how I must get Cannon to trade me back and let me sleep in his guest room. It's not fair to him that I've taken over his bedroom. I've already taken over his life for goodness' sake, his whole focus has become keeping me and Nonna safe.

How did that Mad Max Meralo get through the gates to talk to me tonight? An icy shiver travels down my spine and I push the thought of him away, thinking of something more pleasant. Cannon.

When Cannon walks in a room, he commands respect. When he speaks, everyone listens. When I'm with him, I feel safe.

There's a knock on the bedroom door, dragging me from my thoughts.

I lean up from the bed. "Yes?"

Cannon's voice warms me. "I thought you might like a little champagne to celebrate the end of your first week of work."

Has it already been a week? How time flies. I don't know if I like champagne. I've never had it, but I would like to spend some time with him. "Just a moment. I'll be right out."

"Take your time."

I hop up from the bed, dressing in jeans and a hoodie. After tugging a brush through my hair and running a little gloss over my lips, I join him in his living room. He's sitting on the couch, wearing all black as per usual, his legs spread wide.

On the glass table sit two champagne flutes and a bottle on ice.

"Here, sit," he says, patting the open spot beside him on the couch.

"Thank you," I say.

He leans forward, filling my glass with the bubbly liquid. "I think you'll like it."

I don't usually drink, but I'm still shaken from the encounter with Max. "Thank you." I take the glass from him, waiting to take a sip until he has his filled.

I should tell him.

No, it can wait.

I hold my glass up, clinking it against his. "Cheers. To surviving the first week."

"Cheers to slaying the first week." He tips his glass back, downing half the liquid in one gulp.

I do the same, the fizzy drink rushing down my throat. It's delicious. I sip at the second half of the glass. I don't know if it's fatigue or the alcohol, but my mind feels languid, loose.

He holds the bottle up to me. "More?" he asks.

"Yes, please. Champagne is tasty." I sip the second glass more slowly. "I've never had champagne before. I like it."

"You've had a lot of firsts this week, babygirl." He's staring down into his glass, twirling the stem between his fingertips.

A blush rises in my cheeks at the sound of the pet name, a reminder of our evening together. I think of my other firsts, playing in the playrooms, wearing a French maid costume to work.

I smile. "Yes. I have. And tomorrow night, I'll have another."

"Oh?" he says. "What's that?"

"AGAS." I hold up a finger, trying to remember what Rapture called it. "No, wait, that's not right. ASAG. I'll be able to play with *alll* the staff and this time, it won't get cut short."

"Didn't realize you'd be going."

Am I imagining it, or is his face tightening as he shifts in his seat?

"Oh, I am. I can't wait." I give a little giggle as a hiccup comes bubbling up. "It's going to be fantastic."

"I'm sure it will be." He takes a long, slow drink of his champagne.

13

C *annon*

I COULDN'T DO IT, I just couldn't stomach the idea of having her participate in the All Staff Anything Goes night. I already cut short her two playtimes, the one with Ricky and the one with Rapture. The image of her chained to the wall of the Garden or bent over one of my pommel horses, and me not being the one running the scene? The thought alone makes me want to commit crimes.

Instead of losing my cool and breaking bones, I whisked her away.

I glance over at Kylie curled up against the window, breathing soft, steady breaths in her sleep. She has no idea where she is right now, having not awakened since falling asleep on my couch.

Okay, so, technically, I kidnapped her.

Big deal. I'm the boss.

If I want to give one of my staff members an impromptu, well-earned vacation, that's my prerogative, right? She's been working her ass off. Why not spoil her? She hasn't had to lift a finger for this trip—literally, I carried sleeping beauty onto the plane—and Emilia and Charlie, my co-conspirators, did all her packing.

Who wouldn't want to be spirited away by the man they lost their virginity to? Who, after turning into a sex goddess and unlocking a wild, sensual side of herself somehow in the space of one amazing night, wouldn't want to share that side of herself with that man instead of with other staff members at an all-night anything goes—literally—event?

An unsettled feeling fills my belly as I watch her sleep. God, she's gorgeous. She's going to be pissed when she finds out I've taken her. Every time I look at her, I get this tugging feeling in my chest. I'll be damned if this girl hasn't turned my entire world upside down.

And the craziest part?

I never saw it coming.

All this time, I've been thinking I didn't want another relationship. That I didn't want to risk having my heart crushed under another Louboutin red-soled high heel. But that isn't the truth, is it? Otherwise I wouldn't be sitting next to her now, having dragged her away from Fire.

The truth is that I just didn't want a relationship with any of the other women I've been with. But when it comes to Kylie...

I want it all.

I think back to that moment at the bar at Fire. How I knew in my gut I should send her on her way, not get involved...

And now, I've fucking kidnapped her.

Her dark lashes flutter, her eyes opening. I look away so she won't know I've been staring.

She gives a cat-like purr, stretching her lovely arms above her head. I can't help but pick back up with my staring habit as the sweetest little smile curls the corners of her full lips.

"Did I fall asleep?" she purrs.

"More like passed out."

"Wait... where are we?" She gives a shake of her head, blinking hard as she finally comes to. Her hazel eyes go wide as she takes in her surroundings. When she sees the clouds out of the window of the jet, she grabs my arm, eyes searching mine. "Are we on a... plane? Am I dreaming?"

"We are on a plane." I glance down at my watch. "And you've been sleeping six hours."

Her brow knits together in disbelief. "Have I?"

"Yes. You had a little too much champagne and passed out. I took the opportunity to kidnap you and carry you onto my jet for a little adventure. Didn't think you'd mind."

"Kidnapped. What do you mean? Where are we going?" As reality settles in, her thoughts, as always, go to her grandmother. "And what about Nonna?"

"Nonna approved the trip. She and Booker have facials and full body massages booked at Fire's on-site spa today. She sent you this." I retrieve the note from my breast pocket, slipping it into her hands. It's scented with her grandmother's rosewater perfume.

She opens the paper, reading aloud, translating the Italian to English. "Kylie, dearest. Mr. Cannon has told me he has wonderful plans for you. Please enjoy and don't worry about me for a moment. Love, Nonna."

"See? No harm done. Just a little surprise work break."

She sinks back in her seat. "Thank you. That's sweet of you. I have been working a lot of hours since I took over the ordering of the floral arrangements and candles." She gives me a satisfied smile. "Not that I haven't loved every minute I've been working at Fire."

"I know. You've been an amazing addition to the team." My fingers clench around the arm of my chair, my jaw tightening as I speak. "The whole staff agrees." Especially my straight, single, male staff members...

"And we'll be back in time tonight for ASAG." She gives a decisive nod, knowing I would never tear her away from such an event.

A touch of guilt rises in me. Keeping her from the party is exactly what I've done.

"No. I'm sorry. We'll actually be staying a few nights."

Her jaw drops. "Miss the All Staff? I was so looking forward to it. Tie was finally going to do some ropework on me."

I bristle beside her, my fingers clenching into fists, thinking of Tie's deft fingers looping silky cords around Kylie. "That's too bad. Really. A shame."

There's a hint of mistrust in her pretty irises as she eyes me. "You abducted me."

"No. I... *borrowed* you."

"You got me drunk, then kidnapped me onto your private jet."

"*Nooo...* I gave you your first taste of champagne, good champagne, mind you. Only the best. And then, when you passed out on the sofa for a little catnap, I gathered you in my arms and carried you here to continue your sleep. I thought you'd be more comfortable sleeping in the big leather chair of a private jet, cruising above the clouds. I love this plane. I actually won it from Liam in a bet, but don't bring that up. He's still pissed."

"I won't. You boys and your toys."

"The jet is my favorite possession next to Fire," I say.

She gives a little humph noise, and stares out the window, thinking. A moment later, she says, "This little trip wouldn't have anything to do with the fact that you don't like to see me play with other staff members, would it?" She gives me an accusatory stare.

Jealous prickles dance over the back of my neck. I run a hand over my tingling skin. "No. It would not. That's ridiculous."

She gives a sigh like she's arguing with a child. The tips of her jet-black nails tap at the arm of her chair. "Then what is this?"

I shrug. "Just a trip."

"Cannon Bachman. You cannot just scoop people up and throw them on your jet."

"Shh. You'll wake Emilia."

"Emilia?"

Kylie leans over, peering behind us. Emilia is cozied up, her head tucked against Liam's shoulder, Liam's arm protectively wrapped around her as she sleeps. Liam gives Kylie a nod of greeting.

She offers him a tight smile in return. She turns back to me, hissing, "Is this some kind of couples retreat? When we are not a couple?"

"Nope. Look over there." I point to where Charlie and Tristan sit. Charlie is working on a needlepoint, something floral with bright pink and coral threads. Tristan sits with his arms folded, a grumpy expression on his face. He didn't want to come. "Tristan and Charlie. Two very single people are on board."

"You mean *four* very single people are on board this plane. Last time I checked, you and I were both single and free to do as we wish."

I nod. "Exactly." What I wish is to take her as far away as possible from Fire and the eyes and hands of every adoring staff member and lock her away, keeping her all to myself.

She whispers, "But what if I wish to go back now? To be at Fire tonight for the party? What if I choose to not partake of this mystery trip you've forced upon me?"

I lean over her, my arm pressing against the side of her soft, curvy breast as I glance out the window. She doesn't pull away.

"Hmm...." I say, pretending to examine the puffy white clouds. I turn to her, my lips a beat away from hers as I speak. "Looks like that might be a problem. We are thirty thousand feet in the air right now."

"Is that so?" The tip of her tongue wets her bottom lip, her eyes lowering to my mouth. As much as she protests about this trip, she wants to be kissed. I can feel the heat coming off of her. She doesn't seem too put out to be trapped on this plane with me.

I settle back into my seat. "It's so. And I'm afraid we have no choice but to go through with the visit. I'll do everything I can to make sure you enjoy yourself."

She settles down a bit, her arm pressed against mine. I'll take that as a good sign.

"Well, are you going to at least tell me where you are taking me?"

I stare off toward the front of the jet in fake contemplation for a moment before shaking my head. "Nah."

She rests the back of her head against her seat. "Cannon, you are by far the most exasperating man I've ever met." But she says it with a smile.

God, the Beauties are going to fall head over heels for her. I have an army of well-meaning women at my disposal who want nothing more than to make Kylie happy. And to be happy with me. The Bachman wives love *love* and long for everyone to partake in it. There've been whispers through the family about me for years, horror at my singleness and bachelor ways.

When they set their sights on Kylie... she's not going to have just me to deal with. Perhaps... this trip will be more than just a breather, a chance to have her all to myself. Maybe seeing other happy Bachman couples will make her reconsider her stance on "relationships," and "commitment," words she says with a tinge of fear in her angelic voice.

My jealousy is replaced by hope. Maybe she'll find that being in a relationship isn't so bad. "We're traveling to meet another branch of the family," I say.

She makes a guess. "The Parrish? In Greece? I've heard of that place as well. White stone mansions, sandy beaches—"

"No. Not today." I think of her shapely legs stretched out over a blanket on the sand, tanning in the warm sun. Then I think of all the single Greek brothers who would be admiring her right along with me. "But we should go there. Soon."

"If it's not the Parrish..." She taps a fingertip against her chin. "The Village? In New York? I've heard of that. Are we going all the way to America?"

Ha-ha... the Village, too many single brothers roaming around for my taste. Hellllll to the no.

I shake my head. "America, yes, but the Village, no. Guess again."

She shrugs. "I have no idea."

"We're going to the Hamlet."

Her nose crinkles. "I haven't heard of that. Where is it?"

"Connecticut."

"Connecticut?" After thinking of our branches in New York City and a private island in Greece, disappointment floods her face.

Too bad, princess, it was my safest bet.

I offer a few more details to make the trip more enticing to her. "The Hamlet is one of our family's villages, hidden in Connecticut, bordered by the Housatonic River and surrounded by beautiful, dense woods. To get there, you first cross the river, driving through a dark-red covered bridge. You feel as if you're traveling to a simpler place and time. And you kind of are. The Hamlet is a town lost in time, very little media by way of television or internet make it inside the walls — the families are too busy working, raising kids, and socializing with one another to pay much attention to the outside world."

"Hmm," she says. "So, like their own little mafia world?"

"Exactly. They are completely self-sufficient and have everything they need." I think of the delivery trucks that visit, daily, and correct myself. "Well, as self-sufficient as they claim to be, the women can't seem to live without their internet shopping. But the family grows their own food in a huge, hydroponic greenhouse, raises their own herd for meat and dairy, and even have their own schoolhouse and hospital."

"Umm... compared to the glamor of Fire, this place doesn't sound very," her nose crinkles, "Bachman."

"It is. Trust me. Just in a..." I think of all the families, attached men and women happily married, compared to the completely unattached lifestyle of my club, "tamer way."

"I don't mean to be rude, but it doesn't sound like much fun."

"Says the girl who a few weeks ago was doing crossword puzzles for entertainment," I say.

"Exactly. I've missed out on so much. Why miss a single night at Fire? Especially a night where anything goes." A light shines in her eyes and she gets this faraway look, thinking of the playtime she's missing with the men of my staff.

The flesh on the back of my neck burns, heat coursing through my veins. I shift my weight in my chair, trying to control my jealousy. I manage a gruff response. "I think you'll survive a few nights."

"Hmm..." She eyes my biceps, showing from under my sleeves. Reaching out, she strokes her fingers along my forearm. Her touch sends electric sparks over my skin. She drags her doe eyes up to meet mine, looking up at me from under her lashes. "Well, if we find it too boring there, you and I could always try a few things... no strings attached, of course."

God, is that all she thinks of? Sex?

The thought makes me want to slap my own face. Who am I becoming? A few weeks ago I was a sex club owner with a different woman in my bed every night, literally reading the women first to be sure our evening of pleasure would be one with no strings attached.

Now?

When she says the words, they make me cringe.

What. The. Hell. Has come over me?

Her.

It's her.

Kylie Barone and no one else on this Earth could have changed me in this way. Pain strikes my chest and I have to look away.

She senses my silence, and her fingers stop moving over my skin. She takes my hand in hers, giving it a squeeze. "Did I say something wrong?"

"No, no," I say, surprised by the gruffness in my voice. "You're fine."

What do I tell her? That I want her and her alone. That I want her for my own, and never, ever want to let another man touch her.

That I want every goddamn string in this world attaching her to me?

"How about a drink?" I ask, changing the subject.

She shakes her head. "No way. Not after the way that champagne made me pass out."

"Food?" I ask.

A manicured hand flutters to her flat belly. There's a small chip in the black nail polish on her index finger. "Food, now that sounds amazing. I'm starving."

I raise my hand in the air, signaling a waitperson over. I order us a charcuterie board of meat and cheese and fruit and two coffees — hers with plenty of cream and sugar like I know she likes it.

Trying to make up for whatever bristles have passed between us, she grabs my arm, snuggling up to my side. "Tell me more about the Hamlet. It sounds beautiful."

"It is. The buildings are all red brick with tall, white-cased windows. There're gardens everywhere, tucked in between most of the buildings. And it's very secure. There's a tall wrought iron fence around the entire perimeter of the land, a long and winding, unassuming, private dirt road that leads to a stone wall and massive gate that stretch out across the front of the entrance." Hidden cameras and twenty-four-seven guards keep the Hamlet the amazing secret that it is. That and some very generous political donations to keep our relationship with the local law enforcement peaceful. "Deliveries are made on a separate road, left at a guarded gazebo, the packages then brought to the Hamlet by brothers."

"Deliveries from the online shopping addictions you mentioned?" she laughs.

"I guess when you have kids, you need a lot of stuff. And there are lots of kids in the Hamlet—it's all families, the place created from a time when children weren't allowed in the Village of New York."

"But I've heard there's a school in the Village now."

"There is now, we've got the security and connections we need to keep everyone safe in the city. But we didn't always have those things. The Village was thought to be too dangerous for kids. That's why the Hamlet was created. A safe place for families to run the more legitimate aspects of our business while raising their kids. The married and expecting parents of the family flocked here. Bronson Bachman, a legacy Bachman and our only member to be third-generation Bachman, left the Village to lead the Hamlet. He and his wife, Paige, have a couple kids, Thomas and Kate, that keep him very busy, along with running this branch of our world."

"Hmm..." She taps her chin again, thinking.

"What?"

"Nothing. Just a big change from our current living situation. I mean, next week I'm having dinner at midnight followed by the most amazing hot wax session with Tate—"

Between clenched teeth I interrupt her. "I thought we could use a change."

I can't hear about her plans for the future. It makes my stomach clench into a fist of ice. I run a hand through my hair, trying not to tug it out of my scalp. She tenses beside me. I soften my tone, reminding myself this mess I've gotten myself into is not her fault. I'm the one who's lost my head.

She gets a dreamy smile on her face as she looks out the window. "I wouldn't change a thing."

"*I* could use a change," I say.

She stares at me a moment, contemplating my face. We sit in silence for a moment. Thank God the steward comes with the food. We spend a few easy moments snacking on delicacies from the wooden board that's been placed on a tray between us.

"You know," she speaks gently between dainty nibbles of a seeded cracker, "if you aren't comfortable with our arrangement, you can tell me."

"Why would I be uncomfortable? We made it clear. No strings attached. You know it's my cardinal rule, never to date staff." My tone comes out harsher than I mean it to.

"And my personal rule is never to date at all." She plucks up a grape, popping it into her mouth. Her gaze is far away as she chews, thinking. "But for you to take me from a sex club to a place that sounds almost like a daycare, I can't help but wonder if this trip is your way of telling me that you are not okay with our arrangement."

She eyes me.

What do I say? I hate our arrangement?

That the thought of it makes my flesh go hot, my skin prickle? That I want to murder every amazing staff member of mine who has had the honor of touching her beautiful body? Men that I respect, have worked with for years? I want to wrap my hands around their throats and—

"Cannon? Did you hear what I said? Do you want the last grape?"

"No." I look down at my fingers wrapped around the handle of my coffee mug so tightly my knuckles have turned white. I set the cup down on the tray. Time for a bold move on my part. "Why?" I say. "Why is it that you don't want to ever commit to someone?"

"Because." She stares out the window, lost in thought. When she turns back to me, the look in her eyes dashes every ounce of hope from my chest. "I don't want to get hurt."

"No one does," I say, my throat tight. "Ten years ago, I lost someone very special to me. A woman named Catherine." For the first time in a long time, speaking her name doesn't cause me physical pain. I think of the beauty from my past and can't quite remember her face, or the curves of her body. The vision of her is blurry, fuzzy, pushed further away since Kylie. "That was before I joined the family. I was broke, trying to make my way in the world. I'd misread her, thinking she wanted me, the prospect of our future together, but it turned out she only wanted what I could do for her, and she decided it wasn't enough. She left me for a rich asshole, a yacht broker on the coast."

"I'm sorry," she says.

I continue my story, slightly awed by the fact that I'm sharing it in the first place. "Catherine broke my heart. I thought I could never go through that kind of pain again. I started having one-night stands, telling myself not to get too close." Though now I know I didn't want one-night stands. I was just with the wrong women. "Then, something changed."

"What changed?" she asks.

There is no other time, this is the moment; if I let this go, I might lose my chance. Do I even have a chance? Does it even matter? What do I have to lose — she's already told me there is no chance in hell this thing between us, what I want, what I have to have, will ever happen.

She asks again, her eyes searching mine for answers. "What changed?"

"I met you." I lean forward, needing to kiss her. "You, Kylie, are what changed."

I slip my hands through her hair and bring her to me, kissing her hard, and in the kiss, I take back my fire, my position of control, no longer willing to let her call the shots.

14

K *ylie*

HIS LIPS ARE hot against mine, his kiss growing more demanding with each movement of his tongue. I find myself melting into his kiss, but then remember that Emilia and Liam are just behind us.

My face is heated as I bring my hand to his chest, pushing him away from me. "Cannon. We're not alone."

His voice is hoarse. "I don't care." His fingers tangle in my hair, sending shivers down my spine as he pulls me closer, wanting another kiss.

"This isn't a playroom at the club," I say. "No one here wants to see us kiss."

He looks over his shoulder, finding Charlie giving us a curious stare. Caught, she quickly looks away. He turns back to me. "You so sure about that? I think there're a lot of Bachmans who would like to see us kiss."

His words make the full reality of what he's done settle in.

He's taking me to his family's place, the Hamlet, a secret town where everyone is in loving, committed relationships. He thinks this will change my mind. That seeing his happy, monogamous family members will make me want what they have.

It won't work, though. I won't risk my heart.

He's told me of Catherine, of his heartache. He's told me his truth.

Now it's time for me to share mine.

He's closing in for another kiss.

I stop him. "Cannon."

"What?" His lips brush over mine, a starburst of tingles dancing over me.

"Listen. I want to tell you something."

My words stop him, making him sit back in his seat. He leans an elbow on the armrest, resting his head in his hand. The steady gaze of those deep brown eyes tells me I have his full attention.

"I'm listening," he says.

"You shared your story with me. Now, I'd like to share mine."

"Alright." He pulls back.

I take a deep breath. "My mother was a woman from a simple life with big dreams. She went to college in New York and after graduation she stayed, building a fancy life for herself as an interior designer. Her clients loved the influence she brought from our simple Italian countryside village. Apparently, she was quite successful and even afforded her own high-rise apartment in Manhattan."

This is a story my grandmother told me. This is the first time I'm sharing it. To hear myself say it out loud feels strange, like I'm narrating a film. I have to take a sip of my now cold coffee to continue.

"Let me get you a fresh one," he says, reaching for my mug.

"No, that's okay." I push the cup away. I don't want the flight attendant hovering over us, it's too intimate of a moment.

"Anyway," I continue, "in one instant, everything changed. One beautiful, carefree night spent with a handsome colleague with hazel eyes, drinking champagne on balconies, dancing under the stars, making love in his loft apartment would destroy her dreams."

His brow furrows over his intense gaze. "How?"

My skin suddenly feels cool, a chill passing over me. Maybe I do need that coffee. "She found herself pregnant with me."

"But a child is a blessing," he says.

"Not when you're a single woman with no children in your plans," I say. "The colleague had no interest in becoming a father. Doing all he could to avoid my mother, he quickly found new employment with a company in a different part of the city. She stayed and made it work until I was ten, but then things got hard for her. With no family around to support her, she moved back in with my grandmother, back in our small town, back to the yellow house and the pharmacy job. It was as if she'd never left, the only trace of her other life being the dark hair and hazel eyes I'd inherited from my father, and a set of antique American china dishes she'd painstakingly packed up and brought back with her."

"She couldn't find any happiness when she came back?" he asks.

"I guess not, because..." I get to the most painful part of the story for me. "When we got back, it wasn't long before she took off. She couldn't handle being back in her old life, I guess. Maybe she didn't want to be a mother any more. I don't know, but either way, she abandoned us, and I haven't heard from her since." For some reason, I bare my soul, telling him the most intimate details of my thoughts. "I'm sure Nonna doesn't blame me, but whenever she speaks of my mother, she can't seem to meet my eyes."

"That can't be true." He opens his arms to me. "Come here."

I lean against him, absorbing the warmth and strength of his body as a comfort. I reach up, brushing a tear from my eye. "So you see, I don't want to end up like that, having a man take away my dreams, then growing so bitter I give up on the ones I love."

"How can you think that of yourself? Up until now, your whole live has revolved around caring for your grandmother."

"Yes, because she was there for me when my mother left. So, now I'm there for her. But what if my love doesn't extend past her, what I owe her? What if I was to get married, or have a child, then begin to feel like my mother did, and abandon them?" I shake my head. "I could never live with myself."

He squeezes my arm, his voice going to that deep timbre I love so much. "Exactly. You could never do that. You aren't your mother."

We sit in silence for a moment, then he asks, "What are your dreams, anyway?"

I shrug. "I really don't know. Up until a few weeks ago, my only thoughts were of caring for my grandmother. When I came to Fire," I take a deep breath, thinking of how it felt to walk down that red and gold hallway, to be chained to a padded leather wall, to be with Cannon for the first time, "it's like I woke up from a deep sleep, like my entire life had been on hold and now, it's opening up."

Like a flower just about to bloom.

"What if being with someone doesn't mean the end of something, but the beginning. The start of good things to come?" he asks.

"Or what if letting someone in," I argue, "like in your case, leads to heartbreak."

He goes quiet.

He's done so much for me and here, it seems I keep causing him trouble. "Sorry. I didn't mean to—"

"No, you're right. It's a risk. But you're a brave girl." He sits back in his seat. "Besides, I might not be giving you the choice much longer."

"What do you mean?" I glance over at him.

"Because." He rests the back of his head against the headrest of his seat. Closing his eyes, he runs a hand over his brow. "I'm going to end up killing every man that touches you."

His words are like steel, hard and cold, but they make me giggle for some unfathomable reason.

"Seriously?" I say. "First you kidnap me to take me to some couples-only retreat, then you threaten to kill any man who comes in contact with me?"

"Careful. My Plan C is a convent. There's a precious little nunnery on the mainland, just a five-minute boat ride from the Parrish. Those nuns owe me a favor. They'd have to take you in."

I try to picture myself in the black-and-white habit the nuns at my primary school wore and it only makes me break out into another fit of giggles. "A nun. Me? Can you imagine? Hey, that gives me an idea for a scene—"

The fury of his growl stifles my laughter.

He cracks the knuckles of his right hand. "I cannot watch, talk about, or even think about you being in one of those playrooms, Kylie. I swear to God. I'm ready to commit murder."

I feel bad. He's really struggling with the idea of me with other men. He's doing a terrible job of hiding it. His eyes are still closed, the back of his head resting against his seat. I take the opportunity to stare at the lines and angles of his face, his strong jawline, the dark hair framing his face as it curls just a touch at the ends.

He's beautiful.

He's beautiful and sexy and he wants me. All to himself. I just don't know if I can give him what he wants.

"Cannon," I say.

"Yes."

He's done so much for me, I need to give back to him. Can I? "What if... we just play pretend for a bit. Ease into it. Take this trip of yours. And pretend."

"Pretend to be together?" he asks.

"Sure. Why not."

I've had so much fun taking on roles and playing lately, why not play this game? Let him have a taste of what he wants, enjoy the trip.

His voice chills me, his dark eyes going black as they flash at me. "A game? Do I look like a man who plays games? We've reached a point of no return. Either you're mine, or I'm going to make you mine. No more games. No more playing around."

He doesn't allow me to answer, claiming my mouth with his. The heat of his kiss burns through me, and I realize I have been playing a game this whole time: playing with fire.

How can I win and not get burned in the process?

When we exit the jet, he holds my hand in his with a possessive, domineering energy. He's made his decision. He's going to make me his and his alone.

We've landed on a private landing strip at a small brick airport, the property surrounded by a beautiful wall made of white and gray stone. His bicep flexes as he draws me in closer to his side as we step onto the black, paved tarmac, reminding me just how big and powerful he is.

Will I let him make me his, or will I fight him? We both have fire in us, but his guns are quite a bit bigger than mine. Still, dynamite comes in a small package, doesn't it?

"Kylie. Did you hear what I said?" He gives my hand a reprimanding tug.

I'm buried so deep in my thoughts involving bad metaphors I didn't hear him speak. "Sorry, no."

"Look," he says. "Over there. The women have come to welcome you."

"Me? Why me?" I stand on tiptop to see where he's pointing. "Oh my."

Just past a gate in the wall stands an eclectic group of women from all walks of life with two undeniable things in common. They are all stunningly gorgeous. And they're all impeccably dressed.

I glance down at my jeans and hoodie, the outfit I was wearing when I passed out from the champagne I'd downed after my nerves were shaken by the man on the path. I haven't told Cannon or Booker about Mad Max's visit yet. I don't want to. I've already caused enough trouble. Besides, when am I ever alone now? I'll just be extra careful.

It'll be fine.

My outfit choice on the other hand... is not.

I'm not only underdressed, I'm a mess from sitting so long on the plane. My hair is a fan of tangles around my face and I try to smooth them down, only to have my attention drawn to the fact that I chipped one of my nails on the flight.

"Oh God. Do I look alright?" I tug on the end of a loose lock of hair.

He reaches up, untangling my finger from my hair. "You look stunning. You always look stunning."

The way he's staring at me brings heat to my face. "That's... sweet. Thank you."

Cannon—who never seems to miss a thing and reads me like Booker reads classics—gives me a demanding stare. "Are you okay?"

I go to answer but before I can, I feel a tug on my arm, and Charlie's sweet voice is like the tinkle of silver bells in my ear. "Kylie, come! You have to meet the Beauties. You're going to love them."

Emilia grabs my other arm. "I can't believe you let me sleep the whole way! We could have been chatting that whole plane ride. I was so excited to see what you thought about Cannon's surprise trip."

"The trip he planned in order to lure me into becoming one of you all?" I ask.

Charlie gives an innocent laugh. "Don't be silly! He invited you along as his plus one. Didn't he tell you? We're here for the Benefit Ball."

"What's that?" I ask.

"It's the Hamlet's annual charity auction. The family offers services then does their best to outbid one another. The profits are enough to run a nursing home in the next town over for an entire year. Paige, Bronson's wife, used to be a nurse in her pre-Bachman life but now volunteers at the local homes. Knowing how few resources they have, she demanded Bronson help her do something about it. After the auction, we get all dressed up and have dinner and dancing to celebrate. And that's how the Benefit Ball and Auction began."

"That's amazing. My grandmother would approve. She has a fear of being put into a nursing home, but I told her I would never let that happen," I say. Nonna could be here with us if she wasn't so busy with her fancy new life at Fire.

I give Cannon a passing glance as I'm tugged away. Disappointment lines his eyes at my departure, but isn't this what he wanted? Me to be tamed by these women, to see if this is the life I want?

"Save me a dance?" I call out as I go.

His perfect lips form a stunning grin. "Hell, yes."

Let's hope the night can pass without either of our fuses setting off.

Emilia says, "Would you like to participate in the auction? You must have some hidden talents."

I think of the playroom and hold in a giggle. "Um. No. I've worked in a pharmacy, and I've taken care of my grandmother."

Charlie says, "There must be something. I'm sure you're a woman of many talents."

I remember my focus and passion before Cannon woke the sex monster in me. "Oh, and I love to clean."

"There you go!" Charlie approves. "They aren't allowed to have outside labor come in, so everyone cleans their own houses. I'm sure they would love to have someone come in and clean."

"I love to organize as well. I could offer a closet redo, a pantry makeover." Dopamine floods my brain, just thinking of walking into a messy room and setting it straight. "Everyone has a corner of their home that needs tidying."

"Perfect," Emilia says. "Here's Paige now."

A tiny pixie of a woman with full curves comes rushing over to me, her dark hair cut in a sleek, trendy bob around her pretty face. "Emilia! Charlie!" She greets the women with a kiss on each cheek before turning to me. "And you must be the infamous Kylie Barone." She slips her bubblegum-pink lacquered fingernails into my hand, giving it a demure shake. "I've heard sooo much about you."

Infamous? What can she mean by that? What has she heard? Paige stares up at me with big round eyes, waiting for me to answer.

"Oh, um. Me too. About you, I mean. I've heard a lot about you," I say.

"All good things I hope!" Paige giggles.

"Same?" I say, thinking of her infamous comment.

She gives me a funny look. "Yes, of course, silly. Why wouldn't they be good?"

Charlie, always the one to iron out wrinkles in a conversation, says, "And you're about to hear something even better, Paige. Kylie has a few talents that you might desperately need around here, and they will bring in a good amount for the home."

Paige shoots me a saucy wink. "Oooh, do tell. Maybe some tricks you've picked up in Italy?"

So, she's heard about my sexcapades at Fire. *Stop blushing, Kylie. Deep breaths.* "Nothing too scandalous. Just a little cleaning and organizing."

Paige's eyes light up. "Are you serious?"

"Yes, I love to clean."

"Oh my God, I cannot cook, and I hate to clean. And my cabinets are a disaster. Stuff falls out every time I open a door. I'm gonna win

Kylie's tonight. Bronson better be ready to dish out the big bucks. This prize is mine."

"I'll help you out, Paige," I say. "Even if you don't win."

"Aww, you're so sweet!" She raises a brow. "Too sweet to handle a rifle?"

"I'm sorry?" What's she talking about?

Paige's brown eyes light up. "We're spending the day skeet shooting. A little get-to-know-you activity."

"Oh, um…" I'd pictured the day being manicures and pedicures, or having our hair done. It's fun to be pampered but this is so much better. "Shooting sounds fun."

She continues, "Then afterward we're going tubing down the river, and we have the cutest little insulated wine tumblers for the trip."

"What's tubing?" I ask.

"You've never been tubing?" Paige laughs. "Well, I guess floating downriver in a plastic tube is more of an American thing? It's so fun! And a great way to get tan before an event. You tie these big inflatable tubes together, put a cooler of food and drinks in the middle tube, then just lie down in your bikini and let the river take you on a relaxing ride."

Emilia grabs Paige's arm. "Oooh, Paige, I hate to even ask, but is there any way we can do snowtubing instead of the river tubing? It's my favorite."

Paige shrugs. "I don't see why we can't do both."

The sun shines on my face, a warm breeze fluttering the ends of my hair. "Snow?"

Emilia flashes me a grin. "They have their own sledding hill, complete with fake snow."

"That's amazing," I say.

"With so many kids to entertain, we had the idea a few years ago. A big snowy hill they could sled and tube down. We figured it would keep the kiddos busy and wear them out." Paige laughs. "But then the grownups realized they love it just as much."

"Only we bring cups of spiked hot chocolate for our turns," Emilia says.

We've reached the large group of women. Will they really like me? Or just tolerate me because they're happy to finally see Cannon arrive to a family event with a woman on his arm? *Deep breaths, Kylie, deep breaths.*

I'm passed around, shaking hands and giving hugs. There're so many introductions to make, by the time I reach the last Beauty, my cheeks ache from the smile plastered on my face.

Paige slips her arm through mine. "Ready to shoot a rifle for the first time?"

"It sounds fun," I say. I think of the massive event they've put together for tonight. Surely there are last-minute jobs to do. I want to be helpful and pull my weight. "But what about preparing for the event tonight? Is there work to be done?"

Paige throws her hands in the air, her manner carefree and almost childlike. "Everything's ready! The stage is set, the ballroom deco-rated, the caterers on standby. Even your gown has already been steamed. It's been a long flight. I'll show you to your rooms and you three can rest for a bit, freshen up, then we'll head over to the field."

"My gown?" Before I can ask her for more details, women surround me, asking me questions about me and Italy. As curious as they are about my being here with Cannon, they're polite enough to hold back the questions about him... for now.

I hope they give me more time before their inevitable inquisition. I don't really have any answers for them except that I'm pretty sure he kidnapped me and brought me here because he did not want me at the All Staff Anything Goes.

Thinking of the reason for his abducting me should anger me but interestingly, it has the opposite effect, making a warmth flow through my veins. I'm not 100% sure that I don't like the thought of him wanting me all to himself.

Let's see where the evening takes us.

15

annon

I spend the day keeping an eye on Kylie from a distance. When the women go to skeet shoot, I observe Kylie from the line of trees that hug the field to be sure she puts on the safety ear and eye protection. She aims the rifle in the air, the tip of her tongue wetting her bottom lip as she concentrates. After missing her first target, she hits the second one.

I have to hold in a shout of *Atta girl!* I don't think the Beauties would appreciate finding me spying from the woods.

Later in the day, Kylie lets her fingers drag in the water as she lazily floats down the river in a black string bikini Emilia packed for her. It's torture, watching her in that barely-there swimsuit, not being able to touch her. All I can think is what I would give to be that green plastic tube she's lying on.

When the women go snowtubing, I find myself hovering behind one of the equipment sheds at the top of the hill. *What the hell are you doing here, Cannon? She's fine.* But I can't help this nagging sensation that I need to keep an eye on her every moment to be sure she's safe.

Just as I do—every single night—at the club.

Dressed in black leggings and a hoodie, the most adorable hat perched on the top of her head, a big puff of a pom-pom bouncing as she moves, she gives a laugh as she flies down the snowy hill, powdery snow shooting up from the sides of her big black innertube.

When she reaches the bottom of the hill, she hops off her tube, grabs it and runs back up. "That was so fun! I'm going again."

She's so adorable. I can't take my eyes off her. But my time of spying is over, and she's dragged away in a crowd of women to prepare for tonight. When it's time for the auction, she emerges from Paige's house dressed in a long, fluttering gown, red silk with layers of loose, flowy netting making a tiered skirt over the sleek gown.

The sight of her in the gown makes my chest do that thing and I have to force myself to breathe. Her hazel eyes search the crowd—is she looking for me? But before I can call out, she disappears into a cloud of colorful fabrics.

Fuck this.

I make my way to the group of women, carefully picking my way through them till I see the back of her red dress. "Kylie, wait."

I pull her to me. Relief washes over her face at the sight of me. "Cannon! You're here. I haven't seen you all day."

Was she missing me? I grab her arm. "Come with me."

Paige sees me leading Kylie away. She purses her lips. "Have her backstage in fifteen minutes, please, Cannon."

"Will do." I guide Kylie toward the rose garden. "How about a few minutes of fresh air before we go to the theater."

She gives a sigh. "That sounds amazing."

I slip my arm around her waist. I give the guard at the gate a nod as we pass by. Nikolaos Bachman, our latest recruit.

He stands with his massive biceps crossed over the wide plane of his chest. Dressed in a short-sleeved deep green button-down tucked into black pants, a thick black belt around his waist and heavy black boots on his feet, he gives an air worthy of his military background. He runs his thick fingers over his full beard as he eyes the crowd.

Kylie stares at him as we pass. "Who is that?"

"They call him the Beast," I say. "He's fresh off initiation. Just joined the family last month. One of the brothers from the Parrish got to know him and brought him into our ranks. He used to be an Air Marshal for the military in Greece. He's in charge of all security here at the Hamlet."

"Why do they call him the Beast?" she asks.

"Just look at him. He's huge." She obeys, looking over at him. "On second thought, don't look at him. He's very valuable to us and I don't want to have to add him to my hit list. Half my male staff is already on there."

She gives a laugh, nudging me playfully in the ribs. "I'm not looking for me. I'm looking for *her*." She gives a discreet nod of her head in the direction of the labyrinth of pink roses in the garden.

Charlie Bachman sits on a bench by a pale pink blooming English rose bush, fanning herself with the list of items to be auctioned she's been pretending to read. What she's really doing is staring at the Beast.

"Her face is as pink as her gown," Kylie whispers.

"So it is." I haven't seen Charlie take an interest in anyone since her husband died, and the Beast is the very last man I would have thought she'd want. Charlie is prim and proper, not a hair out of place, always wearing cheery floral print dresses, a casserole delivery machine.

The Beast is... well... the Beast.

"I'm not sure sweet Charlie could handle him," I say.

Kylie disagrees, eyeing the tattooed biceps. "Oh, I think you're wrong. I think maybe he couldn't handle her. Charlie's as sweet as sugar but I'm sure she's got a feisty streak under all those floral prints and strands of pearls."

"Never mind." I wrap an arm around her shoulders, turning her in the other direction as we walk down the path. "I think we've seen enough of his tats for one day."

She reaches out, fingering the delicate petals of a blood-red rose as we pass a line of deeply hued blooms. Something is on her mind. I sneak a glance at her, seeing her brow is creased in the center as it does when she's deep in thought. I wait, knowing it will only be another moment before she asks her question.

"Why didn't you tell me earlier?" She sneaks a peek up at me. "That you were jealous? I would have stopped, you know. I wouldn't have wanted to make you feel that way. Especially after all you've done for me and my Nonna."

"Did I say I was jealous?" I ask.

"You didn't have to," she says. "The kidnapping just happening to be on the night of ASAG says it all. You could have just asked me not to attend. I owe you after all your help."

"You don't owe me anything," I say.

"But why not say something?" she asks. "Why not tell me how you felt?"

I give a simple shrug. "You weren't mine."

She gives me a shy glance. "And now I am?"

"Yes. Now you are." I bring her closer, kissing the top of her head. Her hair is soft as silk and smells of coconut and vanilla. It reminds me of the beaches of the Parrish. "And there's no escaping."

"We'll see, we'll see," she says. But she's smiling as she says the words.

Just as I'm leaning down to kiss her, a business-like Paige comes rushing down the stone path.

"There you are! I've been looking everywhere for you. Fifteen minutes was over twenty minutes ago. We need to get you on stage, Kylie. The families have heard about your organizing skills and they're all clamoring for your services."

"Really?"

Kylie looks surprised. But who wouldn't want her at their disposal?

Paige nods emphatically, her dark hair bobbing up and down. "Yes. I told them to show me how much they want you with their wallets. I'm planning an entire new wing in the Home this year, a spa for our aging clients. Wouldn't that be wonderful?" She slips an arm through Kylie's, guiding her in the direction of the theater. "The touch of a massage can do wonders for a person."

"That's so sweet," Kylie says. "I'm glad I can help in some way."

"Come on. Let's go." Paige offers me an apology as she drags my date away. "Sorry, Cannon. Beauty calls."

"Save me a dance?" Kylie says, but she's gone before I can kiss her goodbye, the faint scent of her perfume lingering in the air.

"God help me," I murmur to myself. "After this auction, she's all mine."

We gather in the town's theater, a mini replica of one of Carnegie Hall's auditoriums, a place Paige commissioned after returning home from a girls' night out in Midtown Manhattan and seeing a child piano prodigy play there. She insisted our children have a similar venue to perform their own concerts and plays. The Hamlet has yet to produce a theatrical prodigy, but I have to admit, the place is pretty stunning.

I sink into a red velvet seat, taking in the Renaissance Revival architecture. The arches and curves sculpted above me remind me of Italy. I think of Fire. I miss my club.

Then I remember what's taking place there tonight and I take a deep breath of relief, knowing I won't have to bear the sight of Kylie and her many partners. I wish she was sitting beside me now. Why does she have to be in this auction, anyway. Can't I have her to myself for a moment? Charity, Cannon. This is all for a good cause.

I sit, bored out of my mind, as we go through endless auction items. A tutoring session for your child, a week of frozen homemade dinners courtesy of Charlie, a salsa dancing lesson. I don't bother bidding; I've already handed Bronson a fat check of a donation for their cause. My eyelids are growing heavy, the darkness of the theater and the cushiness of the chair making me drift off.

Paige's high voice trills through the room. "Kylie Barone! Organizer extraordinaire. Coming to us all the way from Club Fire of the family's Italian branch, Kylie will bring peace and tidiness to any disorganized corner of your home. If you've got junk drawers and overflowing closets, Kylie's your girl!"

I stare up at the stage. Kylie in her red dress stands with her hands clasped in front of her, as if trying to stop those pretty fingers from reaching up to twirl at one of her long, dark curls. She looks out over the crowd, her eyes blinking with surprise as the bids begin to fly in.

Women in the crowd who aren't organizing the auction frantically raise their bidding paddles. The price quickly doubles from the starting bid, then triples. I think of Kylie's work at Fire and know she's worth every penny.

A rumbling voice calls out from beside me. "Ten thousand."

I look to my right to find the Beast calmly raising his paddle. His stoic gaze is trained on Kylie.

What does he think he's doing? Oh... *helll* to the no. I didn't even grab an auction paddle after writing my check—didn't think I'd need it.

I stand from my seat. "Twenty thousand."

Kylies hand goes to her lips, covering a gasp at the amount.

The Beast turns to see who's bidding against him. He eyes me then rises from his seat, his attention back on Kylie. "Thirty," he says.

"What are you doing, man?" I hiss.

His eyes on Kylie, he shrugs. "It's for charity."

"You know I came with her," I say.

He shrugs. "What can I say? My house is a mess. I haven't had time to unpack."

Knowing he's new to the family and hasn't had much time to accrue his wealth, I shout out a number I know he can't match. "Five hundred thousand dollars."

Bronson, acting as the auctioneer tonight, hits a gavel against his podium. "Five hundred thousand dollars. Going once, going twice, sold, to Cannon Bachman. Enjoy your closet cleaning. Next up."

The Beast drops his paddle on his empty seat, leaving the auditorium without giving me a second glance.

"Beast Bachman," I say, envisioning myself scribbling his name on a line of paper. "You just made my hit list."

I put Tie and Tate on there too. Fuck, the list is getting long. I'm going to be a busy man.

I slink down in my seat, waiting for the auction to end. I want her in my arms but she's stuck backstage with the Beauties. My only solace is envisioning her in the cute little maid costume while she redoes my kitchen cabinets.

We're seated beside one another for dinner but Paige is on Kylie's left, talking her ear off. I can't get a word in. I slide my arm around her shoulders, happy to finally have her within reach.

They serve dessert, a ball of hardened chocolate that you tap to break with your spoon, a rich custard flowing from it, paired with espresso martinis, the caffeine to carry us into the late evening. The sound of the town bell rings, signaling it's time for the ball.

As we make our way back to the theater for dancing, I pull Kylie into my arms, guiding us behind a massive oak tree. "I need to steal a kiss."

"That'll be another five hundred thousand dollars," she giggles.

"I'll gladly pay twice that." I brush my lips over her earlobe, nipping at her flesh.

"Why did you bid so high?" she asks, winding her arms around my neck.

"Didn't you see? The Beast was trying to bid on you. I couldn't have you at his place, cleaning his closets. Not gonna happen."

"You can't hide me away from every man on this planet. You know that, right?" She rises up on tiptoe, pouting her sensual lips, begging to be kissed.

"I can and I will. So don't test me." Wrapping my arms tight around her waist, I pull her to me hard and lean down, kissing her breathless.

We go to the dance, her cheeks flushed from my caresses. The bright sound of upbeat classical music flows through the open doors. There's a band comprised of a flutist and several violists surrounding a man playing the grand piano that sits on the edge of the stage.

I hate it.

I was hoping for something slow, sultry, sexy. Low lights and candles. Kylie's body pressed against mine as we sway across the dance floor.

This is *not* that.

People stand in a circle, one man, then one woman, all the way around. As the music plays, they dance into the center of the circle, then back out. As the beat changes, picking up the pace, the men and women turn to one another, linking arms and circling one another, then changing partners.

You've got to be kidding me. I run a frustrated hand through my hair. I can't even dance with her now?

Kylie claps her hands. "How fun! It's like they brought Jane Austen to the Hamlet."

"Jane who?" I say.

"Jane Austen?"

I give her a blank stare.

"Booker would know who I'm talking about." She tugs my arm. "Come on, let's dance!"

I watch the couples prancing around. There's no way I'm going up there. "You go ahead," I say.

She eyes me. "Are you sure?"

"Yes."

She narrows her brow further. "But you know you'll see me dancing with other people, right?"

"Yes. All happily married men. Have at it."

She leans up on tiptoe, kissing my cheek. "Thanks. Be right back!"

I go to the bar, nursing my disappointment with a whiskey sour. Leaning against the bar, I sip my drink, watching Kylie twirl from arm to arm.

Wait... is that...

The Beast?

What the fuck?

He towers over my Kylie, arm linked with hers, dancing her to the center of the circle. He's bending down, that stoic look on his angled face. He's asking her something.

Kylie nods and smiles.

What's he saying to her? What did she say back? I run a hand over the prickles rising on the back of my neck.

I make my way to the stage, reaching him just as they change partners. No longer dancing with Kylie, the Beast has lost interest in the dance. He excuses himself from his new partner.

I grab him as he goes to leave. "A word?"

He gives a grunt and a nod, eyeing me.

We move to the shadows edging the stage. "You know she came with me. Have you already forgotten the code of the Brotherhood? What's a single man doing in the Hamlet anyway? Can't you find somewhere else to work?" My hands clench into fists. "What's your problem?"

"My problem is her." He leans back, nodding toward the floor. There are tables of drinks and finger foods lining the edges of the room. He points in the direction of the champagne fountain.

"Who?" I look over to see Charlie standing alone, sipping at a drink.

Nikolaos' already deep voice drops an octave. "I saw her the moment she stepped onto the tarmac. Charlie Bachman, the widow."

I look from Charlie back to the Beast. He's not taking his eyes off her. "And what did you need with Kylie?"

He shrugs. "She came with Charlie. She seems like a nice girl. Sweet. I thought I could talk to her and see if she would have a word with Charlie for me."

"While she was unpacking your house?"

He shrugs. "We talk about how to organize my books, where to put the pots and pans, then maybe the conversation turns to Charlie."

He still has yet to look at me.

"You're really stuck on her, aren't you?"

"Yes." He nods.

I feel for the guy. "I'll talk to her. I'll talk to Kylie and see if she will talk to Charlie. See if she's interested."

Now his eyes come back to me. "You'd do that?"

I slap my hand against his shoulder, suddenly feeling generous in my relief. "Of course. What are brothers for?"

"Thank you." He takes my hand in his massive one, pumping it up and down. "Thank you very much."

"Don't mention it. Welcome to the family."

I go to the bar to get Kylie a glass of ice water that she'll need after all this dancing. She finds me and I hand it to her.

"Oh God, thank you!" She takes a long sip of the cold water.

"The Beast has a favor to ask you," I say.

She nods. "I know. I'm helping him unpack in the morning. He said has no idea where things go."

"No," I say. "You're not."

She gives me a sweet smile. "You are welcome to come and chaperone," she says.

"No, I mean, he doesn't really need you."

"Oh," she says. "What did he want?"

"He wanted to talk to you about Charlie," I say.

Her eyes go wide. "Charlie? See, I told you! Did you see the way she was staring at him in the rose garden?"

"Apparently the same way he was staring at her when she stepped off the jet this morning."

Kylie's freshly manicured fingers, the black replaced with a bright red to match her dress, flutter over her heart. "That's sooo sweet. Could it be a love connection?"

Obviously, I'm terrible with this stuff. I've spent the past decade alone. I shrug. "How would I know?"

"I'll go talk to Charlie and see what she thinks." She hands me the water glass. "Here. Hold this."

I take the glass. "And I'll stand here. Alone."

She shoots me an apologetic look. "When I get back, it's just me and you the rest of the night. Promise." She kisses my cheek and hurries over to Charlie.

I watch the women talk to one another in hushed whispers until I'm distracted by a ding from my phone. I slip it from my pocket, glancing down at the screen. It's a call from Booker.

I take it. "Booker. What's up? Everything good there?"

His thick accent comes through the other line. "Hey, boss. Everything's fine here but I've got an interesting bit of news for you. I didn't want to interrupt you, but I knew you'd want to know right away."

I turn my back to the crowd, facing the wall for privacy. "What is it?"

"It's Kat. She's not who we thought she was. Not at all."

I glance over at Kylie. She's still whispering with Charlie. Ice crawls up my veins thinking of the blonde woman with the K tattoo and strange behavior. "What does she want?"

"She wants to talk to you. I won't say more now, but consider this a heads up for when you get back."

My gut was right—Kat with a K is going to be a problem. "Alright. Anything else?"

"Yeah."

He goes quiet.

I press him. "Booker?"

"The Meralos paid us a visit. They want what's owed to them."

16

K *ylie*

ON THE FLIGHT HOME, Cannon hands me a hot chocolate with extra whipped cream and sprinkles, then asks me what I think about the Hamlet.

What do I think?

I lick the peak of the sweet cream. The Hamlet was a picture-perfect town, a loving community filled with sweet families. It just wasn't... me. At least, not the new me. The old Kylie might have loved the Hamlet, but the newly unleashed sex kitten Kylie 2.0 craves more.

"It's fun!" I pause, taking a sip of the chocolatey goodness, thinking of the things I liked. "The women are sweet. I really enjoyed the snowtubing."

Sensing I'm holding back, he presses, "But?"

"I don't know," I shrug. "It felt a little... tame to me?"

He gives a sexy laugh. "Trust me. A Bachman bedroom is anything but tame. You'll see when we get home." He gives me a look that melts me to the core.

"But I like *our* lives. I like how it's not just the bedroom that's exciting. Look at where we work, I mean, is there anywhere more fun to be?"

He slips an arm around my shoulders. "Fire is amazing."

"I really, really love the excitement of the club. And, after taking care of my grandmother, I kinda feel like I'm not ready for kids." I peek at him, trying to read his face. "Are you... ready for kids?"

"Kids?" His brow shoots sky high. "No way. Not yet."

"So we are agreed? Fire is the place to be?"

"Yes." He leans over, kissing the top of my head. "Fire is the place to be. And wherever you are, Kylie, that's the place for me."

He's quiet after that, mulling over something. I'm not sure what. When his phone rings, he excuses himself, talking in hushed whispers at the front of the plane, every so often eyeing me in a way that makes me feel like something is up.

When we get home, Cannon leaves me with a kiss, telling me he's got a bit of business to attend to. I sit by the pool, having sandwiches with Nonna while she fills me in on everything that happened at ASAG like she was there. Apparently, the Clamp Tramps have befriended her and love nothing more than to gossip over tea with Nonna and Booker before they start their shift.

She knows everything.

"So," she asks, taking a dainty bite of a chicken and cream cheese sandwich. The cook even sliced off the crusts for her. "What's the news from the Hamlet? I heard there was a near love connection."

Heat flashes over my face. Does she know about me and Cannon? "I wouldn't say love connection, Nonna."

"Why not? Charlie's been alone long enough. If the Beast wants a taste, she should give him a little sugar."

"Nonna!" I shake my head at her, shocked by her language while secretly relieved she wasn't talking about me and Cannon. I'm not ready to tell her that we are a thing. There was a lot of macho talk about "you are mine," etcetera, etcetera, but nothing's become official yet, at least not in my eyes.

She gives a shrug. "What? I'm right. You know I'm right. What's stopping her?"

I think back over the conversation I had with Charlie by the champagne fountain. Wanting to find a balance between respecting Charlie's privacy and sticking up for her, I give up some information. "You know Charlie was widowed and lost a fiancée before that. It was very hard for her, to lose her husband after being married for such a short time. She's having a difficult time moving on."

"Pfft!" My grandmother dismisses my words with a wave of her hand. "Nonsense. She's just scared, that's all. You know what they say, stop focusing on what could go wrong and dream of what could go right."

"True, true," I say, lifting a berry from the tray.

"And what about you, sweetheart? Have you had any luck in love recently?" She eyes me suspiciously. "People talk, you know. They've seen you and Cannon together."

The strawberry gets lodged in my throat. I give a cough. "He's my boss."

"Hmm... my boss never swept me away on a last-minute trip across the world."

"Well, you worked at the pharmacy. I work at Fire."

She gives a naughty wiggle of her brow. "You're working overtime. That's what I heard."

"Please, Nonna. Let's speak of something else." I hide my face in my hand, wrapping my fingers around my forehead.

"Of course, of course, sweetheart." She pats my hand. "So, you know Carlos, he's single. And only five years younger than me. Cute as a button too. Booker's my wingman. A real cupid, that one. He's going to spread a little hot sauce on the tamale of love for me, help me make my own love connection."

"You and Carlos?" I can't picture my grandmother dating, but I never imagined myself working at a kink club, either. I want to be supportive. "Could be a match."

"We'll see, we'll see." She turns her focus back on me. "Just promise me you won't follow in your mother's footsteps."

I'd so rather be talking about her and Carlos. I shift my weight in my chair, uncomfortable by the turn in the conversation. "That's exactly what I'm trying not to do. Why do you think I don't date?"

"You misunderstand me, *tesoro.* I don't mean for you to be afraid to love. I mean, don't make the mistake your mother made of not realizing that you have everything you need to be happy, right here in front of you." She gives my hand a squeeze. "Everything you need, love, happiness, work, it's all right here. You've been blessed, my child."

"Nonna..."

Her soft tone turns to a mumble. "Blessed by a man who might take after his namesake and explode if you don't open your eyes and see what's right in front of you, my dear."

Oh my. "I'll try to keep my eyes open, I promise."

"That's all I ask. Don't be afraid of what could go wrong, of how you'll react. Know that you are full of love to give and if you find the one who's worthy, lavish them with your love."

Thank God Booker chooses this moment to approach us. I don't think I can handle much more heavy conversation on a topic I'm so confused by.

"Sorry, Miss Kylie," Booker says. "Can I steal Ouma away for a moment? The chef wants her to show him how to make the perfect bread with wine and sugar."

"I did promise him, didn't I?" Nonna rises from her chair. Booker takes her arm to help her.

Booker gives me a parting nod. "Good day, Miss Kylie, and oh — Cannon has something he needs to discuss with you. He asked if you could meet him at his house."

"Sure." I stand, wanting to clear the dishes away, but it's not my job and as strange as it feels to leave them on the table, I do. I hum as I walk toward the guesthouse. Cannon probably wants to sign off on the final decision for the floral arrangements for Extravagance, the annual party Fire hosts where tickets must be purchased for an extravagant fee, the proceeds going to a local charity.

I've gone with fresh roses sprayed with black acrylic paint, the ends of their leaves and petals then brushed with a pewter silver. I hope he likes them. My humming evolves into singing at the thought of the party. It's going to be an epic night.

I open the door to find Cannon standing in the foyer, his arms crossed over his chest, storm clouds brewing in his dark eyes. He must be having some staffing issues. Nothing makes him grumpy except for staffing issues.

"Booker said you wanted to meet," I say, closing the door behind me. "What's going on?"

He narrows his gaze, the hard look in his eyes making the hair on the back of my neck stand on end. "You have something you want to tell me, babygirl?"

Those storm clouds are directed at... me?

I rack my brain, trying to think of what he could be upset about. "No, no, I don't think so. Why?"

"Let me try to refresh your memory." His words are a growl. "The other night, did anyone special come visit you?"

Mad Max.

My stomach does flip-flops in my belly. He knows? But how can he know? Surely I would have heard something about this earlier if someone had found Maxim Meralo wandering the property. I sneak a peek at his face. His jaw is clenching and unclenching as if he's fighting to keep his calm.

Do I tell him?

Because I'm pretty sure when he told me I was his, that meant his in the way a Bachman woman is a Bachman man's. And that involves punishment when she puts her safety in jeopardy.

Will he...

I get my answer when he closes in on me, his hand slipping along the back of my neck, bringing my ear to his mouth. The heat of his words warms my skin as he whisper-growls, "I can see you battling with yourself, whether you want to tell me the truth or not." He brings me even closer, his lips now brushing my skin as he speaks. "Let me give you a little advice. Never, ever, lie to me." He pulls his face back so he can stare into my eyes, but his hand remains on my neck.

My tongue is glued to the roof of my mouth. I don't know what to say, what to do. His patience wears thin, the slow raising of his brow like the ticking of a bomb about to go off. I need to say something, anything.

"I, yes. I'm sorry. I did have a visitor."

"Mad Max?"

"Yes."

"The man is as mad as they say if he thinks he can get away with this." He releases me, pacing across the floor, his heavy boots tromping as he goes. "And you didn't think to tell me? You didn't think that I needed to know the fact that Maxim Meralo, the head of the family that has been leaving you threatening notes for weeks, somehow eluded my security and approached you?"

"I didn't want to tell you... yet." I plead with him. "You'd already done so much for me and Nonna. I knew it would just cause you more work, more problems, and—"

He turns to face me, his eyes filled with hurt and anger. "A problem? Is that what you think you are to me?"

I shrug. "I don't know. I mean, look at how I've turned your life upside down! You've gone from a bachelor to a... to a... I don't know. Babysitter? All because of my family problems that have nothing to do with you."

"I know about your problems, your uncle, the way the Meralos got him addicted to that nasty shit, always upping his debt. It has nothing to do with you, either. You owe them nothing and I've told them as much."

"You've spoken to them?"

"Twice. Once when you first came here, I asked the amount owed, to pay it off. Then a second time today. They came to the Club when we were at the Hamlet, asking for me. I met with them this morning. That's when I found out you'd been visited by Mad Max."

"Did you pay it off? The debt?"

He gives a frustrated shake of his head. "No. The bastards won't take money."

"They want me," I say. "My hand in marriage in exchange for my family's debt."

"Over my dead body. Even if it means starting a war, I will not let you be married to that man." He runs a hand through his thick hair, leaving it sexily disheveled. "And I'll tell you what else is not going to happen. You will never, ever let something like this happen again and not tell me."

A comforting warmth creeps through the cloud of nervous energy that surrounds me. He cares for me. He'd... kill for me. "Okay, okay, *bene, bene.* I promise."

His dark eyes flash with anger. "Your promise means little to me. I have other ways to be sure you obey."

The warmth is short-lived, replaced by the chill of his promise. I could run out of this room, tell him I want nothing to do with him or his twisted lifestyle. But I'd be lying.

I think of Nonna's words, of her advice, to not be afraid of what could be, but to embrace it. Staring at Cannon, the fire in his eyes when he speaks about protecting me, the heat that emanates from him at the thought of me putting myself in danger — they dull the chill, turning the ice in my belly to molten lava.

I want to be punished by him. I want to see what it's like to truly be his girl.

"I accept." I give a nod.

He grabs my arm, tugging me toward the living room. "As if you had a choice."

He pushes me over the arm of his black leather sofa. I cringe as I hear the unlatching of his metal belt buckle. The leather swishes as it leaves the loops of his jeans. My ass clenches at the sound. How much is this going to hurt?

His voice is a rumble. "Tell me, babygirl. Have you ever heard of edging?"

"Edging?" I rack my brain thinking of that one night on my computer, doing my research on all things sex. The word doesn't sound familiar. I think back on the steamy staff conversations I've overheard. Nothing about edging...

My throat feels tight. I swallow, hard. "No, I don't think so, why?"

He snaps the belt together, making a loud popping sound that makes me jump. "Edging, my dear, is just what it sounds like. Taking you to the edge of what you think you can handle."

"Okay..." My stomach clenches, a cold sweat prickling under my arms.

"Tell me." He taps the rounded end of the folded-over belt against my ass. "Do you trust me, baby?"

I do trust him. "Yes?" That doesn't mean I trust his belt.

He lifts the belt in the air, snapping it together again. The sound alone makes my knees go weak. "I want to hear *yes, sir*."

"Yes, sir. I trust you."

"Good. Then let's begin." He drags the belt over my ass. "And Kylie?"

"Yes, sir?"

"This isn't the club. There are no safe words."

"Yes, sir." My teeth clench together, my eyes shutting tightly. *Deep breaths, Kylie, deep breaths.*

He lifts the belt from my ass again. My fingers sink into the leather cushions, bracing myself for the belt. He brings it down, striking my ass across the seat of my jeans. I cry out as a fiery line of pain dances over my curves. I'm shocked at how much it hurts. I suck air in between my teeth, shifting weight from one foot to the other.

This hurts! Is this really what I want? A man who punishes me?

I consider calling it off, running from the room before he can strike again. But I've committed to this. I'm going to see it through. As for edging... one smack and I feel like I'm already clinging to the edge of a tall building, my fingernails digging into the leather to keep me from spiraling downward.

"No more secrets, Kylie."

"No, sir."

His words are soft, sincere, reminding me how I ended up over this couch in the first place. I put myself in danger. I held back information from him.

He brings the belt down again, another line of fire dancing just above the last one. I raise up on tiptoe, a cry lodging in the back of my throat as another spank from the belt rains down. My pain tolerance is so low, I don't think I can take much more...

I like playing, but I don't like this. I feel bad I've disappointed him. And... I hate his belt.

"I think you've had enough." The sound of the belt hitting the floor makes relief rush through me.

He reaches down, stroking my ass over my jeans. His hand dips between my thighs, rubbing my pussy over the thick denim. I give a low moan, my hips rolling. His fingers reach around my waist, undoing the button and lowering my zipper. He yanks my jeans and panties down at once.

He steps between my legs, forcing the denim to the floor, then takes his hands to my thighs, spreading them. He undoes his own clothing, there's the crinkle of a condom wrapper, then I feel the force of his cock entering me from behind. My pussy is slick from his belt, even though I didn't like it, still, his control over me and my body makes me soaking wet as it always does.

He grabs my hips, his fingertips digging into my flesh deep enough to leave bruises tomorrow. He brings me against him, slamming his cock into me hard. My eyes pop open, my jaw going slack as a strangled moan rises in the back of my throat.

"You're mine, Kylie Barone. You get that?"

"Yes, sir," I manage to choke out between hard fucks.

He pulls me back against him, giving a powerful thrust that leaves me standing on the balls of my feet, a strange sound coming from me as the full length of his cock fills me. "And that means you tell me everything."

"Yes, sir." My pussy clenches around him, a brutal climax rising in my core. He fucks me again, harder this time. I cry out, my palms damp against the leather of the sofa. My eyes shut tight, perspiration dotting my brow as my heart rate increases.

The orgasm is so strong, it causes me discomfort, my insides clenching too tight, the strength of the climax tearing at me, demanding release.

He fucks me again and again, and I'm coming hard. "Cannon!"

"Give it to me, babygirl. Give me everything you've got." He gives my ass a smack that leaves my skin burning as I shudder through the climax.

He reaches his own peak of pleasure, calling out my name as he comes. "Kylie. Kylie."

Afterward, cleaning me with a warm rag, he leaves my pants and panties down and sits on the couch, pulling my naked ass down onto his lap, unbothered by the damp spot I'm leaving on his thighs. He holds me to his chest, crooning, "There's my good girl" in my ear as he strokes my long hair, his palm making circles along my lower back when he reaches my waist.

I snuggle into him, totally content and at peace.

"Now, I have something to tell you." He strokes his fingers over the bare skin of my back. "I wanted to be sure you heard it from me." It feels good, his light touch. But something in his voice makes spidery legs crawl across my skin.

Whatever he wants to tell me, it's not good.

17

K *ylie*

I SIT DUMBFOUNDED. It can't be. Does this change everything between us?

Kat, the blonde woman with the bad hair extensions, is Catherine, the woman who broke his heart.

That night, my very first evening at Fire when I sat at the long table, dining with him, there was a strange blonde woman who was doing everything possible to get his attention. I remember joking with him that theirs wasn't a love connection.

But it was, wasn't it?

It was his Catherine.

He stares at me, concern etched in his features as he lets the news sink in.

His precious Catherine has come back...

Of course she acted strange, showing up out of the blue all these years later. I mean, personally, I wouldn't have pretended to be someone else to get into his bed, I would have been honest about who I was, but I've never been in her position before. Maybe she felt she didn't have a choice.

"Why do you think she lied and hid who she really was? Why wouldn't she just tell you straight up?" I ask.

"She saw how much I'd changed, joining the Bachmans, owning the club. She was intimidated, knowing I wasn't the same Cannon she left ten years ago. She wasn't sure I would want her anymore. And," he reaches out, tucking a lock of hair behind my ear, "she was one hundred percent right. Even before I found out who she was, something about her turned me off, made my skin crawl."

"Fair enough. But tell me," I say, needing more confirmation, not wanting this to be true. I stand up from his lap, tugging up my panties and jeans, zipping and buttoning them up over my still stinging behind. "How did you not know it was her?"

"Her hair was much lighter and longer. She's made some changes to her body, enhancements, she calls them," he says. "Between that and the fact that it's been a full decade since I saw her, I had no idea."

I think of the woman at the table. She had a perfect nose, impossibly high cheekbones, and what looked like the outline of amazing breasts in her low-cut blouse. Looking back, it's quite possible she had some cosmetic surgery done which would make it harder for him to recognize her.

Still... the two of them had been intimate back in the day. I think of Cannon and our time together. I wouldn't forget how it feels to be with him, not in a million years.

"There had to be some familiarity between you," I say, wanting to know more and wanting to never talk about her again, all at the same time.

"Maybe. But it doesn't matter. Her coming back was a gift. It made me realize that the person, the thing I thought I was wanting, was all wrong for me." He reaches out for me, grabbing my hand in his. He tugs me back to his lap. "Come here."

"Or maybe you just need to give it time," I say, crossing my legs. "You two have been apart for a very long time."

"Kylie, I need you to listen to me." He grabs my chin in his fingers and stares at me long and hard. I have to look away, unable to take the heat of his gaze in this moment. He won't allow it. "Look at me."

I force myself to meet his eyes.

"She means nothing to me, Kylie. I swear it to you. I just wanted you to hear this from me."

I nod. "Of course, of course."

"Trust me. Please." He kisses me in a way that's meant to be reassuring but even his perfect lips can't quiet the storm brewing in my mind.

There's a knock at the door. "Go away," he calls.

I take the opportunity to hop up from his lap, to have a moment away from him and clear my head. "It's fine. I'll get it." I smooth down my shirt and my tangled hair as I go to the door.

He grabs my hand as I go, tugging me back to him. "Kylie, don't use this as an excuse to build your wall back up. Please."

He's pleaded with me over both of his last requests. He's fearful I'll let Kat come between us. I try to give him a smile of reassurance but I'm afraid it probably looks more like a grimace.

"Don't be silly," I say, my voice as tight as leather spread over the top of a drum. "I'm fine."

His brow knits together as he tries to read me.

I work my hand out of his. "I've got to get the door."

Booker stands on the stoop, the usually playful light in his eyes replaced by a flash of fear, his hand over his heart. "Kylie. Thank God I've found you. You've got to come with me. It's Nonna."

"Nonna?" My heart sinks in my chest.

He nods. "Yes, I'm so sorry. I went to wake her from her afternoon nap, and I couldn't rouse her. She's breathing just fine and when I took her pulse, it seemed normal but still, I've called a doctor in to take her to the hospital and then came straight here to get you."

Cannon appears over my shoulder. "Has anything like this happened before?" he asks.

"No, no." I shake my head. "Nonna's been lucky. She really hasn't had any health issues before." I grab my sweatshirt from its hook on the wall, no time to even shower. "Take me to her, Booker, please."

"Of course."

As I pass through the kitchen of the spotless guesthouse, I notice the fresh flowers I ordered sitting in the center of the kitchen table. Back in her room Nonna lies on her bed, completely still, the color gone from her face, a sheen of perspiration covering her forehead. The doctor sits beside her, a stethoscope pressed to her chest.

I hover over her, waiting for him to finish. "Oh, Nonna."

Her eyelids flutter open at the sound of my voice. "Is that my Kylie?"

"You're awake!" I move past the doctor, excusing myself, and take her hand in mine. "How do you feel?"

"Just fine. So I slept a little late. Why all the fuss?"

"Nonna, Booker couldn't wake you." I stare up at the doctor, looking for answers.

The doctor stands from his chair. "Pleasure to meet you both."

"Same, thank you for coming. What's wrong? Do you know?"

"Everything looks good, strong heartbeat, good breaths. We will go to the hospital and run a few tests. I'll have more answers for you at that time."

Nonna frowns with disapproval. "I hate hospitals."

Booker steps in. "I'll go with you. We'll bring a deck of cards to pass the time."

Cannon wraps his arm around my shoulders. "I'll drive you behind the ambulance."

"Thank you, Booker. Thank you, Cannon." I think of what would have happened had Nonna and I been on our own with no support, and the thought is so jarring, I have to push it away. "Let's go."

Cannon doesn't leave my side for a single moment at the hospital. They take Nonna away, running tests. When they're done, they settle her into a bed to observe her for the evening. I sleep with my head against Cannon's chest, his arm wrapped around my shoulders.

In the morning, we're visited by the doctors, who found nothing wrong with Nonna with the exception of a little low blood sugar.

"One more question, though," the doctor says. "What about alcohol consumption?"

Nonna dismisses him with a wave of her hand. "Meh, a glass of red wine here and there."

Booker eyes Nonna. "And a shot of whiskey every day before her nap," he tells the doctor.

"Ah, I see." The doctor looks at Nonna. "Alcohol can lower blood sugar. Let's stay off the hard stuff for now, Nonna, and see how you're feeling."

"Fine, fine," she says. "Just don't take my bread away."

"Bread is not an issue," the doctor says.

"She likes it soaked in wine," Cannon offers.

"Of course." The doctor nods. *Pane vino e zucchero.* Yes. Let's keep that to a once-a-week treat, shall we? In the meantime, we have a medication that will help you keep your sugars where they need to be."

The shot is once a week, in her stomach or thigh. The nurse shows Booker and me how to administer the medication. Booker makes it clear he'll be happy to be the one responsible.

The big man is very attached to my little grandmother. He's so gentle with her, smiling softly and telling her to squeeze his hand if it hurts.

Grimy from our evening sleeping in chairs, we're all very much ready to go when they hand us the discharge paperwork.

"Thank God she's alright. I cannot wait to get a hot shower." Cannon twirls the ring of his car keys on the end of his finger. "Let's go home."

"Actually," I glance down at my sneakers. I've thought a lot about this, and I've made up my mind. "I was hoping you could take us to our home. I think Nonna could use the rest, somewhere quiet."

I tell myself that my decision has nothing to do with Catherine.

He stops twirling his keys, catching them in his fingers and closing his hand into a fist. I can feel his eyes on me, but I don't raise my gaze.

There's a tightness around the edges of his words. "Are you sure?"

Finally, I look at him. "Yes. I am."

"Okay. We'll go by and pick up the things you need from home—I mean my place—and bring them back. And I'll have a couple guys outside overnight." I start to protest, but he lifts a brow. "That is non-negotiable."

"Thank you."

We pull up to the little yellow cottage and it takes me a moment to realize some changes have been made. The lawn is freshly mowed, the flowerbeds have obviously been weeded and watered in my absence, the blooms thriving. And no more peels of paint hang from the corners of the porch.

I turn to Cannon. He's been watching me take in the house. "Did you have the house painted?"

He shrugs. "A little. And I had the creaky gate fixed and the yard done, just a few things to maintain it while you were away."

"Thank you. That's very thoughtful."

"Anything for you, Kylie. You know that." He brushes a kiss over my cheek before exiting the car to open my door.

Booker takes Nonna in to get her settled, leaving Cannon and me alone on the front porch for an awkward goodbye.

I have to ask the question that weighs so heavy on my mind ever since he told me about her. "What about Catherine? I don't want to come between you and the one person you were meant to be with."

"Catherine who? As soon as you came into my life, she was forgotten." He gives a wicked grin. "Besides, she's off to Rome."

"Why? How?" I have to admit it's a relief knowing she's gone. Even if he says he doesn't want her, having the space between us helps.

"I don't know. Maybe someone gave her a little bit of what she really loves—cold hard cash—to make herself scarce."

"You paid her off to leave?" I ask.

He reaches up, tucking a lock of my hair behind my ear. "I couldn't have her here. I knew it would leave room for doubt for you and I want you to know, with certainty, you are the one for me. I love you, Kylie Barone." He leans down, kissing the surprised gasp from my lips. "I love you."

And with that, he turns on his heel, leaving me with only one backward glance, a sad smile on those soft, kissable lips of his.

I quickly close the door behind me, my heart racing in my chest.

"He… loves me?" I feel stunned, my mind numb, like I'm trying to process shocking news. But his confession shouldn't come as a shock, should it? Not after the way he's cared for me.

And the fact that I'm in love with him too.

After showers and a meal and a long nap for us both, I sit on the sofa, a cup of Earl Grey resting on a saucer in my hand, an afghan Nonna crocheted years ago covering my lap.

A warm, thrumming string of words keeps winding its way through my mind and my heart. *I love you, Kylie Barone. I love you.* Deep breaths, deep breaths, I tell myself, trying to relax, but it doesn't slow my racing heart.

Nonna sits beside me, sipping chamomile tea. We have the television on, tuned into our favorite gameshow. One we watched together every night before Fire came into our lives. She's quiet tonight. She's usually animated during the show, talking back to the host, shouting out wrong answers.

I glance over at her. "You feeling alright?"

"I feel just fine. That's the problem. I can't believe I'm missing the weekly poker game for this nonsense." She gives a rude gesture to the television, mumbling Italian curses under her breath.

"You need your rest." And a night off from the cigar smoke and open bar of hard liquor. I take a sip of tea. "It's better for you to be here, where things are calm..."

Where life is simple and just makes sense. Where beautiful women don't come back into the life of your man, making you wonder if you've gotten in the way of what could be true love.

But he told you he loves you, Kylie. How can you not accept the words?

"The only true love you're getting in the way of is your own," Nonna snaps.

"Huh?" I shake my head. Is my grandmother a mind reader? Was I talking out loud?

"I hear you mumbling over there. And don't think I don't know about Catherine who changed her name to Kat and got a K tattoo and came back from the past, like a blonde bombshell in a time machine," she says.

"I don't want to talk about her," I say.

"Well, I do. You love someone for real? Let me tell you something, Kylie. You don't disappear for ten years."

Quiet falls over us, her words instantly bringing the thought of my mother into the room. A woman who's been gone almost ten years. The presence of her memory is so strong, it's as if she's sitting here with us.

Nonna reaches over, patting my hand. "I'm sorry, Kylie. I wasn't thinking when I spoke. Your mother loves you. Of course she does.

I only meant that if Kat left him, the two of them have had their chance. He loves you, now."

"Loves me..." I'm careful to keep my thoughts in my mind this time, as I ponder her words.

Does Cannon love me? He says he does. Why can't I believe him?

If love is an action, then yes, he does. He'd do anything for me. But if it's a feeling, a fleeting emotion, I have no idea. After Catherine, he stayed single for ten years.

Ten years. I could never have that kind of hold over someone, could I? I mean, if your own mother doesn't love you, doesn't stick around for you... how can you expect anyone else to?

Nonna takes the remote from my hand, clicking the TV off. Silence buzzes in my eardrums.

"Kylie." Her voice is soft. "Why are we really here?"

"I told you, Nonna," I say. "So you can rest. I thought you'd like the comfort of a familiar place and the quiet of being home."

She gives a heavy sigh. "Home. It's a funny word, isn't it?"

"What do you mean?" I take another sip of tea.

"Well, a home can be a building, or it can be something else. This little yellow cottage we are sitting in is as familiar to me as the back of my own hand." Her gaze holds mine. "So tell me, Kylie, why is it that I feel homesick right now?"

"I don't know," I say, blinking back the tears my own yearning is making well up in my eyes. "You tell me."

"I'm homesick because a home is the people inside of it. When it was just you and me, this was home. But we've grown, Kylie. We have others in our lives now. And we need to be with them. You need to be with your Cannon. Don't let fear keep you from him." She flops back against the cushions of the sofa. "And for the love of

God, I'll cut the booze, but don't let this make you keep me from Booker and Carlos and my poker nights."

It is quiet here. A little too quiet.

I miss my new friends at the club. I miss the beauty of the property, the buzz of the nightclub.

I miss... him.

Two yellow headlights shine into the living room as a car's tires crunch along our short gravel drive.

Nonna pops up from her seat. "Oh, thank God. He's here."

"Who's here?" I crane my neck to see whose car is outside the window.

"Booker. I have him on speed dial. I texted while you were getting the tea. I'm sorry, Kylie, but I want to go back." She moves to the center of the room, looking at me to follow. "I'll go batty if I'm stuck here another moment."

"Nonna! This is our home."

"Not anymore, it's not. We belong at Fire, Kylie. Fire is where we burn bright. This?" She waves a hand around the living room. "This was a waiting room."

A waiting room... an interesting metaphor for the quiet life we led before I stumbled into Fire with that package of powdered sugar.

"We spent almost a decade waiting quietly for your mother to come back," Nonna says. "Now grab your things and let's go."

The door opens. I look over at Cannon. He's waiting for me, arms crossed over his chest, his eyes, as always, on me. Looking at him makes me feel warm all over, like everything good is possible and waiting for us outside of that door. As long as we step out into the world, arm in arm, everything will be alright.

I glance around the little cottage, taking in the familiar needle-points and doilies, the knitted blankets and the crafts my grand-mother spent long, lonely hours making to pass the time while she waited.

Hope fills Cannon's gaze as he speaks. "What's it going to be, babygirl?"

"Nonna's right," I say, going to him, embracing my future. "It's time to go home."

18

K *ylie*

IT FEELS SO good to be back at his place, home, as Nonna calls it. I'm snuggled up on the leather couch, recalling fond memories we made here, a thick, cozy blanket wrapped around my shoulders. "I'm so glad you came for me," I say, blowing on the hot tea he brought me.

"Like I was going to let you stay there. Please. I gave you as much time as I could."

"I thought Nonna texted Booker to get us."

"She did," he says. "But we were already on our way."

"That's funny." I think back to the shower and nap I took at the yellow house. "You didn't last very long."

"There's just one thing." He does that oh-so-sexy thing I love, running a hand through his dark hair.

I take a sip of the cooled tea. Sweet and milky like he knows I like it. "What is it?"

His eyes lock on mine. "Look. I can't date an employee. I just can't."

My stomach falls. I should have known this would not be a smooth transition. I think of my cleaning closet at Fire, the orders I've put in for my black and silver roses for Extravagance. I must be firm with him.

I hold his gaze. "I'm not giving up my job. It's my greatest love."

He eyes me, a dark brow rising dangerously slowly over one eye. "I'd like you to think about that last statement."

"My greatest love next to you, of course," I say, teetering on spilling the words, I love you.

I set my tea on the table beside me and secure the blanket around my shoulders so I can pop up from the sofa. I stand on tiptoe and plant a kiss of reassurance on his cheek. "So what's your solution?"

"I can't date an employee of mine," he repeats.

I hold the blanket tighter, waiting for him to fire me. Instead, I'm surprised and confused by what he says next. "But I could date the co-owner of Fire."

"Co-owner? Me? You can't be serious."

"Why not? Everyone loves you and since you've come, the place has been way more organized. You could manage the facility, and I could keep managing the staff."

Is it that crazy of an idea? The man is obviously attached to me for the long haul, he's made that clear. And we both adore the club and love our jobs.

"I really do love Fire," I say.

"And Fire loves you. You're amazing. You even remember to have them water the plants. My Monstera has never looked better since you came along."

"It's not me," I say. "It was easy to help out when you've cultivated such an amazing staff."

"It's you." He brushes a kiss over my lips.

He's already done so much for me. Can I let him do this too? Make me part owner of his club? "Let me think about it," I say.

"Think about it, but I already know you'll say yes." He gives me a teasing smile, nipping my bottom lip between his teeth. "And I only have one little demand in exchange."

"What is it?"

He says, "You'll find out tomorrow night. At the party."

Butterflies of excitement tickle my belly, a slight sheen of nervousness settling over me. What could he possibly want from me? What do *I* have to give *him*?

As I ponder, I fall asleep on the couch, only to find myself snugly tucked into his bed in the morning. He must have carried me as I slept. He's already gone to work; today is the busiest day of the year for him.

He's left me a love note, a fresh muffin, and an iced coffee in an insulated tumbler. He knows I like to start my day with a little sugar. He says it makes me sweeter.

I read the note, my heart skipping a little beat when I get to the last line.

Babygirl, hope you slept well. I know I did, holding you in my arms. See you soon.

Love, Cannon

"I love you too, Cannon." It feels good to say the words, even though I don't have the guts to say them to him in person. I slip the note in my pocket, knowing I'll tuck it somewhere safe and cherish it forever.

There's an assault of knocks on the door. I grab my coffee, taking a deep sip of the delicious brew. "I'm coming!" I take the cup with me to answer the door.

Keisha stands on the other side of the door, strands of silver streaked into her hair. "There you are! I've been searching everywhere for you. Everyone's already at work. I'm honestly shocked to find you still here."

"I slept in. It was a long night with Nonna at the hospital last night." I tip the cup, drinking more of my rocket fuel. "But give me five and I'll be ready to go."

I have her sit on the couch. "You want anything?"

"No, no. Just hurry. Please. I have ten Hombre Hermosos ready to move furniture for me but with no direction, they'll just end up shoving everything to the edges of the room."

I leave the bedroom door open, quickly getting dressed in jeans and a tee. Later, Keisha will help me dress in my elaborate costume but today we'll be working, making sure Fire is perfect for tonight. "Thanks for coming to get me. I'm almost ready!"

"We were all so worried about your Nonna when we heard what happened. Thank God Booker kept us all in the loop on a group text. She seems fine this morning."

"You've already seen her this morning?" How is it that my grandmother got up before me? I slip my sneakers on my feet. "Where was she?"

"She's working on her tan." Keisha laughs. "She said she needed a little color for tonight."

I pop my head out of the room to eye Keisha. "Are you serious? The woman just got out of the hospital."

"Yes, I am. She's currently lying out in the center of the pool, floating on that giant pineapple float of Booker's, enjoying a virgin mimosa. Booker insisted on no alcohol, so Cheffie laced it with some sparkling apple cider." Keisha pops up from the sofa. "Are you ready to go? You look ready."

"Hang on. Let me just grab my breakfast. I'll eat it on the run." I grab the muffin from the counter, splitting it in two. I hand one half to Keisha. "Half-sies?"

"Sure. Thanks. I haven't even had time to think about breakfast." She nibbles on the treat as we step into the cool morning air and walk to the club. My flowers have arrived, tall silver vases filled with the black and silver painted flowers, the soft scent of roses filling the foyer.

Kiesha goes to a vase, gently feeling a petal between her forefinger and thumb. "Oh, Kylie! You've outdone yourself with this. We've never had arrangements this unique. They're gorgeous."

"They did come out good, didn't they. It wasn't me. The florist just brought my vision to life." I bend down, getting a deeper scent of rose.

She makes a *tsk* sound, clicking her tongue between her teeth. "Kylie, Kylie, always deflecting praise. Can't you just say, 'I kicked ass,' for once?"

"I kicked ass. For once," I joke.

"You know that's not what I meant. You're totally kicking ass here, ladybug. I mean things were always good, but now they're great. You're a big part of that." She loops her arm in mine. "Come, come. Help me boss these boys around. I want the ballroom completely transformed in one hour, max."

I remember Cannon's proposition from last night. Doubt plagues me. Have I brought a lot to Fire? Would I be a good co-owner? And what is Cannon's one requirement of me...

"Keisha..." I want to ask her what she thinks about Cannon's idea but we're stepping into the ballroom and she takes off like a shot, going after a group of men who are pushing the grand piano into a corner of the room.

"No! No! No!" She rushes over, stopping them. "The center of the room, please. There's going to be a pianist, some fancy guy from Rome, playing for the guests as they enter. How can you shove someone so important into a corner?"

I leave her to manage the ballroom, and find my team, the Clean Beans. The other staff groups all had special names, and I thought we should too. I even changed our cleaning uniform. When there are no clients present, we're in sweats and tees. The ridiculous but very sexy maid costumes are now only for the crew working evenings.

The Clean Beans, like me, love tidiness and order. We do a walk-through to be sure every inch of chrome and glass in the place is totally spotless and perk up any spots we may have missed. Being a group of naturally type-A clean freaks, we find very little work for ourselves.

As we make our way through the club, my eye searches for Cannon but our paths don't cross. The day flies by and Keisha finds me performing a few final adjustments on the floral arrangements, grabbing my arm, her eyes wide and excited.

She squeals at me, tugging me toward the stairs. "It's finally time to get dressed! *Let's gooo!*"

An hour later, I assess my look in the mirror.

The elegant floor-length black gown I wear is completely sheer. Underneath I wear a bra and panty set made of a thick silver satin material. My hair is swooped up on top of my head in a high pony-tail. My dark hair streams down my back, strands of silver woven into thin braids. My eyelids have been done up in silver, long fake lashes framing my eyes.

"It's pretty hard to believe that just a short time ago, I showed up here in jeans and a hoodie," I say.

A never-been-kissed virgin overwhelmed by trouble, desperate for a job, searching for protection. Now, I've experienced the world of sexual pleasure firsthand, and I even have an IUD hidden inside me, when a few months ago I didn't know what one was.

My gaze drags over my reflection in the mirror. "And now... look at me."

She beams at me. "Cannon will love it."

"I hope so." After all, he's the catalyst for the change in me and waking up the sensual energy that laid dormant in my body. And he's the reason I don't fear for Nonna and myself anymore. He's my knight in black armor.

"Last piece." Kiesha clips a heavy metal clasp around my neck. A long, shimmering, sheer silver cape flows from it behind me. She throws an arm over my shoulders, admiring our reflections. The green and sparkling silver corset of her dress pushes up her amazing breasts. "You look like the sex goddess that you are, babe. Now let's go!"

The ballroom has been transformed. The grand piano sits in the center, and a handsome young man with a thick mustache, wearing a black tux, sits perched on the piano bench. Rich music fills the room as his long nimble fingers dance over the keys, a look of determination melded with passion on his face.

My hand flutters to my heart, taking him in. "He's amazing." I lift my gaze to the sheer black net of fabric that has been stretched across the ceiling. Thousands of white and purple lights are woven into the material, twinkling above us like little clusters of stars.

"If you look closely, you can make out the constellations." Cannon comes to my side, pointing to a line of three stars. "There's Orion's Belt. And over there," he gestures to a thick grouping of lights, "the Milky Way."

"It's unbelievable. So beautiful." I turn to him, taking him in. He wears a black suit, a black shirt underneath. At least the necktie is silver, and there's a little silver kerchief peeking out of the breast pocket of his suit jacket. "And you look amazing as well."

"No." He smooths a hand down my side, cupping my waist. His gaze travels from the top of my head to the toes of my strappy sandals. "You are the amazing one."

"It's all Keisha's doing. She's a genius with fashion and makeup."

"But you bring her ideas to life. You give them beauty." He leans down, brushing a kiss over my cheek. "Now come with me. I want to play with my little toy before the guests arrive."

"Huh?"

His mouth is by my ear, his words hot as fire against my skin. He gives a growl. "Finally. It's my turn to play. I didn't think I'd survive, watching you with those other men."

"Don't be jealous. They're just friends." I think of the heat of his hands when they touch my body, of that first night in the Garden of Eden, the way electricity traveled through my body when he touched me. I glance up at him through my thick lashes. "Besides, you're the one I really wanted to play with."

"Good. You're all mine. Let's go. Which room would you like, my love?"

My love...

Those words on his perfect lips, said in that deep sultry voice I love so much... they shake me to my core. Is this my life? Is this my man?

Am I truly worthy of either?

He demands an answer. "Which room, babygirl? We don't have time to waste but I have to get a taste of you before this party. I would die of frustration if I had to watch that perfect body of yours sashaying around in that see-through gown all night. Remind me to thank Keisha, by the way."

I think through all the rooms of the mansion. There's one I've never been inside of, only hovered at the entrance. I know what I want.

The Velvet Bed.

It's a large room, black and gold paper on the walls, the thick wood trim all painted gold. There's a massive chandelier hanging over the center of the room, one of Cannon's creations with the candles made to look like real flickering flames.

There's a large, square bed in the center of the room, no frame or headboard or pillows. Just a huge, gushy-looking square of red velvet. The thought of the room makes me tremble, my teeth sinking into my bottom lip just at the idea of telling him I want to go into that room.

The entire far wall of the room is a mirror. An absolutely thrilling, terrifying wall of smoky glass you can see your reflection in. And on the other side of that mirror are voyeurs. Staff members will know if we go into that room. Word travels faster than wildfire at this club, and they will come, and they will watch us, whatever it is we do in that room.

The thought of hungry eyes taking us in during our most intimate moments...it makes my knees go weak, my stomach clench into a tight fist. But it also makes my clit pulse and my pussy clench so hard, I fear I might come right where I stand.

He's staring at me, waiting with a curious smile on his lips. He won't allow it. He'll refuse. I raise a hand, gently cupping his cheek. "I know it might be a stretch for you... but I want the Velvet Bed."

His jaw clenches, his brow knitting together. "That room? But the entire staff will see us fucking. They'll see you."

I think of my play times in other rooms. Though they were cut short, there was plenty of time for staff to see my bare breasts, my ass covered only in fishnets. "They've already seen me."

He shakes his head. "Not like that, they haven't. I won't have it."

"Please? It's what I want." I run my fingers over his beard.

He contemplates my face for a moment. "Here," he says, "come here."

He drags me into the shadows of the hall. "Let me see how wet you are, just thinking of the Velvet Bed. Then I'll make my decision."

A hard shiver tears through me as he lifts my dress, stroking my pussy over the thick, slippery material of the silver panties. He dips his hand past the stretchy waistband of the panties, finding my vulva.

I gasp, grabbing onto his shoulders as an anchor as I shoot up on tiptoe. My eyes close, my head lolling, the long ponytail swishing across my back. He dips two thick fingers inside me. "My God, babygirl. You're positively soaked."

He pulls out, stroking my pussy. With a few gentle pets from the slick pad of his finger over my folds, I'm shuddering, a tiny, weak orgasm traveling through my body, my mind too busy with thoughts to focus. He finds my clit already engorged and pulsing from the thought of people watching us as we fuck, and strokes it.

His lips find my ear. "Come for me, babygirl. Come now."

His words, his voice, they do something to me, and my body clenches tight, a fierce climax tearing through me, leaving a wet patch in my panties. I'm shaking, still holding onto his shoulders.

I'm ready to play now, my head where it should be. "Was I wet enough, sir? Wet enough for you to take me to the Velvet Bed?"

"Hell, yes." He leans down, kissing me, his hand still on my sex. He pushes two thick fingers inside of me at the same time and forces his tongue into my mouth. More arousal pools between my thighs.

I'm ready, so ready for this.

He tears away from our kiss, his hand leaving my pussy. He straightens my clothing, grabbing my hand in his. He gives a groan as he leads me to the stairs. "You better know how much I love you, sharing you like this."

"I do." A smile of pleasure warms my face. "And I love you, too, Cannon."

My words make his face beam. He kisses me. I know he's jealous and possessive, and letting me fulfill my fantasy like this... I know it's a lot for him to take. But I couldn't lie. When he asked me where I wanted to go, this room called to me like a siren.

We enter the room. The dim glow of the flickering candlelight instantly calms me. My silver vases of black roses sit on tabletops accompanied by other sweet-smelling bouquets, the soft scent of rose and jasmine lingering in the air.

He takes my hand and for the first time, I step over the threshold, entering the gorgeous room.

The piano music is being piped in from the ballroom. It's in every room of the mansion tonight, and I can almost picture the pianist and his grand piano in this room, playing off in the corner as we make love.

He leads me to the bed and I stand, for just a moment, staring at the wall. My eyes are wide, shining bright with fear and excitement as I take in my reflection. The hair, the sexy, teasing dress, the makeup, the natural flush in my cheeks.

I look... stunning.

I lift my black fingernails, giving a little smile and wave to the mirrored wall. I can't see anyone, but I know they're there, cheering me on.

annon

I CAN'T BELIEVE I'm allowing this. She belongs to me, yet I know there's at least a dozen sets of hungry eyes behind that mirror, ready to watch her, to see her, to experience her from a distance.

This is what she wants. And I'll give it to her. Just this once.

"I want to teach you a lesson," I say, turning her to me and away from the mirror.

Her arms slid up my chest, linking behind my neck. She gives me a naughty grin. "What have I done?"

"You don't accept how truly awesome you are. And I'm going to change that. I want to hear you say you know how much ass you kick."

A nervous giggle bubbles up from her throat. "Kick ass? I don't know about that."

I reach down, grabbing her ass in my hands and squeezing it. "Let me hear you say it. I want you to say, 'I'm amazing at what I do.'"

She gasps as I dig my fingers into the soft curves of her flesh. "Okay. I... kick ass?"

"Not convincing enough." I lift my hand, bringing it down on her ass with a hard spank. The sound of my palm striking her ass echoes through the big room. "Everyone just saw me spank you. And now, they're going to see me take you over my lap on the Velvet Bed and punish you until you convince me you've accepted how amazing you are."

I grab her, pulling her over to the bed. I sit, my back to the wall, and tug her over my lap. They can see us, but with us on this side of the bed, they're not getting the full show, only a taste.

I'm only human after all, I can only accept so much.

She's spread out across my thighs, her chest resting on the bed, her cheek laying against the back of her hand. Her legs stretch out behind her, the sheer dress draped across the lovely curves of her body.

I grab the thin material, inching it up till the dress rests across her lower back. Smoothing my hand over the silky panties, I say, "Try again. Tell me what a good job you're doing here at Fire."

She manages to squeak out, "I... I really love my job?"

"Wrong answer." I bring my hand down, spanking her ass.

She gives a little hiss, the pain dancing across her curves. "Okay! I'm good at my job."

"And tell me how much everyone adores you here." I rub my palm over her round curves, ready to punish her again.

"Come on, Cannon," she moans. "You know I can't say that."

"Then the panties will have to come down." I hook my finger in the waistband of her panties, tugging them slowly down till they rest at the tops of her thighs. I spank her ass, once on the right side, watching a pink handprint bloom on her skin. I give her a matching spank on the other side.

She moans, rocking her hips side to side. She gives a little whisper, her voice quiet, but her tone sincere. "They adore me."

"That's right." I smooth a hand over her naked ass. "And so do I."

I help her up from my lap, putting her onto her knees before me. "If you want to put on a show, then suck my cock. Right here, right now, for everyone to see. Show everyone how you use that pretty mouth to pleasure your man."

She peeks over my shoulder at the wall, like there's people standing there.

Her fingers are trembling as they reach for my waist. She undoes my belt, unzipping my pants. I help her free my cock from my clothing. It stands proud and tall, waiting for her. I turn my body slightly, so the voyeurs can partially see her going down on me. I want this to be a memorable experience for her, I want her to get what she came for.

She gives me a sheepish grin, then wets her lip with the tip of her tongue. She's loving every moment of this.

"God, you're so fucking beautiful," I moan, reaching around and grabbing the end of her long ponytail. "So. Fucking. Beautiful."

She wraps those full, rose-red lips around the head of my cock. The warmth and wetness of her mouth on me almost make me come. I take a deep breath, running my fingers down the length of her silky hair. "There's a good girl. That feels so fucking good."

She takes my balls in her hands, stroking them as she lowers her mouth further down my cock. She gives a little swirl with her tongue over the head of my cock, sending a surge of electricity down my spine.

Fuck. I can't let her continue like this. I'm going to come.

And I have plans for her that last much longer than this.

I give her hair a tug. "You want to really put on a show, babygirl?"

She looks up at me with heat in her eyes, her lips even redder and swollen from going down on me. "What do you have in mind?"

I lie down on the bed, pulling her up beside me. "Why don't you ride me? Sit on top of me and show the world how sexy you are when you fuck your man?"

My cock stands tall and ready for her. She slips off her panties, shyly straddling me on the bed. I give a deep moan as she lowers her sex down onto mine, her muscles gripping my cock tight. I grab her hips, holding her still on top of me and just take her in for a moment.

The look on her pretty face is sweet and shy, but so fucking sultry, heat rushes into my core. Knowing I'm the one who showed her this world, I'm the only man she's been with, I'm the man she wanted to be with on the Velvet Bed, my chest nearly bursts with pride.

I give what I can reach of her ass a slap. "Ride me, babygirl. Fuck me good."

She starts out slow, moving up and down gently as she sneaks a peek at the mirror. She gives a little whimper and moan as her pussy tightens around me, she's so turned on, a tiny hint of an orgasm already traveling through her.

She closes her eyes, gaining confidence, gaining momentum, going after what she wants, what she so desperately needs. I lift my hips, shoving the full length of my naked cock inside her. It feels so good, skin on skin, no condom this time. She gasps, throwing her head back in her pleasure.

She reaches up, tugging the ponytail from her hair. Her dark hair cascades over her shoulders and her back, the silver strands woven into tiny braids. Her hair moves with her as she delves into the moment. She gives another deep moan, her palms flat against my chest, fingernails scratching at my skin.

"Oh my God, Cannon. I'm loving this so much. It's such a turn-on. To know all those people are watching, getting turned on too."

I reach up, grabbing her breast over her clothing and squeezing. "They're so turned on by you. You're so fucking gorgeous up there, every woman wants to be you, every man wants to fuck you." I release her breast, my fingers dipping along her slick folds. I find her clit and press as I growl, "But you're mine. All fucking mine."

She whimpers, another orgasm running through her. This one is stronger, her pussy clamping down on my cock until I too know I will come soon. I rub her clit, rub her pussy, milking another orgasm from her as she fucks me. She cries out, screaming my name over the piano music, "Cannon! Cannon," riding me hard until my balls tighten, my core clenches, and I know I'm going to come.

She's so damn gorgeous, and caring and smart and funny and so... damn...sexy, and the fact that she wanted this, and asked for it, makes me love her all the more. I grab her hips, shoving mine up so I'm deep inside of her and I hold her tight to me as the climax takes over. My cock spurts, hot and wet, filling her with my cum. It leaks out of her, running down my thigh.

When I can finally breathe again, I say, "You did good, babygirl. You did so good."

She stays sitting on me, her breaths coming in bursts as she recovers. "Oh my God. That was so sexy. I loved it." She leans down, her hair brushing over me as she kisses me. "Thank you, Cannon."

"There's one more thing." I pull her from me, sitting her beside me on the bed. I tuck my cock back in my pants, fixing my clothing. I haven't even taken off my jacket, I realize, and reach into my breast pocket. I hand her the little red leather box, the words Bachman's Jeweler swirling across the top in gold lettering. "My one condition."

She takes it from me, a curious look coming over her flushed face. "What is it?"

"Open it."

She flips the lid open, giving a little gasp as she sees what's inside. It's a two-carat princess-cut diamond set in platinum. I lift the ring from the box. I slip down off the bed, pressing my right knee into the hardwood floor. "My one condition is that you marry me. I want you to run Fire with me, as co-owners, husband and wife."

She stares from the ring to me, then back at the ring again.

The moment hangs in the air like a decade. My heart stops beating in my chest. "What do you say?"

She stares at the ring. "It's just... I'm still afraid of Max Meralo. He thinks I belong to him." She shakes her head. "I can't accept with full joy in my heart till I know it's over with him, that he doesn't think I'm owed to him anymore."

"I'll take care of it. I promise. Then will you say yes?"

She nods.

Max Meralo has finally met his match.

I will end him, even if it means starting a war.

20

K *ylie*

I STARE DOWN at the diamond on my left hand, watching it sparkle under the lights. After all these weeks, I still can't believe it's mine.

The morning after Extravagance, Cannon came to me, ring in hand.

"It's all taken care of." He slipped the diamond on my finger. "So, what do you say?"

"Yes. Of course, I say yes!"

"You're officially mine." He kisses me.

Joy and relief filled me. "How did you resolve it?"

"You let me worry about that, babygirl." He looked down, twisting the diamond back and forth over my finger. "It's not your concern."

If we were to be married, he needed to know we're going to be a team. Not just at Fire, on everything. "Tell me, Cannon. I need to know," I said.

"Well, for starters, someone else caught his eye..."

"What do you mean?"

"I mean, when he first got involved with your uncle, Max had seen you at the pharmacy and already decided to make you his. You are just that beautiful, a perfect stranger wanted to trap you into marrying him."

"Stop it. I am not." I shake my head. I think of the intensity in Max's gaze as he stared at me, a little shiver running down my spine. "I'm grateful he's moved on. Who with?"

Cannon gave a laugh. "It's a small village. I guess when Kat was making her way out of town, grabbing a coffee as she was heading back to Rome, the two of them bumped into one another. Literally. Apparently, Max ran into Kat, spilling the cinnamon dolce latte she held all over her wool coat. Max is known for shooting up to ten espressos a day; maybe the over-caffeination aids in his intensity. Anyway, she demanded he pay for a new coat. For Max, like with you, it was love at first sight. For Kat, it was probably dollar signs. The Meralos are known for their empire of cash."

"Seriously? Mad Max and Kat are... a thing?"

"From what I've heard. Though their relationship is in the early stages. I'm not sure how stable either one of them are. We'll see if it lasts." He runs a hand through his hair. "Still, I needed reassurance that he'd given up on the idea of you for good. I gave him something. Something to keep him away from your uncle, and you, and your Nonna, forever."

"What is it? What did you give him?"

"I wanted to give him a silver bullet straight through his heart." Cannon ran a frustrated hand through his hair. "But that would only have started a war. And I refuse to put you in harm's way."

"So, what did you give him?"

"I gave him the jet."

"What? You gave him your jet? You love that thing!"

"It was easy to part with." He shrugged at me. "What do I need it for? You and I never want to leave Fire."

"Cannon... you didn't have to do that for me..."

"I did. And I wanted to. It means nothing to me. You, Kylie, mean everything." He kissed me and our kissing evolved into more. Tears filled my eyes, the ring, the sign of the promise of his forever love catching my eye as we made love.

There's a knock on my door, dragging me from the warm memory. It's Keisha. "I have the most epic surprise in the universe!"

Keisha grabs my hand in hers, tugging me down the long hall of the main floor of Fire. "No peeking, Kylie! Do not ruin this surprise for me." My fingers go to the wide black satin ribbon she's tied around my eyes.

"How can I possibly see when you've blindfolded me?"

"I don't know—maybe you can peek out the bottom?"

"Good thing I trust you," I laugh. "Otherwise I'd be tripping over my feet right now."

And I do trust Keisha. We've become so close over the past few months, she's the closest thing I've ever had to a best friend. My ballet-slippered feet dash over the rug as I follow behind her, my world a blank, black canvas with who knows what at the end of the journey.

Her voice sings with notes of reverence as she announces, "We're here."

I stop, standing still, waiting for whatever it is they have in store for me. I hear a door opening; the sound seems crisper with my vision taken from me. The scent of jasmine floats through the air.

I just put fresh bouquets in the staff dressing room. "The staff dressing room? Is that where we are?"

"Just a moment and all will be revealed." I feel her fingers tugging at the ribbon behind my head. She whips the ribbon from my eyes with a dramatic flourish. "Ta-da!"

The most gorgeous wedding dress I've ever seen hangs in the center of the room, every inch of its mastery on full display. It's an off-white halter-neck gown, solid fabric beneath an overlaid netted layer of lace and beads.

It's... mine? How can something so beautiful belong to me?

My hands flutter over my heart. "Oh my gosh! You guys bought me a wedding gown."

Keisha focuses on me, reading my expression. "I hope you don't mind. I know most brides-to-be go all Godzilla on people, having to have everything exactly how they want it. But you, sweet Kylie, I just couldn't let you do what I thought you might do and try to pluck something off a sale rack last minute."

"You know I've been wearing a hoodie and jeans almost every day of my life. I never could have picked out something like this for myself." I walk around the dress, in awe. My fingers reach out to touch it but I bring them back in, for fear of ruining it in some way.

Keisha hovers at my side as I make my way around the dress. "Do you love it? Oh my God, I've been so nervous to show you. Please tell me you love it."

I tear my gaze away from the gown just long enough to meet her eyes and reassure her. "Keisha. I love it. And I am so touched you all would do this for me. Thank you."

"Look closer, at the bottom." She points to the bottom half of the skirt. I take a closer look. The intricate beading rises up from the hem of the dress, dancing into swirls of what looks like flames and the wings of angels.

"Fire," she says. "And angels. Cannon said you like angels."

Of course my friends, my people, would go so far as to make sure the dress was one hundred percent... me.

"Oh, Keisha. It's perfect." I throw my arms around her, hugging her tightly. I stare over at the dress. "I can't wait to wear it."

"Let's try it on." She goes to the gown, and I can't help but to cringe when she touches it. It's so perfect, I almost hate to put it on and risk ruining it somehow.

"Now? Are you sure?"

She focuses on her task, carefully lifting the gown so it doesn't touch the floor. "What else do we have to do today? Cannon closes the club on Sundays now, remember?"

"True, true." My husband-to-be, wanting a little more Kylie to himself, decided that Fire could operate six nights a week instead of seven, leaving Sundays blissfully free.

She helps me with the dress. The silk feels like cool water slipping over my skin; the weight of the beadwork surprises me, but it feels good, anchoring me. I stare in the mirror and can hardly believe it's Kylie Barone staring back.

"I look..."

"Amazing. Stunning. Gorgeous. Fucking incredible!" Keisha dashes off to the corner of the room, returning with a long, beaded veil. "May I?"

"Of course."

She pulls a few locks of hair from either side of my face back toward her and attaches the comb of the veil to the back of my hair, securing it with hairpins. "And how about a gift from Cannon to complete the ensemble?"

"A gift?" I smile. "What's he gotten me now?"

Ever since our engagement, Cannon's been showering me with surprises. Clothing, jewelry, furniture, an expensive phone so fancy I can't even work the thing... my favorite tall, beautiful stone statues of angels for the gardens, and...most recently... a car. The sleek silver Mercedes in the driveway belongs to me, silver angel wings stitched into the black leather headrests.

Her grin is giddy as she hands me a large, square, black velvet jewelry box. I flip open the lid to find dangling blue sapphire earrings and a matching bracelet.

"Your something blue and something new," she says, taking the bracelet from the box and clipping it around my wrist.

"It's beautiful." Twisting my wrist under the lights, I watch the gemstones as they sparkle. There's a knock on the door. I look up from the gift, calling, "Come in!"

Nonna's at the door, Charlie at her side. They're both dressed beautifully, their hair and makeup done like they're headed to a glamorous wedding. Nonna's dressed in a gown of soft, silvery purple. She comes rushing over to me, a jewelry box in her own hand. "I'm not too late for the something old, am I, Keisha?"

"Not at all, Nonna."

Nonna hands me the jewelry box. "This was the necklace I wore on my wedding day when I married your grandfather. I want you to have it."

My grandmother has very little jewelry from her past. I'm very familiar with the necklace this box holds. I spent hours admiring it when I was a little girl, two silver strands that twist together at the bottom, a diamond pendant hanging from them.

It touches me that she would give me such a sentimental gift.

"Nonna, are you sure?" I think of my mother's white and rose china dishes she and Booker surprised me with just yesterday. "You've already given me the dishes."

"Of course, *tesoro*. Who else would I give it to?" She pats my hand. "And now Charlie has your something borrowed."

"But why all these gifts now? I haven't even set a date for the wedding."

Being so enraptured with my new job as co-owner of Fire, I really haven't put much thought into wedding planning. To the point that Cannon has gotten a little grumpy over the fact that we still don't know when we'll be getting married.

I eye Charlie's elaborate updo and shimmering, sleeveless floor-length gown, big pink flowers on black silk. "And why on Earth are the two of you so dressed up?"

Charlie gives a nervous giggle, turning to Keisha. "You haven't told her yet?"

Keisha shrugs. "Sorry. I got a little carried away with the dress."

"Told me what?" I look at Nonna's smiling face, teeming with excitement. "What is it, Nonna? Tell me."

Nonna bursts. "Oh, *tesoro*, my sweetheart. It's so romantic. Your husband couldn't wait another day to marry you!"

"Huh? What are you talking about?" I say.

Keisha throws a hand on a cocked hip. "Why do you think he closed Fire on Sundays?"

"So we could have more time together?" I say.

She rolls her eyes at me. "Yes, but why did he demand that we start this new schedule now, this week, today?"

Charlie giggles giddily. "Because he couldn't take it anymore. He had to marry you. Today. It really is so romantic."

"And a little grumpy of him," Keisha adds. "But cute."

I stare back at my reflection, overwhelmed. "I'm getting married… today?"

"Yes." Charlie points at the door. "In one hour, right down that hall, in the ballroom, there'll be four hundred people waiting to see you get married."

"Oh my God." Can this be real? "And you all planned everything for me? It must have been so much work."

"Please." Keisha rolls her eyes. "Ever since Extravagance ended, Grace has been itching to event plan. She was over the moon when Cannon came to her with the idea of a surprise wedding."

"Oh, wow, if Grace had a hand in this—"

"Yup. It's going to be the most gorgeous wedding. Ever," Charlie chirps, hearts practically filling her eyes. "And afterward, while the guests are having lunchtime cocktails and appetizers, we'll have our own private Bachman-family-only ceremony. Then we'll join the others to celebrate with an entire evening of festivities."

Emotion washes over me. I feel overwhelmed but in the very best way. "All the people I love have come together to do this for me, for us. I'm touched."

They whisk me away for a snack and makeup and a few last-minute things to prepare their bride. I spend the time in a euphoric state, a serene smile plastered on my face. I'm about to walk down the aisle to marry the love of my life. And I didn't even have to lift a finger.

A whole team of people did the work for me, out of love. *Deep breaths, Kylie. Don't cry. You'll destroy your mascara.*

Our pianist is back. When the chords come, signaling my time to enter the ballroom, I feel nothing but happiness as I take those steps into the room. My gaze searches for Cannon, but I'm momentarily distracted by the amazing transformation of the place and the elegance of the beautiful music as it fills the hall.

Flowers, real live flowers, thousands of them, all colors and shapes and scents have been woven into a netting and hung overhead, pink and peach and burgundy roses, coral and yellow and sunset pink peonies, dotted with little starbursts of white jasmine. It's breathtaking to see—I can hardly believe it's real. Crisscrossing over the flowers, strands of white twinkling lights illuminate the room. On the back of each chair hangs a bouquet of plump pink peonies.

No decorations or music or beautiful dress could match the sight of my man, standing at the end of the aisle, waiting for me, his eyes only for me. He stares at me with such intensity, his gaze so full of love, I feel as if my heart will burst from my chest.

He wears all black.

As I get closer, he holds his hand out to me, pulling me into him. "My God, Kylie. I swear I've never seen anything so beautiful in my life as you, walking down that aisle." He breaks all the rules in the wedding playbook, wrapping his arms around me, kissing me.

A cheer rises from the rowdy crowd. I break away from him, laughing and looking out over the sea of people. All my friends from Fire are here, some dressed in fishnets and leather, others in formal wear. The Bachman Beauties are all here with their husbands, wearing couture and dabbing the corners of their eyes with tissues to save their makeup.

I give a little wave to the crowd. "Thank you for coming!"

"Do you like your surprise?" Cannon asks.

"I love it. So much. Thank you." I dab at my own tears.

He murmurs into my ear, "It was selfish, really. If I had to wait another day to make you my wife, I was going to go crazy."

"I'm all yours," I say.

He leans forward, wanting to kiss me again, but he's stopped by the clearing of the priest's throat.

We exchange classic vows, slipping platinum wedding bands on one another's fingers. It's a beautiful ceremony but in my mind it's just a gesture. The real vows will be exchanged in private, when the Bachmans gather to welcome me into their fold.

The priest proclaims us husband and wife, saying, "And now, you may kiss your bride, again."

The crowd stands, cheering and throwing the bouquets from their seats up in the air, over and over, peonies flying as we kiss.

The time I've most been looking forward to comes. The private Bachman ceremony. Cannon holds my hand in his, leading me to the Garden of Eden Room.

Tingles of sexy memories play between my thighs. "We're having the ceremony in here?"

"I had to have it here," he says. "The family ceremony makes us official, and I needed it to be in the room where I first touched you."

"I love that," I say.

Two staff members open the doors for us. My breath catches as I take in the room. The chandelier flickers overhead, filling the room with soft, warm light. Above that, the glass ceiling tiles have been opened, the starry night above us, the cool night air breezing through the room. The plants are lush, pushed to the sides, lining the walls with flowers and green leaves.

The room is filled with family, all standing, women on one side, men on the other, the gap between them forming an aisle.

"Ready?" he asks, dark eyes resting on my face.

"Yes." I give his hand a squeeze. "So ready."

Rockland, the head of the family, a handsome man with a deep tan and cropped, dark hair, stands in the front of the room, the black leather wall making a dramatic background for the ceremony. "These words spoken today are sacred and celebrate a lasting bond that already exists between Cannon and Kylie, who have already joined their hearts and chosen to walk together on life's journey. Today, as Bachmans, we bear witness to the pledge of a sacred, eternal bond. One that may not be broken. Ever."

Cannon slips his arm around my waist, pulling me closer into him.

Rockland says the vows and as Cannon repeats them to me, I can barely believe he's making this pledge to me. I'm the luckiest girl in the world. The look in Cannon's eyes melts my heart, my knees going weak as he speaks, the deep timbre of his voice warming my chest.

"I, Cannon, take you, Kylie, to be my wife; to have and to hold, from this day forward; for better, for worse; for richer, for poorer; in sickness and in health; to love and to cherish; until we are parted by death."

I repeat the words back to him, my voice a shaky whisper.

He leaves me with a kiss. The room goes dark. I stand in the front of the room with Rockland, all eyes on me. Where is he going? What is he doing?

He returns with a white pillar candle in his right hand, the flame flickering as he makes his way to me. In his other hand, he holds a small red leather jewelry box like the one that held my engagement ring.

Cannon stands before me, his voice thick with emotion. He flips open the lid, revealing a silver chain with a tiny sword pendant hanging from it, green and brown gemstones laid in the metal. "All Bachman women wear this necklace. It is a symbol of our creed, the way we live our lives, the eternal care of a man for a woman. For as long as the stars have lit the sky, men have cared for and loved the women they have pledged their lives to. And women have loved and obeyed those men, accepting them as the headship of their family. Choosing to give the gift of their submission to these men — men who would lay down their lives for the ones they love. The sword is our symbol — the length we are willing to go to, the sacrifice we would willingly make."

Liam comes forward, taking the box and candle from Cannon. Cannon lifts the necklace from the jewelry box.

Cannon says, "Kylie, I freely give you this symbol, and pledge my very life to you. Do you accept?"

Everyone looks to me, the room buzzing with quiet as they wait for my answer. "Yes, of course."

He brings the necklace around my neck, clasping it in the back. The little sword rests just below my grandmother's pendant, the metal a cool weight against my skin. Cannon brushes a kiss over my cheek.

Rockland says, "Fire, also as timeless as the Earth, symbolizes the Bachman family's pledge to one another. To guide, care for, and protect one another above all others."

Now, all the guests are passing out unlit white candles like the one Cannon had been holding. Liam hands Cannon his still-lit candle. He reaches over, lighting his brother's with it. The flame spreads through the room until everyone holds a burning candle, their soft flickering glow brightening the room, the earthy scent of fire reaching me.

Rockland asks, "Bachmans, do you accept this union of bride and groom?"

The crowd gives a reverent, "We do."

"And Bachmans, do you pledge to care for and protect bride and groom, as you would your own blood?" Rockland asks.

"We do," they respond.

Rockland says, "And how long will you hold bride and groom in your care?"

"Forever."

It's overwhelming, all these people who want me to be a part of them. Rockland turns to me as I'm wiping tears from my eyes. "Welcome to the Bachman family, Kylie Bachman."

"Come here, babygirl. I want to kiss my wife." Cannon takes me in his arms and kisses me, deeply.

We join our guests for dinner, dining in the same seats where we sat my first night at Fire, Catherine now a distant memory. Afterward, the party moves outdoors. We dance under the stars, twirling over a parquet dance floor that's been laid over the grass.

Nonna dances the Cha Cha Slide with Booker. The music slows and Carlos approaches her. He looks dapper in a dark gray pinstriped suit and... does his silvery purple tie just happen to match her dress? He asks her something—for a dance? She gives a nod, and he takes her in his arms. When she looks up at him, her whole face lights up. Her smile makes my evening that much more special.

I watch as the Beast approaches Charlie, asking for a dance and, as timid as a mouse, she accepts. Liam holds Emilia in his arms, swaying to the music, his brothers all around him, dancing with their own beautiful women.

Even Antonio is here, hiding in the shadows, a whiskey in his good hand. I give him a little wave, excusing myself from Cannon's arms. "I'll be right back. There's something I need to do."

"I'll let you go, but only for a moment," my husband says, giving me a passionate kiss before releasing me. I can feel him watching me as I make my way across the dance floor.

I go to Antonio. "I'm glad you came. I have you to thank for this night."

He raises his glass. "To the happy couple."

He looks so sad and so beautiful all at once, I can't help but to rise up on the balls of my feet and peck a kiss on his cheek. "Thank you. For what you did for me."

"*Non è niente.*" He shakes his head, raising his glass to his lips and taking a long sip. "It's nothing."

"One day, Antonio, I hope you will find love like I have." I leave him with a smile.

At midnight, we all stop and stare up at the sky, watching a thrilling show of fireworks Carlos had flown in from Mexico, followed by the release of hundreds of floating white paper lanterns — Madam Funai's wedding gift to us, flown in from Japan, their soft glow rising and disappearing into the inky black sky.

Cannon makes a champagne toast. "To my beautiful bride. May everyone have a heart as pure as hers." He raises his glass and everyone cheers. The bright taste of the bubbles reminds me of that night I fell asleep on his sofa and woke up to find myself kidnapped on his private jet, the jet that now belongs to the Meralo family.

All the memories we've already made surround me, making me the person I've become today. And I know there will be many more happy memories as we grow together in love. Nonna's words come to me and now, I know them to be true.

Everything you need, love, happiness, work, it's all right here. You've been blessed, my child.

And I have been blessed, blessed by fire.

EPILOGUE

harlie

IT WAS ONE NIGHT. And if I'm being honest—apologies to my dead husband, God rest his soul—it was the best sex of my life.

I mean, they call the man *the Beast.* Would you expect anything less?

Six-foot five ex-military giant with a face meant for Hollywood and a thick head of hair you want to run your fingers through... I have had the privilege.

He wanted things to continue, but I couldn't risk it, I couldn't bear the pain of another relationship gone wrong. I've already lost two men I've loved. Why risk losing a third?

I've decided I'm cursed. After losing a fiancée and a husband, I know that any man who tries to marry me will surely perish. I couldn't do that to him. He's the biggest man I've ever seen, stronger than anyone I know, and tough as iron. But he has a sweet side too, buried beneath all that muscle.

I just don't want to get to know it. Don't want to get attached. Don't want my heart, that's already hanging by a thread, to be in any more pain.

There's just one problem...

I have a secret. A huge, massive secret that's even bigger than him. And if he finds out what it is...

This Beauty is going to have to answer to one seriously ticked-off Beast.

READY FOR THE NEXT BOOK? **Grab Mafia Beast on Amazon**

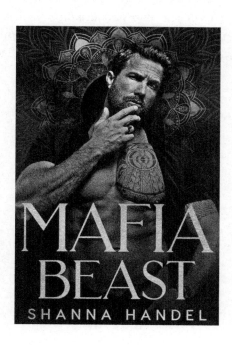

BONUS SCENE
THE SCHOOLROOM AT FIRE

K ylie and Cannon just couldn't keep their hands off one another. I had to write one more naughty little scene for my newsletter subscribers. Please go to this link in your browser to get the bonus scene: https://BookHip.com/RLNBVKJ

FREE CHAPTER ONE OF VOW TO THE KING

VOW
TO THE
KING
SHANNA HANDEL

E milia

TONIGHT IS *that* night in my house. The one terrible night of the year that the men in my family lock themselves in my father's study and drink too much whiskey, thereby avoiding their emotions. Not that the other nights around here are great or anything. This one is just particularly disturbing.

It's the anniversary of my mother's death.

They won't talk about their feelings or admit they miss her. Instead, they pour one another deep, cut-crystal tumblers of the amber liquor. I, on the other hand, do my best to avoid them. I choose to cry my eyes out alone, hiding in the library, my face buried in one of the last few things I own of my mother's. Her books. They're the only things of hers my father didn't remove from this house in his attempt to scrub the place of her memory when she died.

These aren't *quite* all of her books. One rainy afternoon I was exploring our dusty old attic and I found a bunch of paperbacks hidden in a corner behind an old chair, stacked neatly in brown paper grocery bags. Pages and pages of dark romance, the women falling for men with harsh hands and handsome faces. Those books found a new hiding place.

Under my bed.

Holding my mother's leather-bound book in my hands makes me ache for her.

A single tear trails down my cheek, falling from my chin and dampening the page. My brothers hate when I cry. They see it as a woman's weakness, to shed tears. They like to punish me when they find me crying.

My heart falls as I hear heavy footsteps headed right to me. Ignoring the closed door, Antonio, my oldest and most vicious brother, disturbs my peace. With bold green eyes, straight dark hair down to his shoulders, and high cheekbones, he'd almost be handsome if his heart weren't so charred. He throws open the heavy door.

The hard look on his angled face berates me before he even opens his mouth. His green eyes glitter with meanness. "Ah, the little bird is reading."

I'm slight but strong and he calls me little bird. It's his joke about me being small and held in this cage that is our crumbling mansion.

"You know I hate when you call me that." I dip my nose deeper in my book. "Please, go away."

He rips the book out of my hands.

My chest tightens at the sight of him holding such a precious belonging. Antonio has a habit of destroying beautiful things.

"Don't!" I grab for it, terrified he'll toss it in the fire.

He holds it just out of my reach, a cruel smile curling at the corners of his tormenting lips. He tosses it to the floor. It flutters open, landing facedown. I scoop the book up, grateful it's safe in my hands and not in the fireplace.

"There's a special place in hell for people who disrespect books like you do." I smooth the pages, close it gently, and lay the leather-bound book on the table beside my wingback chair.

My brother moves in close. Too close. I can feel heat and anger coming off him. The scent of whiskey pours from his mouth.

The tips of his fingers dig into my skin as he pulls me from my chair. I try to pull myself from his grasp but he's too strong.

He grips my upper arm, holding it tight. "You need to get over her."

"I'm fine. I was just reading, minding my own business—"

"No," he sneers. "You were crying."

"Get over her? Is that what you're doing with all that whiskey? Forgetting her?" I stare at Antonio, remembering when we were kids how he begged my mother to tell him stories about her child-hood, growing up in the countryside. "Why do you all drink your-selves silly on this night, then? Is it random, or are you hurting too?"

My words anger him. How dare I suggest that he, too, is weak in the absence of our mother. I see venom rising in his face. Fury flashes in his gaze.

"Shut up." He gives me a hard shove, his hand returning between my shoulder blades as he pushes me out of the library. "And go to bed. You don't need to be down here."

"Fine. I'm going. Enjoy your poison." I move toward the stairs.

He watches me briefly to be sure I obey. I turn my face away, grabbing the smooth banister. I release a deep breath when he finally leaves me, turning down the hall to rejoin our brothers.

The door to my father's study closes, the lock clicking behind him. Deep voices rumble down the long, dark hall. Funny. Usually when they drink, they get loud, laughing or fighting. Tonight, their tones are dull, serious. What are they discussing? Leaving the stairs, I creep down the hall, pressing an ear against the wood.

My heart hammers against my ribcage, fearful of what Antonio will do to me if he catches me. I focus on their voices, but I can't make out the words. Maybe the surname Bachman? They're another mafia family, more powerful than mine, that recently moved to the lakefront.

The men are talking so low, I can't be sure that's what I heard. The only sound I hear clearly is the blood whooshing past my eardrum. They're up to no good, I'm sure.

Hate and nerves prick at my skin, making me uneasy. I need to get out of this prison. I need to feel the night air on my skin, release some endorphins. I need a run. Time for this little bird to fly from her cage.

I'm wearing biker shorts and a cropped tee from my earlier bodyweight workout in the garden. I just need to grab my shoes, and I'll be gone. I'm experienced at going unnoticed.

Leaving the door to my father's study, I tiptoe toward the massive foyer. My worn sneakers sit ready by the front door. I slip them on. I grab the ornate metal doorknob, its carvings cold in my hand. The door creaks as I open it.

I flinch, squeezing my eyes shut tight and freezing in place like a little kid. If I don't move, they can't see me.

No one comes.

I glide through the door, pulling it softly closed behind me.

Please let them all be passed out by the time I get home.

The cool night air wakes up my skin as I jog down the gravel drive, pebbles and stones crunching beneath the thin soles of my shoes. Picking up speed, I run through the tall iron gates they've left open. I make it to the paved road, the feeling of my long ponytail swishing behind me, swinging like a pendulum as my feet hit the road, one after the other. It's a steady rhythm and it lulls me into a sense of peace, even though my life feels anything but peaceful.

The moon is almost full, and it lights my way, casting a blue glow against the dark pavement. It's my own world. There's no one out here but me. I push myself a little harder, chasing those endorphins I'm lusting after. I love a good runner's high. My family keeps me locked away from the world. Working out is my only joy.

I'm so lost in keeping my pace, it's not till the car is right behind me that I hear it.

My impulsive decision to take this run settles heavy in my stomach. Out by myself on the road at night. Not smart. Who's out this late? Very few people use this road. We live deep in the forest, hundreds of untouched acres in our name. Ours is the only house for miles. The road leads to the lake, to the gorgeous estates that dot the shore.

Please pass me. My skin crawls as the car slows.

It pulls up to my side, keeping time with me. I try to pretend it's not there. Ignore it and it'll go away. I peek at it out of the corner of my eye. A black SUV with dark, tinted windows.

Staring straight ahead, I keep running.

I don't know what else to do.

Please don't let it be men sent by my father. I'd been so quiet. The study door was closed. They were all drunk and engaged in whatever they were talking about. Surely, they didn't hear me leave.

There's the whirr of the motor of a window rolling down. My body goes tight, as rigid as a wire drawn taut from two ends. I keep running.

A low voice comes to me, rumbling through the night. "Little girls should be safe at home. Don't you know the kinds of men that prowl through these woods?"

Ice flows down my spine.

"Yes," I say, keeping my eyes forward and my voice steady. No one knows I'm gone from home, but this man doesn't know that. "My brothers prowl these woods. They're terrifying."

I keep my pace, one foot in front of the other, trying to ignore the hammering of my heart he caused. I can feel his eyes heavy on my body as I move.

To my horror, the SUV pulls to a stop.

There is no other choice. I take off. My legs burst into an all-out sprint. I listen for footsteps, but the only sound is my feet slapping against the pavement. I don't look back, pulling heavy breaths into my burning lungs.

Hairs stand on the back of my neck, perspiration prickles at my underarms. How many times has my father warned me not to come out here? How many enemies has he warned me of, telling me they'd love nothing more than to deflower the Accardi princess?

Now the footsteps come, heavy with determination.

I glance at the thick, dark woods to my left. They're my only hope. I can't afford a backward glance over my shoulder to see if he's gaining on me. I dart off the road, my feet hitting the soft earth.

Strong forearms dig into my belly, knocking the wind from me. No! My assailant holds me tighter, my back pressing into his chest. I can feel the muscles beneath his shirt shifting.

His arms lock around me, creating a prison around my ribcage.

"What do you want?" I hiss, grabbing at his arms, trying to push them away.

His mouth finds my ear, his breath hot against my cheek, and it tickles my skin, making the bits of hair that loosened from my ponytail flutter. "To teach you a lesson."

It's the same deep voice that reprimanded me from the SUV.

His hard palm runs over my trembling midriff. My cropped shirt rises, his hot skin caressing my cold torso. My muscles constrict, my belly going hard as a rock. Fear and remorse fill me.

What have I gotten myself into? What is he going to do to me?

One big hand presses into my belly, holding me against him, pushing my ass against the tops of his hard thighs. I dig my fingers into his forearm, a feeble attempt to dislodge him.

Heat from his body travels through his clothing, warming my skin. The clean scent of him hits me, cedar and man. This is the closest to a stranger I've ever been. My mind goes to my mother's other collection of books, the ones that hide under my bed. The spicy romance novels that I've dog-eared, re-reading my favorite scenes time and time again.

Is it the cool night air or the feel of his body that has my breasts heavy, my nipples tightening against my sports bra? A shiver tears through me, making me shudder and as I do, my hips roll, my ass accidently circling his lap.

Who *am* I, responding like this? I'm acting like one of the women in my books, wanting this and fearful of it all at the same time. My body is at war with my mind.

He lets out a low groan. The hand on my breast becomes his pinning hand, the one on my belly changing position, sliding up around my neck. He holds it lightly in his hand, his mouth so close to my ear now, his lips are touching my skin.

"What," I say again, my voice shaking, "do you want?"

"I told you." He drags his hand upward, smoothing over my curves, the pad of his thumb brushing ever so slightly over my traitorous nipple. "I want to teach you a lesson."

"I'm all good on lessons, thanks." Why is my ass pushing harder against him? My hips moving with a mind of their own... What is wrong with me?

"There are bad, bad men out here. Men that would take an innocent little girl like you and destroy her." He cups my breast in his palm, squeezing. "Let me tell you what you're going to do now..."

Is he one of the men my father warned me about...?

The idea and his touch cause my body to go to war with itself. Fear and adrenaline unite, wrapping around my spine. At the same time, dampness creeps between my thighs.

He continues, breath hot on my skin. "You're going to turn around and run home. We'll follow you in our car to be sure you get home safely. And don't let me find you out here again." His hand moves from my breast, slowly palming my belly, my hip.

He turns me slightly and snakes his arm around my waist, grabbing half my ass in his hand. A gasp, sharp and shocked, comes from me as he clutches my curves, the tips of his fingers pressing into my crack, one wandering middle finger pressing hard against my rear entrance.

This stranger has his finger pressing into my asshole...

His intrusion makes me shoot up on the balls of my feet, my fingers clutching at the forearm of the hand that holds my neck. His touch becomes more aggressive, his finger pushing harder through the spandex of my shorts.

I can't breathe. I can't think.

His words tear me from my cloud of shock. "I don't ever want you on this road alone again. Do you understand?" His finger pushes harder through my clothing. The unspoken threat of where he'd punish me if he found me out here again hangs between us in the air, heavy and cold as a block of ice.

His fingers tighten around my nipple till I squeal. "If you understand, say 'yes, sir.'"

Should I try to kick him, stomp on his foot, run away? I look to the SUV. The door in the back is open. He has a driver, so at least one other man is with him.

What can I do other than obey?

I force the shameful words from my mouth. "Yes, sir."

He gives another groan like when my ass rubbed against him. He likes that. When I call him sir, when I obey.

"Now run home to daddy and tell him what you've done."

"Like hell I'll do that. I'd like to live to see another day."

His response is a dark, rumbling laugh, one I feel against my back.

His hands move to my shoulders, turning me to face him. My gaze flits up to his. Eyes so dark they glitter like cut onyx. Dark, wavy hair. Olive skin. A short, well-trimmed beard, lighter than his hair.

A face too handsome to be forgotten.

"I'm going. Now," I say.

"Good choice," he says, another laugh echoing in his chest.

I take off running, my feet moving as fast as the beats of my heart. I hear the car door close behind me and for the entire quarter-mile run home, I'm terrified that the car will stop again.

That he'll change his mind and climb down from that big SUV and...

I reach the gravel drive, sneakers crunching against stone. The car stays on the road. I can't see inside the tinted windows, but I know he's watching me all the way to the front door of my house.

As soon as I open it, a slice of dim light from inside creeping over the porch, the car pulls away.

I'm left alone with my hammering heart, its beat pulsating all the way down to my melting core.

I close the door, pausing only a moment to lean my head against it and breathe.

Shaking, I slip off my shoes, the rubber of the toe pulling away from the fabric, then set them neatly where they were before I left.

Alone in my room, I take a long, lukewarm shower in my tiny ensuite bathroom, wishing our old hot water heater could keep up. My calves ache. I press my palms against the chipped tiles of the shower, stretching my legs and feet out behind me to relieve the pain.

I dress in sweats and a tee, sit on my bed, and dry my hair as best I can with a towel. I stare out the window, over the small balcony off my room, taking in the huge moon that looms over this night.

The very moon that witnessed what happened to me on the road.

What's this?

A small, blinking red light catches my eye as it floats toward the balcony. I move closer to the window, picking up the whirring sound of a small motor or something. I open the balcony door, a cool breeze chilling my freshly showered skin.

A white and black machine flies my way. A drone, I think? I've seen my brothers and their friends messing around with one, a light, plastic model, taking turns flying it in the backyard with a controller.

This one looks more heavy-duty, expensive, as it moves closer and I get a better look. A white parcel hangs down from it, tied by thin ropes. Who's flying it? I move out onto the balcony, looking down. There's no one in sight.

I stand in the center of the moonlit balcony, my wet hair lying down my back, the towel draped over my shoulder. The drone hovers above my head, just out of reach. There's a small, steel claw holding the twine. The claw opens, releasing the ropes. The box drops.

My arms fly out, catching the box as it falls. It's fairly light in my arms. What could it hold? I stare down at the lid. There's a note attached. Should I open it?

Curiosity wins out over safety concerns, and I pull back the lid. Nestled in the white paper is a gorgeous pair of pink and gray Brooks Aurora running shoes, something I could never dream of owning. I check the tag beneath the tongue. Six and a half. They're my size.

They can only be from one person. The man on the road. But I've only been home, what? An hour? How could he pull this off? He's got to be crazy rich with a team of minions at his disposal.

I slide a nail under the edge of the envelope, pulling the creamy cardstock from it.

NEXT TIME KEEP *your runs at the gym, little girl. There are wolves in these woods.*

Liam Bachman

GRAB Vow to the King NOW on Amazon

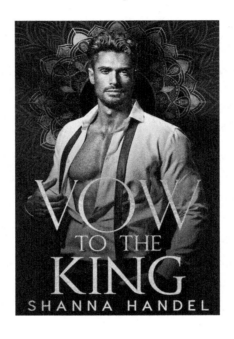

FREE CHAPTER ONE DARK CROWN

SHANNA HANDEL

 elicity

I'VE DREAMED of my wedding day since I was a little girl. I knew I would wear a white dress with long sleeves and a full skirt. I would dance with my father to his favorite song, *Figlia Mia: My Daughter*, and I would carry a bouquet of deep red roses.

And my groom—my prince charming, my knight in shining armor —I didn't know who he would be, but I knew *what* he would be. A warm, funny man with a crooked smile and an easy laugh. One that would hold me tight, kiss my forehead, shower me with his love.

A kind man. A gentle man.

Now, as strangers surround me, preparing me for what should be the happiest day of my life, I find myself swallowing back bitter tears. I watch them in the mirror as they curl my dark hair, blush my cheeks, and pin my veil into place, smiling and laughing with one another as they work.

After all, a wedding in the family is a joyous occasion.

I take in my reflection. Other than the flashing terror behind my hazel eyes, I'm the picture perfect bride. They've thought of everything, no detail has been overlooked.

He's thought of everything.

My keeper, my dark king. And by the end of this day, my husband.

I will be his.

His will be done.

The youngest member of his staff, seventeen year old Esme, hovers at my side. She's eight years my junior, impulsive and flighty, but there's a deep wisdom that resides within her. With her light hair and contrasting dark eyes, they call her *perla negra*, the black pearl. She longs to please, to prove her place in the ranks. She can read this unhappiness in my face and she fears she's the one who's put it there.

Placing a birdlike, fluttering hand on my shoulder, she says, "Miss Felicity? Is there anything else I can do for you?"

Catching her worried eyes in the mirror, I try to reassure her with a smile. It comes out forced and tight. My voice breaks as I speak. "No, my darling. You've done everything perfectly. Thank you."

Her face etched with concern, she gives me a timid nod. I've noticed she can be a bit distracted and seems somewhat boy crazy, but now, sensing my need to be alone, she gathers the other women, shooing them out the door. For someone so young, she's extremely perceptive and helpful.

I tuck the thought in the back of my mind. Perhaps Esme will be of assistance when I plan my inevitable escape. Because though I may be legally bound to this man in a few short hours, there's no way in hell I'm staying here.

Where will I go?

I've no idea.

And to complicate matters, I must save my father as well, even though he was the one who put me in this hell. After borrowing money from the Russo family that he couldn't pay back he sold the only thing he had left of value.

Me.

His only child. His precious daughter.

There's only one thing I take solace in on this day. Marrying this man means my father will live out his days in safety. And thanks to my husband gifting my father a monthly stipend, he won't be living in the streets.

My groom is generous with his wealth to those who are tied to him. For that, I cannot fault him.

Vincenzo Russo.

I've heard his name plenty of times, but never seen the man in person. Everyone calls him Vincent. Sophia, the matronly woman who's been employed by his family all her life tells me his name means to win, to conquer.

And he does. In every avenue of his life. He always gets what he wants.

And he wanted me.

Apparently, a few months ago, he visited my father's shop before we had to close it down due to money troubles from Dad's gambling addictions. I must have made an impression because he took me for his own, plucking me from the store, like a can of dry goods from the shelf.

I've racked my brain, wondering what possessed him to choose *me*. Surely there were other girls whose fathers were indebted to him?

Girls more beautiful, or interesting. Girls who longed to be the queen of the mafia, to live the lavish lifestyle he offers.

Why choose me?

As a shy bookworm, I often kept my nose stuck in the pages of a fairytale as I worked the counter at my father's shop on the main street in the village. I'd often spent lonely afternoons gazing upon, watching the members of the Russo family as they made their way home from the village to their chateau in little clusters. *Talking. Laughing. Happy.* I'd envied them their lives.

The irony grows bitter in my mouth.

Sophia briskly enters the room, shuffling over to my side, her generous, floral-covered hips pressing against my arm. "Get up, *il mio amore*, my love. It's time."

It's time.

I find myself frozen to the chair, unable to move.

She grabs my shoulder, gently tugging at me to stand. "Come, come. You mustn't keep him waiting. He's not fond of delays."

"I'm not fond of being forced to marry."

My words make her face fall and I instantly regret them. I soften my tone, putting a hand over hers where it rests on my shoulders. "It's not your fault, I don't mean to take it out on you."

She sniffs as if I've complained of my hairpins being too tight. "I understand. But my dear, things could be worse. In my day, our parents had the say in who we married. And it was difficult to move up in this world other than through marriage. At least in Vincent, you will never want for anything."

Anything, other than love.

Though her demeanor is tough, in her gaze I can read her apologies. She's not the one at fault. I give her the same tight smile I braved for Esme.

Patting her hand, I say, "I know. He's been more than generous."

She gives a grateful sigh, as if I've taken the weight of guilt from her shoulders. "I understand this isn't the way you envisioned your life heading, but you will grow to love him. I have a sixth sense about these things and I've not been wrong yet."

There's a first time for everything, Sophia.

I will never love him.

As soon as I can break out of the castle walls safely, I'm going to flee. Grab my father, and get us out of the country. Maybe we can go back to New York, where we lived before coming to Italy.

But first, I must play the part of the bride.

Standing, I smooth my shaking hands over my dress, a slinky white silk slip gown, the seaming hugging my curves, the back rising into baguette-encrusted halter straps that lead to a black grosgrain bow-topped T-back. It's nothing I would have chosen for myself, but as I gaze in the mirror, I find it suits me.

"How do I look?" I offer Sophia a smile I hope is kind. She hemmed this dress for me, painstakingly making every stitch by hand when I arrived the other morning, telling me if she left it up to the castle's tailor, he'd snag the silk with his rough hands.

Tears brush up in her eyes as she gazes at me through her wire-framed glasses. "Dear, you look lovely. Vincent is a very lucky man."

Taking my arm in hers, she leads me from the room. We make our way through the castle.

It's a truly beautiful building, a structure built for fairytales. I've read so many books, and in every one pictured myself walking along the halls of the castles on the pages. But now, it's real.

Deep red rugs line the halls. Paintings of the Italian countryside, and the regal ancestors of the family hang from the walls below black iron sconces that hold burning candles. Servants flutter behind me, ready and willing to meet any need I may have.

I've dreamed of castles like this.

And now, my dream feels like a nightmare.

Together, we walk down the back stairs of the castle, beneath an arched entrance. My feet pad over the soft green grass of the rolling hills toward the Gothic cathedral style church that sits on the property.

Shaped topiary trees twist up from the ground, lining our path to the stone building. Above the elaborately carved archway, the front of the church curves into five sharp points that seem to be reaching for the clouds, the center one wider than the others, a massive cross rising from its peak.

Where hundreds of curious eyes are waiting.

I will walk down the aisle alone—my father was not invited.

As we walk under the warm sun, a breeze blows by, fluttering my veil. The weather is so pleasant, I almost smile, but then my gaze goes to the dark wooden doors of the church and I tense.

The doors are flanked by guards.

Are they here to keep us safe from rivals, or to keep me from running?

My shoulders stiffen as the guards eye me, their gazes heavy, their jaws clenched.

The guards open the doors, and my knees go weak. *So many people.* The church is packed, the guests standing shoulder to shoulder, dressed in crisp suits and satin gowns, their faces turning toward me.

Overwhelmed by their gazes, my eyes turn upward. I focus on my breath, taking in the architecture, the domed ceiling with its carving and paintings of angels with feathery gold wings. I've dreamed of visiting this *duomo*, built in the eleventh century and an integral part of our village's history, but only the Russo family and their guests are ever allowed on the property. If I was here under other circumstances, I would stay for hours, taking in the beauty of this place, lighting a candle for the spirits of my mother and my grandmother.

But this is not a day out.

This is my wedding.

And I must move my body, force my legs to obey me, make my feet glide down the cold, stone aisle, where, at the end of this sea of people, I will get the first glimpse of the man I am to marry.

The music is beautiful and full, as it echoes through the church. The organ plays the notes of Wagner's *Bridal Chorus,* but in my heart it feels more like a funeral march, reminding me *this is not the happy day I dreamed of.*

With trembling limbs and not even a bridal bouquet to hide my shaking fingers, I somehow manage to force my way down the aisle, the sound of the magnificent organ thrumming through my chest.

There he is.

It's...him?

His jaw is cut from stone, his eyes as dark as his soul. His lips, though full, rest in a line, a near scowl. There are a few strands of early silver woven through his thick, chestnut hair. He holds his shoulders as if he's going into battle.

An icy tremble runs through me, a chill running down my spine.

I remember him.

I was working the store, my nose stuck in a book when he first walked in with his posse. He was buying a bouquet of purple roses. For a special lady, he said, his accent a blend of Italian and American, like mine.

His eyes lingered on my face. He brought his finger to my cheek, running it down the curve of my face, leaving a line of fire behind from his touch. The move was so exciting, so possessive, I felt a welling in my chest.

But this was a stranger. And judging by the men in dark suits that flanked both his sides, a dangerous one at that.

When I went upstairs to our home that night, I found the roses in a vase on my front steps. No note. No sign of him.

I took the flowers into the apartment, leaving them on the center of the table. When my father saw them, his face blanched. He scurried from the room without a word.

I figured the gift had made my father uncomfortable, a case of him not wanting his little girl to be all grown up, receiving gifts from strange men. I gave the beautiful roses to a neighbor, but kept the vase.

My father said nothing in the morning, but acted strangely for days. Then the money ran out, our suppliers no longer making deliveries. He confessed his lifelong gambling addiction.

And I forgot about the man with the purple roses.

That was weeks ago.

Now, I stand before him, realizing his gift of flowers was simply a prelude to him claiming me as payment. I want to turn, to run. But I think of my father, and do the only thing I can to keep him safe; put one foot in front of the other and close the final distance between us.

I reach the front of the church, and I stare straight ahead past his looming presence, focusing my eyes on a bouquet of white lilies resting on a table just behind the priest.

The mass is in Italian. The Russo family has ties to Italy as well as America, and like me, are bilingual. I let the words flow around me, unable to focus. Vincent stands beside me, his arm a hand's length from mine. I feel heat emanating from his body, making my spine rigid, my muscles tense.

The priest drones on. My feet pinch in my shoes. Dread creeps through my body, weighing heavy in my stomach. My heart thumps in my ears. Tears burn at the backs of my eyes.

I will them away.

Do not cry, Felicity.

The language changes to English, I assume for the benefit of Vincent's friends who have flown in from the states. They will want to hear the words, to understand what is said as we bind our lives to one another for all eternity.

Only there will be no exchanging of vows today. My hands shake as I realize *I can't do this.*

His dark eyes lock on mine.

And he begins to speak.

He's saying the words by heart. He's taken the time to memorize them.

"I, Vincenzo, take thee, Felicity to be my wedded wife, to have and to hold from this day forward, for better, for worse, for richer, for poorer, in sickness and in health, to love and to cherish, till death do us part, according to God's holy ordinance; and thereto I pledge thee my faith."

For one bizarre, fleeting moment, I'm touched.

Then, I remember the monster in the man that stands before me.

The priest turns to me. "Now Felicity, please repeat after me. 'I, Felicity, take thee, Vincenzo, to be my wedded husband..."

The priest awaits my response, dewy perspiration forming above his brow.

My throat feels tight and I clear it so that my words will be heard and there can be no mistaking of my response.

"No."

The single word echoes through the church like the sound of the guillotine crashing down on the block.

All eyes are on me.

Including *his*.

They smolder with flames from the depths of hell. Fear and fire fill my belly as his hand reaches toward me. I flinch as he grabs my hand in his. His touch surprises me. *Strong. Warm. Possessive.*

He turns to the Priest, murmuring, "You'll have to excuse us for one moment."

The haunting silence finally breaks in the crowd as hushed whispers fill the church. He drags me past the altar to the side. He opens a door, guiding me down a long hallway.

Terror pierces my heart. I try to tug my hand from his. "Where are you taking me?"

He ignores my question, opening another door, pulling me inside.

"Let me go!" I struggle to pull away, but his strength overpowers me.

We're standing in a small, rectangular room, what looks like a butler's pantry. A window overlooks the gardens, the walls are lined with shelves of food, and a counter runs down the length of the room. It reminds me of the store, adding sadness to my anger.

He shuts the door, facing me.

His words come, harsh and fast. "It's time you received your first lesson in respect. You are nothing without me. Penniless, homeless, left with your father's debts. No education, no career, you have nothing."

How dare he. Anger rises in me, looming so large I'm briefly no longer afraid of him.

I lean in, pressing my fingertip into his chest. "Let me offer you *your* first lesson in respect. You, sir, are wrong. I may *have* nothing, but that does not make me nothing. I'm bilingual and highly educated from books I've read. I have a community that I served every day, before you brought me here. And yes, though I am burdened with my father's debts, I am also filled with his love."

His gaze lowers to my hand, my finger still poked into his chest. He takes my hand in his, removing it. It drops limply to my side.

His jaw tightens. His eyes flash. The muscles in his shoulders tense.

He leans in, close, his voice lowered to a dangerous rumble. "Well played. But no one, *no one,* tells me no."

I've crossed a line. A dangerous one. And I'm going to pay for it.

Fear swirls around me, fogging my mind, making me numb. No other defense, I back toward the window like a caged animal. There's no escaping him—his broad shoulders block my way.

My voice shakes. "Why are we here?"

"Why do you think?" he asks with the growl of a tiger, stalking toward me as if I'm his prey.

"You plan on...punishing me?"

"You *are* smart, aren't you?" he sneers.

What will he do to me?

Though I'm terrified, my sharp tongue breaks through the shock. I shoot my words at him like arrows. "You're such a strong man, but you can't handle a woman speaking her mind. Can't tolerate someone not bending to your will?"

He grabs me roughly and as his fingertips dig into my flesh, I find my tongue going dry, my mouth, my words disappearing like sawdust in the wind.

"I've no need to bend you to my will. I'll break you."

With that, he turns my body, forcing me to bend at the waist. My hands reach out, grabbing at the edge of the counter for stability. His left arm wraps around my torso, pinning my left hip and side to his hard body.

His hand comes crashing down on my ass with a sharp sound that echoes through the small room.

The pain is like lightning, flashing and spreading over my skin. My teeth sink into my lip, holding in my cries. But his hand comes down again, harder this time, and the pain is too much to bear. "Stop!"

"You don't tell me when to stop." His hand comes down again and again, punishing every inch of my silk-covered curves. "The sooner you learn that, the better off you'll be."

Is he speaking of his rough punishments...or more?

The way he handles my body with such confidence, such force; will he be just as commanding when he takes me as his wife for the first time?

I hope so.

A shameful thrill runs through me at the thought, my insides becoming liquid.

A white heat flushes my cheeks as my stomach turns to knots. My confusing thoughts are forgotten as he brings his hand down again. My only thoughts now are of the stinging, painful fire that's spreading over my skin.

I loathe this man. I hate him.

And yet...the assault on my ass has ceased and now, his big, open palm strokes over my stinging curves. As his hand runs from my waist, sliding down the silky material of my dress, caressing the cleft in my bottom, a warm heat begins to grow in my core.

A pool of arousal gathers between my thighs.

Shame covers me like a blanket, my varnished fingernails digging into the soft wood of the counter. I've been with men...a few...no serious boyfriends, just an evening or two with an admirer from the village. Nothing about them kept me coming back for more.

They were all good men. Nice men. Sweet men.

Men not at all like Vincent. After only a few moments alone with him I'm charged with desire, lust filling my veins like it's been injected into my bloodstream.

This can't be.

How can a man I despise, one that's just violated my pride as well as my body, make me react like this? My breasts ache, my nipples strain against the thin silk of my dress, as if they are begging for his touch.

He pulls me up, holding me, my back pressed against his hard, broad chest. His arm tightens around my waist. My hands clutch at his arm trying to pull it from me, but his mouth finds the base of my neck.

And he kisses my delicate flesh with a harsh punishing kiss on that soft spot just a finger's length below my ear. His lips press, his teeth nip at my tender flesh. Despite my best efforts to harden my will, my head lolls back, my eyes close, and I let out a soft moan.

The sound of surrender.

And it feels so fucking good.

One brutal kiss on my neck and suddenly every man I've been with, every perfectly pleasant evening of gentle lovemaking evaporates from my mind, disappearing forever, making me forget that warm, kind man I dreamed of marrying.

This man, to his core, his very nature, is the thing I've secretly been craving.

Blame it on reading too many medieval fairytales, or too many hours alone...or just the way I'm wired, but I've laid awake dreaming of an encounter like this for a long time.

Why am I so weak? Why am I melting in the arms of this monster? I should fight, I should kick, I should scream. But now his hand slides up my belly, palming and squeezing my breast. *Hard. Punishing. Possessive.*

My nipples tighten, peaking further against the fabric of my dress. He takes one in between his fingers, pinching as his mouth moves down, sucking and biting at my shoulder, marking my flesh with his harsh kisses.

"You fight me, little girl, but I know down here," his hand dips below my waist, his fingers cupping between my thighs with the lightest of pressure, "you're wet and aching for your husband to take you."

Damn him to hell for being right.

Damn him for making my body crave him, his rough touches waking up my deepest desires.

I've no weapon against him, only my tongue. "You're not my husband."

"Not yet. But unless you want a repeat of what happened in this storeroom out there in front of the curious eyes of all of our wedding guests, you will walk down that aisle and say your vows like a very good little girl." The pads of his fingertips stroke my pussy over the dress as his thumb brushes over the tips of my nipples.

He presses against my swollen, pulsing clit. And I come undone. My breath catches in my throat as a pool of moisture gathers below his caresses.

"More." Shame fills me as I utter the word, begging for my captor's touch.

He gives a dark chuckle. With a nip of my earlobe, the warmth of his body is gone from mine.

Leaving me standing with weak knees, my eyelids heavy, my breasts aching, my panties damp. My slick sex throbs for more of his touches. My ass still stings where his hand rained down.

He gives me a look of triumph. "Come," he commands, his dark eyes locked on mine. He holds his hand out to take mine.

And in this moment of madness, I give it to him.

GRAB Dark Crown NOW on Amazon

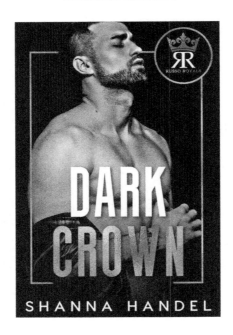

Printed in Great Britain
by Amazon

37979639R00155